THE
LAVA
WITCH

The Dark Paradise Mysteries
by Debra Bokur

The Fire Thief

The Bone Field

The Lava Witch

THE
LAVA
WITCH

DEBRA BOKUR

KENSINGTON
PUBLISHING CORP.

www.kensingtonbooks.com

KENSINGTON BOOKS are published by

Kensington Publishing Corp.
119 West 40th Street
New York, NY 10018

All Kensington titles, imprints, and distributed lines are available at special quantity discounts for bulk purchases for sales promotion, premiums, fund-raising, educational, or institutional use.

Special book excerpts or customized printings can also be created to fit specific needs. For details, write or phone the office of the Kensington Sales Manager: Attn.: Sales Department. Kensington Publishing Corp., 119 West 40th Street, New York, NY 10018. Phone: 1-800-221-2647.

The K with book logo Reg US Pat. & TM Off.
First Hardcover Edition: June 2022

First Paperback Printing: June 2023
ISBN: 978-1-4967-3836-3

ISBN: 978-1-4967-3786-1 (ebook)

10 9 8 7 6 5 4 3 2 1

Printed in the United States of America

For the sibs, in order of appearance:
Robin Bokur-Lambert, Raymond Bokur,
Ronni Bokur-Linville, and Kynewulf MacGowan.

ACKNOWLEDGMENTS

With sincere thanks to Leo F. Kennedy, Deputy Chief (Ret) CFD, EFO, for his assistance sorting out fire and explosion details; and to T. Kuʻuipo Alana for her essential help with the spelling and pronunciation of Hawaiian words, names, phrases, and places.

CHAPTER 1

The path snaked uphill, hedged in on either side by dense vegetation and endless forest. A heavy, soaking mist cloaked the rim of everything, forming a cloud canopy that blurred the tops of the towering redwoods and pines. The ground was slick with mud, and Detective Kali Māhoe slipped, grabbing for a branch of an ʻaʻaliʻi shrub that jutted into the trail in front of her. The branch of the hopbush dipped as she grasped it, her weight dragging it toward the ground. As she turned, scrambling to keep her footing in the thick muck, her hair, woven into a long braid that reached nearly to her waist, swung out and became entangled in the shrub's smaller branches.

"Damn this place," she swore, pulling at her unraveling braid.

"I thought," said a voice from just behind her, the words punctuated with heavy wheezing, "you were a nature lover."

"Yeah, but not when there's a storm system lurking off the coast and everything is soaking wet," she said. She swore again as a tall, broad man moved up beside her.

"Stay still for a second till I get you loose," he instructed, his tone businesslike despite the unmistakable hint of breathlessness.

The voice belonged to her uncle, Maui Police Captain Walter Alaka'i. She glared at him, then down at the mud streaking her lower legs, fidgeting slightly as he gently worked at the snarl of hair and branch.

"Don't pull!" she said, wincing as he separated bits of leaves and the shrub's thin branch from her braid. She wasn't sure why, but she felt deeply agitated and out of sorts.

"I'm not pulling. You are," he said. "And don't be such a baby. I have three daughters, remember? I know how to untangle hair."

She did her best to stand still as Walter deftly finished freeing her. As he stepped away, she took a deep breath. "Sorry. I don't know what's gotten into me. It's like this place . . ." She hesitated, then continued, "It's like this place has something dark pressing down on it. It feels . . . wrong."

"To me, it just feels cold," said Walter. "I guess I don't have your mystical sixth sense, or whatever it is."

She turned and took a few steps forward. "Let's just call it intuition."

They resumed their trek. Kali agreed with Walter about the air. She rubbed her arms, berating herself for not having grabbed a heavier jacket than the light rain shell she wore. Even in Hawai'i, the higher mountain paths could be chilly. The trail they were on was a segment of a network within Polipoli Spring State Recreation area, part of the greater Kula Forest Reserve in the southwest region of Maui. The wooded slopes approached the summit of Haleakalā volcano, soaring over six thousand feet in elevation. The damp, chill air had added to the significant drop in temperature that came with the additional ground height.

"Do you know how much farther we need to go?" she asked, looking up and through the mist-shrouded forest ahead of them. "We've got to be pretty close to the summit."

"Here's hoping," Walter responded, clearly winded by the effort of the climb. "The body's supposed to be about a half mile in from where we turned onto this trail."

"That's pretty remote. I think the old caves and the crater cone are just south. Do you know if they're going to try to land the chopper there?"

"Can't get it in," he answered. "It's not safe. They're going to have to carry her out. We've got mountain rescue on the scene to help."

They continued through the trees. Kali was going to respond, but they'd just reached a slight rise that opened into a clearing, and could hear conversation. She recognized the voice of the coroner, Dr. Mona Stitchard, known privately to her colleagues as "Stitches."

The conversation came to a halt as Kali and Walter stepped into a small, grassy space beneath a towering rainbow eucalyptus tree. The tree's trunk was covered with narrow strips of peeling, papery bark that ranged in color from deep orange to purple and multiple shades of green. Several people dressed in white plastic crime scene gear were gathered beneath it, staring upward. Their gazes were held not by the startling natural colors of the massive trunk, but by the lone figure that dangled about seven feet off the ground from one of the tree's thick branches.

The suspended figure belonged to a young woman. She was naked, and a rope was looped around her neck. Her face was tilted forward, obscured by a mass of curly brown hair. Her lifeless arms hung limp, fastened together with rough twine behind her back at the wrists. The fingertips of both hands were badly scraped. The soles of the girl's feet, clearly visible from where the watchers stood, were partially charred and blackened.

Kali and Walter walked slowly toward a taped-off area surrounding the suspended figure, glancing at the ground at the base of the tree. A faint impression that might have been drag marks could be seen disappearing into the undergrowth on the north side of the clearing that ultimately led to the edge of a steep slope.

They stayed where they were in order to avoid contaminating the space. Stitches walked up to meet them. Like the others, her clothing was covered by a white jumpsuit and a white cap that confined her hair. She was wearing gloves and holding two packets that contained disposable outfits identical to her own. Two sets of booties rested on top of the packets, and she passed them to Walter and Kali. She said nothing, waiting for Kali to speak.

"A Eucalyptus deglupta," said Kali, gesturing at the tree.

"Yes," said Stitches. She removed her glasses, wiping a layer of condensation from the lenses. "The rainbow eucalyptus, though I didn't think that would be the first thing you commented on." She looked back at the tree. "Mostly native to the Philippines, I believe. Such an odd thing, isn't it?"

Kali nodded. "There aren't that many in Hawai'i. You kind of have to know where to look for them."

"Do you think the choice of tree might be significant?" asked Walter.

"Possibly," said Kali slowly. She looked around, then back at the body. There was no shortage of other trees that would have served equally well, with thick, lower branches. Many of them would have been far easier to access.

Kali and Walter opened the packets and slipped on the thin plastic garments, covering their shoes with the booties. They ducked beneath the tape, moving toward the body. This close, Kali could smell the burned flesh of the girl's feet and see the scratches that marked the skin of her torso and limbs. There were small bits of twigs and leaves snagged in the thick curls of her hair, as though she may have been dragged. The brown tresses were streaked with golden highlights, and the twigs seemed almost like small earthy ornaments that had been deliberately placed. Reaching up unconsciously to finger the end of her own bedraggled braid, Kali stared at the body, hanging close enough to the tree's trunk to suggest—from the right angle—that the dead girl was merely leaning against it, poised in exhaustion for a moment of rest.

Kali did her best to remain dispassionate, but it was no good. That the woman had been tortured was clear. Pausing at the body's side, Kali considered her immediate impressions. The woman's physique was athletic and toned. The legs and buttocks were muscular, the biceps and shoulders well-defined. A thought flitted through her mind that the dead woman might have been a regular in a local gym, or an avid hiker.

"Who found her?" she asked.

"She was discovered by that park ranger over there," said Stitches, nodding toward the group of people on the edge of the clearing. "He said he hadn't been up this way for the past three days, but that there was nothing out of the ordinary in this area the last time he came through. He led us up from the ranger station at the midpoint on the trail." Stitches stepped away. "I'll be waiting over there with them while you make your initial observations. We can talk more once they've taken her down and I've had a better look."

She left Kali with Walter by the body and walked away to where a small team had assembled with a stretcher, a ladder, and the necessary equipment for getting to a point in the tree that would allow them access to the girl. A gust of wind blew through the clearing, and the body swayed slightly as the branch from which it hung moved in the current. As the air shifted, the scent of death and charred skin swirled, renewed. The wind briefly lifted the hair off the woman's face, and Kali stepped back, unable to look away from the open, staring eyes, their pale blue fading, no longer registering the surrounding world. Marks around the eyes and lips suggested that birds had already discovered the body and begun to take advantage of the soft tissues. She felt a wave of irritation that on top of everything else this person had been through, she was now being slowly and meticulously picked apart.

Walter edged closer. "You okay?" he asked. "You've suddenly got that intense look on your face that shakes everyone up. Kind of unnerving."

She turned to him. "Yeah, I'm okay." She gazed up at the tall tree and its peeling, multicolored bark. "I wonder if she got to see this tree. It's magnificent."

Walter shook his head. "What?"

"It's extraordinary," said Kali, her voice thoughtful. "I just hope that she got to see it. You know—maybe her view was filled with something beautiful as she took her last breath."

"Now you're just being weird." Walter looked at her sideways. "You worry me sometimes."

Her eyes swept the clearing and the surrounding forest, taking in the giant Cook pines whose crowns rose above the other trees, and the wondrous layers of greens that swept in leafy, undulating waves down the slopes into the valley below the clearing's edge. She could hear the rush and tumble of water from a nearby fall, just out of view, and myriad gatherings of birds engaged in song. The girl in the tree had clearly died an agonizing death. Was it too much to hope that the beauty around her had offered some small measure of solace?

Kali could feel Walter's stare. "Feel free to piss off," she said.

"That's no way for you to address an elder family member, who also just happens to be an officer who outranks you."

"Nevertheless," she said.

Walter looked up again at the lifeless body. "Noted," he said, his voice quiet and suddenly serious. "At any rate, it's time to get her out of here. If you're through, I'll give the go-ahead."

Kali nodded her assent. "Okay." She looked in the direction where the drag marks seemed to have led from. Several officers she recognized from the scene-of-crime crew were visible just beyond the border of the clearing, also looking at the ground. "I'll go see if they know where she was brought here from, then catch up with you for the trek back down." She watched him as she spoke. "I know the downhill part of a path is always your favorite direction."

"Only you could make that sound like some kind of a character flaw," said Walter. He turned away toward the waiting crew, gesturing for a ladder to be brought forward.

Kali no longer felt cold. Her mind was racing. She looked again at the girl, at her scratched body and disfigured feet. She was far higher off the ground than would have been necessary to cause death by hanging. Someone had gone to a lot of effort to get her into that tree. As Kali stepped away across the clearing, she made a silent, fervent vow to find out who that someone was—and what had made them do it.

CHAPTER 2

The girl's body was lowered carefully to the ground. Kali watched, her expression solemn, as Stitches stepped forward and placed her medical bag on the ground beside the rescue litter that was being used as a stretcher, and began a cursory examination. After a few moments, she signaled to Kali and Walter to join her.

"First, while she was hanging, she wasn't hung," said Stitches. "You understand the distinction?"

Both Kali and Walter nodded.

"Next, while it will take an autopsy to sort out the details, I think it's clear she was dead before she was hoisted into the tree. Look closely at her nostrils. They're packed with something dark, like thick dust. And," she continued, opening the girl's mouth slightly, "the same substance is filling the oral cavity, all of which suggests asphyxiation."

Kali moved to the end of the stretcher, bending slightly to peer closely at the girl's scorched feet. "What about these burns?"

"Her feet may have been held over an open flame," said Stitches, her voice thoughtful. "Or some other devilry, such as a blowtorch, was directed at her. Exceptionally unpleasant, I'm sure. I highly doubt the damage was self-inflicted, though it's also possible she was burned after she was no longer alive. I would suggest that at least some of the scratches and other marks on the limbs and torso may have been the result of an unsuccessful attempt to defend herself—or escape."

Walter looked up at the tree, considering the thick branch. One of the more athletic members of the scene-of-crime team was stretched partially across it, one hand grasping the bark surface as he searched for any possible clue, his feet anchored on the rungs of the ladder.

"Then why all of this?" asked Walter. "If she was dead already, why the effort to get her into this tree?"

"Theater, perhaps," said Stitches, still moving slowly around the stretcher. "A killer with a sense for staging."

"I'm not so sure," said Kali. "There may have been an element of that, but this feels more like a warning, or a statement of some kind—as though whoever it was who killed her wanted her to be seen."

"This path isn't one of the more commonly frequented ones," argued Walter. "And, as you may have noticed, it's ridiculously high. As far as I can tell, there's absolutely no reason in the world to be here unless you're a bird—especially when there are plenty of perfectly good paths at lower elevations. Those paths are where the tourists usually head, so if someone wanted maximum exposure for their work, it seems like this spot is a little bit out of the way."

"Plenty of visitors come up here," said Kali. "A lot of people actually enjoy hiking, you know. And who's to say that someone wanted her found by a tourist? There may be a very local aspect to this."

"Yes. Early days," said Stitches. She turned to them, grasping the handle of her medical bag. "I'm going to estimate time of death as having occurred within the last thirty-six hours. We'll all know more once we have her safely in the lab. It's still early, so I'll be in touch this afternoon or sometime tomorrow morning." She glanced away, waving briefly to the mountain rescue team who were waiting silently at the edge of the clearing. She walked over to join them. "All yours, gentlemen. Let's be careful with her, shall we?"

Kali's eyes briefly met Walter's. It struck her as unusual for Stitches to add such an addendum. She saw Walter shrug his shoulders almost imperceptibly in agreement. They stood, watching as the body was covered and strapped into place and carried into the mist along the lush trail. Stitches stepped onto the path, following close behind in the cheerless parade.

Another exhaustive search of the ground in and around the clearing picked up in momentum. Numerous soil samples were gathered to examine for evidence of the same dust that filled the girl's mouth and nostrils. Kali and Walter moved away from the tree and joined Senior Scene of Crime Officer Ren Santos where he stood waiting at the point where the drag marks disappeared into the underbrush.

Ren gestured toward the path. "The girl was brought through here. Whether she was conscious, unconscious, dead, or alive is anyone's guess at this point, of course. There's no clear sign of a struggle, but since her hands were bound, that would be a tough call to make. We've got some footprints, and we did find this."

He lifted a branch and held it out of the way as Kali and Walter walked past him into a small glade next to the larger clearing, separated by a swath of thick bushes and tall grass. It was about thirty feet from the tree where the nameless woman had been left. In the center of the glade was a firepit that had been crudely constructed of irregularly shaped stones. Burn marks marred the surface of the circle's rim. From its edge, a narrow path of flat stones led away for a distance of about ten feet, then stopped abruptly. The surface and sides of the flat stones were blackened. Crime scene tape had been stretched along either side of the stone path, about three feet out from either side.

"This looks like someone staged a firewalking ceremony," said Kali to Walter. She knelt beside the tape, peering at the ground and the surface of the stones. On each side, she could see a line of footprints running parallel with the line of rocks.

"If she was made to walk on the surface, these footprints were probably made by two people, each holding on to her from either side so that she had only one way to go," said Kali. She looked up at Walter and Ren. "Do either of you see anything here that contradicts that theory?"

"Nothing," said Walter.

"It's what I'm thinking as well," said Ren. "But why do you suppose someone made a path of stones leading away from the main pit?"

"If this was set up for firewalking," she said, "which is what it looks like, then the stones leading away from the pit would have been heated in the main fire, then laid out as a route that the fire-walker would travel across." She moved to where the last stone had been placed, slightly out of line with the others. The drag marks began there, and the ground on either side of the marks was beaten down as though it had been trampled by multiple feet. "I'd say there were more than two people here," she said.

Ren nodded. "We've identified four sets of foot-prints leading here, and three sets beyond the last stone, separate from the drag marks. None of those three sets is of bare feet, like the girl. Thanks to all this rain, they're too indistinct to get accurate tread marks or trace them back to where they began on the path; but based on their size, my first guess would be three people of various sizes who dragged or carried her. We'll analyze the prints further to see if there's a chance we can determine height and weight ranges."

Kali took a deep breath, looking from the small clearing in the direction of the larger space where the rainbow tree stood. She got up slowly, consid-ering the surroundings and wondering why a mur-derer—or murderers—would choose to make the

difficult climb when other options must surely
have been available.

She turned to the two men. "Okay. I'd like to
talk to the ranger now."

Ren nodded. He led her to where a short, fit-
looking man dressed in a park ranger's uniform
was waiting.

"This is Ranger Mark Shore," said Ren. "Mark,
this is Detective Kali Māhoe and Police Captain
Walter Alaka'i. You up to answering some questions for them?"

Mark nodded. He stood awkwardly, holding his
hat in his hand. He looked ill at ease.

"Hello, Ranger Shore," said Kali. She gestured
to the clearing. "Thanks for your help. Can you
tell us if this is an official campsite?"

He shook his head. "It's just Mark, please. And
no—this is definitely not a sanctioned camping
spot. This entire area, from the ranger station to
the peak, is off-limits for campfires. It's too difficult to get assistance up here if a fire breaks out."

"So this fire pit was deliberately constructed,"
Walter said.

"Yes," said Mark.

Kali looked closely at Mark Shore. She guessed
him to be in his early fifties. His uniform shirt was
smeared with mud and grass stains.

"I expect you know this park pretty well," she
said.

He nodded. "Twenty-two years here." He looked
around at the thick, damp undergrowth. "Seen a
lot of things. Couple of suicides, one from a gun-
shot. Pretty messy. One death by exposure from

someone who got lost during a storm and fell into a ravine. He'd been there weeks by the time we found him. And there have been two hikers—different times—who crashed to their deaths on the rocks along the slope. One was just a kid." He looked back to where the body had been left. "But this? I've never seen anything like this." He looked directly at her. "I guess maybe cops get used to it?"

Kali considered his question. She looked at Ren and Walter, and then back at Mark. "No," she said. "You never get used to it. You learn to manage it, but . . ." She chose her words carefully. "I think it's the kind of thing you should never allow yourself to become unaffected by."

He nodded slowly. "I guess that makes sense."

Walter sighed. "I remember that young hiker case, you know. High school kid. Turned out later he was having a rough time at school, getting bullied. He'd put himself on a physical training program to make himself stronger—all his own idea—and used to come up here to run the trails." He shook his head at the memory.

"Yeah. It's when you hear those details that it becomes more than just a story," added Ren. He turned to the ranger. "You've been a big help so far, Mark, and if you could think a little bit about what you've noticed up here lately, it might be vital information that helps us track down the people involved in this girl's death."

Kali chimed in. "For instance, if you've noticed the same people coming up to this area, or onto the paths, during the past few months—or if you've heard anyone say anything that sounded even the least bit suspicious or odd. Anything that struck you as out of the ordinary. And the same goes from this point onward. If you can just pay attention to what you notice, and let us know, that would be truly helpful."

"Sure. Of course. Nothing occurs to me right now, but my small staff and I have been up to our ears with clearing paths from that last storm. There were branches down everywhere, blocking the trails."

"How many people are working with you?" asked Kali.

"Three." Mark looked rueful. "I could use two dozen, but I've got one community volunteer and two part-time rangers."

"Please check with them to see if they've noticed anything, and call me right away if any of these people has anything to share," said Kali. She smiled reassuringly. "Sometimes, it can be the smallest anomaly that jumps out and points us in the right direction."

As Ren and Mark walked away, Walter looked hopefully toward the trailhead. "You ready to take off these fashion suits and go?"

She regarded him appraisingly. "I was born ready. It's you I'm worried about."

He grinned. "You saying you'd miss me if I toppled over the edge of that cliff?"

"Most likely." She set off at a brisk pace, then looked over her shoulder. "I've gotten pretty used to having you around."

CHAPTER 3

Walter moved his chair closer to Kali's desk. In the back of the main room in the Maui police department's satellite office on the island's southeast coast, Officer David Hara was hovering, wiping down a countertop that supported a coffeemaker and a selection of cups, spoons, and other coffee break paraphernalia, including a large platter that held a half-eaten pineapple cake. Tall, dark, and exceptionally handsome, Hara looked like a film star in a well-pressed police uniform costume, instead of the rookie cop whom Walter was training. Kali watched him, knowing he was waiting hopefully for Walter to invite him over to listen in on the conversation they were about to have with the coroner.

Hara looked up briefly, catching Kali's eye. She

winked at him, and he blushed and turned back to tidying the counter.

"Stop encouraging him," Walter growled.

"Stop harassing him," answered Kali. "He's trying to stay engaged, and he really wants to learn. Aren't you supposed to be teaching him, not scaring him?"

"He shouldn't be that good-looking."

"So you've noticed?"

Walter scowled. "Kind of hard not to."

Kali sat back in her chair and linked her fingers behind her head. "Oh, I see. Clearly, what we have here is a case of a middle-aged guy with a wife and three kids suppressing an internal jealousy of a younger, much better-looking man who still has his freedom."

"If I remember correctly, your fancy degree is in cultural anthropology, not psychology, so stop trying to analyze me."

"I don't have the time or the energy for a project of that scale, Walter. Your anxieties are for your poor wife to deal with, but you know as well as I do that Hara's got a good—exceedingly well-shaped—head on his shoulders, and it would be smart to let him help."

"Fine. He can help you with interviews. Right now he's going to help me by making me a fresh cup of coffee and bringing me a nice big slice of that pineapple cake." He looked at her, on the defense. "And don't you dare start lecturing me about calories. That hike this morning was all uphill."

Kali shook her head as she turned back to her

desk. "It was only uphill one way," she said. "You go ahead—I'll dial up Stitches for our video conference call while you put your lunch order in." She lifted a piece of paper from her desk and scanned it, then pulled her keyboard forward and began typing.

Walter ignored her sarcasm and got up, crossing the room to Hara. He returned with a plate of cake and a cup of coffee, and sat back down next to Kali and watched the computer screen, where the face of Stitches came suddenly into view.

"You received a copy of my preliminary findings?" said Stitches, by way of greeting.

Kali waved the paper she'd been looking at. "Right here," she said.

"I haven't yet completed the autopsy, of course, but I thought you might have a few questions at this stage based on what I know so far," said Stitches.

"Lots," said Kali, her voice wry. "Not that I expect you to have the answers that I want." She sighed. "Maybe you can just tell me if I understand the details of your initial findings."

"Of course. I'll go over them for clarification. First, as you already know, the girl was positively identified this morning as Maya Louise Holmes, age twenty-four years, single."

"Yes, and we have the missing persons report filed two days ago," said Walter. "She was a full-time employee at the Center for Marine Mining and Research—or CMMR—and lived with her younger brother, Charles Jason Holmes, who is a former student at the University of California, where he studied marine biology. He's working with some group here that studies sea turtles. He's the one who reported her missing after she didn't come home. They shared a condo."

"Yes. We couldn't get clear fingerprints off the girl's damaged fingers for a legal identification, so the brother had to come in to provide that. He was very . . . distraught when he viewed the body," said Stitches. "We only allowed him to see her from the neck up, of course, but the effect was quite grim."

"He's just a kid," said Kali. "It's unlikely he prepared for a day when he'd have to be the one to say, 'Yes, the naked, tortured woman in the morgue is my sister.' "

"That's very true," said Stitches.

There was silence. Kali watched the doctor on her screen, seeing her glance down at the floor before raising her head to look back into the camera.

"He's apparently the only family in the area," said Walter.

"Yes. According to him, his parents live on the mainland. They've requested that the body be returned to them there once we're able to release her." Stitches exhaled. "Now, as to cause of death. Rather fascinating, taken independently of the act of murder. The girl's nostrils, mouth, and throat were filled with what has proven to be very fine lava dust. Pulverized scoria, to be precise. It's relatively pure, in that nothing chemical or artificial was added to it. There's also a significant amount in the lungs. Based on this, I would postulate that she was forced to breathe it in, and that a certain amount made it into her lungs before she succumbed to asphyxiation. Forced asphyxiation, to be precise."

Kali felt a sense of horror well up within her. "That's hideous," she said. On her screen, she saw Stitches nod curtly in agreement.

Walter, who had been reaching for his plate, withdrew his hand. There was a look of revulsion on his face.

"Are you saying that someone shoved her face into this dust and made her breathe it in?" he asked.

"That's not an unlikely scenario," said Stitches. "As I pointed out in the report, there are marks on the back of her neck distinct from the rope wounds that suggest bruises left by fingers. There are also significant finger bruises on both upper arms."

There was silence as they each imagined how such a scene may have unfolded, wondering if the girl had had a chance to cry out, or if she knew what was taking place.

Finally, Kali said, "I've spent a fair amount of time around volcanoes. I'm having a hard time picturing anything like the dust you've described. There are always plenty of lava rocks and stones of various shapes and sizes, and those otherworldly expanses of rock from the lava flow—the stuff that cools in those undulating, wavy formations; but nothing as small and fine as what you're describing."

Stitches shrugged. "I'm giving you the cause of death. I'll be able to tell you more in a day or two, but the why and how and all the rest of this unfortunate affair is your department."

Biting her lip, Kali nodded. "So—the lava dust

and neck bruises aside, what can you tell us about the other wounds?"

"As for her fingertips," said Stitches, "she may have grasped at rocks along the pathway or in some other location prior to arriving in the forest, perhaps before her hands were bound. We'll do sample comparisons, of course. We'll have to surmise that the burns on the soles of her feet occurred just prior to death, as the depth of the burns indicates that she walked across the stones with her full body weight at play, even if the act was unwilling."

"The drag marks from the end of the stone path to the clearing with the tree would also support that theory," said Kali. "It's unlikely she would have been able to walk normally after treading across the hot stones. So she was probably dragged to the clearing, and then made to breathe in the dust or sand before she was hoisted into the tree." Beside her, she felt Walter cringe.

"That's a reasonable hypothesis," said Stitches in agreement. "The other marks—the cuts and scratches—were also inflicted prior to death."

"Is there any pattern?" asked Kali. "In your opinion, did someone cut her deliberately to form any kind of specific marking, or is there repetition of certain marks?"

"Not that I can determine. I think we can safely say that the marks don't have any clear pattern to them, as would be expected if there were a ritualistic significance to their placement, which is what I assume you're getting at."

"Yes." Kali grimaced. "Okay—so, if nothing else,

she most likely got scratched up along the pathway, and put up a good fight . . . hopefully."

Stitches nodded. "I would agree that that's consistent with what I've found."

Kali looked back down at the report. "We've searched the area for clothing, shoes, and personal items, but nothing's been found. We're going back in for additional soil samples to see if we can find any residue from the lava dust. It must have been carried there in something, and chances are good that some will have scattered. No sign of any yet, but if we can find some, that will prove a few things."

"Agreed," said Stitches.

"I guess now the big question is why," Kali mused. "I'll go and talk to the brother this afternoon. Maybe he can tell us something useful, like whether she had an insane ex-boyfriend or had recently become involved in something weird. I guess even science researchers occasionally get into trouble."

"I couldn't speculate," said Stitches. "And I have to end this call now. I've just had a bicycle fatality delivered that I must go deal with. Another daredevil riding on our busy roads without a helmet, surrounded by people driving while texting or talking on their phones. Let me know what you find out about the dust."

Kali was about to agree, but the screen had gone blank.

"Guess she's through talking to us," said Walter. "That's definitely not a woman who's big on chitchat."

"That's an understatement." Kali handed the printed report to Walter. "I'll head over to talk to the brother. I hate to stress him more, but I'd like to see where the girl lived."

"SOC has gone through her belongings and living space, but the sooner you see them as well, the better."

"Right. It's going to be about a thirty-minute drive. I'll need to stop by my place first to feed Hilo. You want to come along?"

Walter shook his head. "I'll organize the additional soil collection up at the crime scene and let you handle the interview, if it's okay. But go ahead and take Hara with you—or go alone if you feel it might be less traumatic for the brother to talk to just you."

Kali weighed her choices, aware that Hara, who had returned to his own desk, was still trying not to show that he was listening. "I think I'll make this trip alone," she said. She lowered her voice. "Why don't you send Hara up there with the SOC team? It will be educational for him."

Walter tilted his head, looking from Kali to Hara and back to Kali. "You think he has a detective badge in his future?"

She thought before she answered. "I do, yes. If he wants it. But I guess there's always the chance he might become a film star instead." She got up. "Try to be nice to him, Walter. Maybe someday he'll invite you to a big premiere party."

CHAPTER 4

Charlie Holmes sat across from Kali in the small living room of his condominium, his head in his hands. His distress filled the room—a blend of anger and despair that was so strong Kali could feel it physically pulsing against her. She took a deep breath, watching him closely as she spoke.

"I can only imagine what you must be feeling right now," she said, her voice as calm as she could make it. "Thank you for helping us go through your sister's belongings. And I apologize for the questions I'm going to have to ask you. Please understand that our goal—my goal—is to find out who was responsible for what happened to your sister, and to make sure that person, or persons, faces justice for their actions."

He looked up, his swollen face streaked with tears. There was a wild look in his eyes. "Do you realize I had to supply an alibi to prove I didn't do this thing?" He shook his head. "And justice? What does that mean? Jail? If these people are found, and if a jury even convicts?" He laughed, the sound somewhere between darkness and hysteria. He began to bang his fist on the table, over and over.

Kali sat without speaking, waiting for him to be ready to continue the conversation. He stopped his pounding and took a deep breath.

"You think I don't read the news?" he asked. "That I'm unaware of how many depraved people get away with doing terrible, unspeakable things to others?" He swore. "Justice. There's no such thing. Even if someone is rightfully convicted and goes to prison, they still have their life. They still have breakfast, and dinner, and a place to sleep, and maybe even the prospect of release to look forward to someday. Justice."

"I can promise you . . ."

"Promise me? Promise me what? That you'll find who did this to Maya and make sure they're tortured and then strung up from a tree like a piece of meat? As if they didn't matter?" His voice broke, and he turned away from her.

She could see that his whole body was trembling, his anger and grief enveloping him. "I do understand," she said quietly. "Please believe me. And I know that there's no way to make up for what's happened." She watched him for a few moments, gauging whether it was time to go on. "If you'd like to wait for a day or so before we talk, we can do that, but I have to tell you that the longer we delay . . ."

"The less likely it is that you'll pick up a trail, right? Isn't that the lingo they use in the movies?"

She nodded. "Yes. Something like that," she said. "But I'm afraid it's actually true—the longer the head start a criminal has, the more time they have to go into hiding or develop an alibi. If it was someone from off-island, I don't want them on a plane or a boat. I want them here, where I can find them."

He seemed to recognize the sincerity in her words. He wiped at his face, the gesture automatic, as if he were unaware of the action. "I appreciate that. I . . . I guess I just don't understand any of this. Why someone would do this to Maya. Or to anyone."

"Let's start there, then. Can you tell me about your sister? Anything and everything. Her daily life, her hobbies, her friends and enemies. Tell me about her work, and her favorite places. What she liked and didn't like. What was important to her."

Charlie nodded, the gesture slow and sad. For the next hour, Kali listened as Charlie stumbled over his memories, trying to describe to Kali who Maya had been. He told her how his older sister had been an avid hiker and trail runner, and a proficient surfer. He said that she loved animals, especially cats, and had planned to adopt one from the local shelter. They'd grown up in San Diego, and Maya spent hours on weekends and during summer breaks volunteering on beach clean-up committees. She'd left San Diego to earn her bachelor's degree from the University of Hawai'i's Hawai'i Island campus while he'd stayed on in California to finish high school and begin his studies in marine biology

through a program at Scripps Institution of Ocean-
ography. He'd missed her, and had decided to leave
the program in order to move to the islands to be
close to her. For the past year and a half, they'd
shared this small condo close to the research facility where she worked and the sea turtle conservation center where he was employed.

"We're just a year apart in age, and we've always
been close," he said. "Our parents each worked
two jobs so that we could go to college without having the burden of student loans, so my sister and I
were on our own a lot. Maya was . . . well, in-
domitable is a good way to describe her. She wasn't
afraid of failing, you know?" He sat quietly for a
moment, some of his emotion spent. "If someone
told her, 'That will be really hard,' or 'You can't do
that, you're just a girl from a poor family,' it would
make her even more determined to do it. Some
jerk she worked with told her she'd never be able
to get through the Ironman competition in Kona,
but she just kept training for it and competed in it
last year." He smiled, the expression conveying an
infinite sadness. "She'd never raced in a triathlon
before, but she finished in the top fifty. She was my
hero."

Listening to Charlie describe his sister, Kali felt
a sense of loss that was unrelated to having personally known her.

"I'm really sorry," said Kali. "The world needs
people like that. People who aren't afraid." She
waited a minute, allowing him to gather his thoughts,
then continued. "You mentioned that this person
she worked with was giving her a hard time. Can
you tell me more about that?"

"Oh, that wasn't really anything except some arrogant guy who was intimidated by her." He looked up at Kali. "Not physically, that's not what I mean. But she was the most focused human being I've ever known, and I think her colleague judged himself against that, or something. And she was brilliant, always thinking up things that no one else had ever considered. It got her top honors in college, and a lot of job offers. Plus a scholarship to begin her graduate work."

"But she chose to accept a position here on Maui?"

"Yes. At the end of her senior year, she did a summer internship with the National Oceanic and Atmospheric Administration—NOAA—and had been hoping they'd offer her a permanent position in the fall. But then she got a better call from someone she knew who'd been named the director of an important research group and wanted her to join his small staff."

"She was a researcher?"

"Yeah, partly. She loved research, she loved inventing things. I mean, really loved it. She was always coming up with new ideas, and won some pretty prestigious awards for innovation in college. But her degree was in mechanical engineering technology, and she specialized in the sonar field."

He explained that his sister had accepted a position at CMMR on Maui after her former course advisor had been named director and had reached out to her about a job opening.

He hesitated. "She thought it was a good opportunity, given that she'd only just started her master's program. She really just wanted to stay in school and go on to get her doctorate degree, too, but it's so expensive. She had that scholarship to start, but we both learned from our parents about not taking on long-term debt, and she thought if she could work at the research center for a couple of years and save up while working on her master's, she could continue on with her studies and eventually get the PhD she wanted. She . . . she would have been the first person in all of our family to get an advanced degree."

"What about you?"

"Me? I don't know. Maybe someday. Right now, it doesn't seem important. But I want to have some kind of career in the marine life field." He gave a short laugh, a rueful sound. "I don't really think I have much of a head for hard science, but I really love sea creatures, especially octopuses. I guess if I'm honest with myself, what I'd really like to do is work in a marine rehabilitation center, helping injured animals before setting them free. Right now I'm getting a lot of satisfaction working with a group that rescues and studies sea turtles."

"I like that," said Kali.

"Yeah. I also volunteer a few hours a week at the rehab facility we have at the aquarium. Maya used to like to come there with me."

They sat for a few moments as Charlie gathered his thoughts. Kali looked around the room. There was nothing remarkable about it. The television screen seemed larger than necessary, but the furniture was basic and generic. There were a few shelves on one wall that held a mélange of items— a set of speakers, a few film DVDs, a pair of headphones, and several cookbooks. On the small table at the end of the sofa next to where Charlie sat was a lamp and a framed photograph. Kali wandered over to the shelf, looking more closely at the display. Next to the DVDs was a decorative set of tarot cards and a stuffed octopus that looked like a child's toy. Kali waited until she felt he was ready to go on talking, then sat back down. She leaned toward him and spoke gently.

"Are those tarot cards yours?"

He shook his head. "No, I think someone gave them to Maya. Some woman she worked with." He looked introspective. "She didn't have any interest in that kind of thing. You know, the occult or stuff like that. But the artwork on the cards was done by some famous contemporary artist, and she thought they were too nice to just throw away or donate."

"Have you ever used them?"

Again, he shook his head. "I wouldn't have a clue what to do with them."

She watched him, trying to evaluate his present capacity to discuss the more personal details of his sister's life.

"Charlie, did Maya have a boyfriend or a partner?"

He looked at her. When he spoke, his voice was hesitant.

"No. You were looking at that stuffed toy on the shelf a minute ago, right? She gave that to me on account of how much I like animals." He turned his gaze momentarily to the shelf, then back to Kali. "I guess this might be hard for some people to understand, but she wasn't really interested in romantic relationships. Part of that is because of the way she was always treated, especially by men.

All through childhood and school, everyone always made a fuss about her looks. How beautiful she was. She used to hate—really hate—when people called her striking or exotic. As if it took away from her intellect or something." He reached over to the end table beside him and lifted the framed photo, handing it to Kali.

In it, Maya and Charlie were standing side by side in front of a large glass wall. Behind the glass, an enormous, graceful octopus was poised in the act of swimming by. Charlie was grinning, and Maya was gazing at him, a wide smile on her face. Kali studied the image. Charlie was correct: Maya had been a truly stunning woman. Kali looked at her long neck and delicate cheekbones, at the rich browns in her thick hair, at the tall, graceful figure. It felt odd to see her this way, filled with life and vitality, and to remember the bruised, silent body she'd encountered in the forest.

She handed the photo back to Charlie.

"No romantic interests?"

He shook his head. "No. She's had a couple of boyfriends, but nothing serious. She maybe went out with them a few times, but there's been nobody for a few years. Definitely not since I've been living here with her."

"What about friends in general?"

Charlie frowned. "No one really close. There were a couple of women from work that she'd see for lunch now and then, but she trained mostly alone and was really involved in her research. She used to meet one of those women now and then to run or swim, but she preferred to do those things on her own. It used to worry me that someday she'd wind up all by herself, surrounded by nothing but awards for her work and a bunch of sports trophies."

"Okay," said Kali. "That's all really useful." She waited a moment. "If you could give me the name of her boss, those people that she dated, her lunch friends, the jealous colleague you mentioned, and anyone else you think might be able to tell us anything about her movements over the past few days, it would be a great help. Also, we'll need her cell phone and computer. Do you happen to know where those things might be?"

Charlie thought for a moment. "She had two computers. One for work, and one for personal stuff—both of them were laptops. I guess her work computer might be at the lab, but I don't know where the personal one is since it doesn't seem to be in the house. The police who were here before you asked about that, too, but they couldn't find it."

"And her car?"

"Oh." Charlie seemed genuinely surprised. "Her car. I never even thought about it." He looked up at her, a bewildered expression on his face. "I guess I don't have any idea where it is."

CHAPTER 5

Kali got Maya's phone number and car plate information from Charlie and called them in so that tracing could begin. She left him sitting on the sofa and stepped into Maya's bedroom. It was tidy and well organized. Clothes hung on racks in the closet, the bed was made, and the curtains were drawn back from the windows, allowing sunlight to illuminate the small space.

Feeling like an intruder, Kali went through the closet, dresser, and desk, finding nothing that seemed out of place or in any way connected to an interest in Hawaiian ceremonies, or anything dark that might have suggested her involvement with people given to violence. There were no letters or cards, except for two birthday cards. One was from her parents, and one had been signed by Charlie. Both were sitting on top of the chest of drawers.

The SOC team had been thorough, and there was nothing obvious to be discerned beyond an apparent loyalty to certain clothing brands, and an interest in difficult jigsaw puzzles. Maya had amassed quite a collection, including several wooden puzzles that had been hand-cut and looked satisfyingly complicated. They were stacked on the floor next to the bookcase, the top box displaying the image of a jewel-handled sword. The bookshelves were filled with textbooks and thick tomes on ocean mining. Kali had a fleeting thought that she would have enjoyed the puzzles, but that the book choices looked intensely boring.

She stood in the middle of the room, feeling vaguely voyeuristic—the same feeling she had experienced in other rooms that had belonged to strangers who were destined never to return to the spaces they'd filled with meaningful belongings. She looked around again. Every choice—from the worn denim jacket with the embroidered flowers on the back, to the shade of yellow of the bedding, to the hairbrush resting on the top of the chest of drawers next to the birthday cards—had been made by a woman who no longer had any use for them.

Kali closed her eyes, trying to still her mind. She breathed deeply, controlling her exhalations, letting herself be open to any small stirring or nuance that might suggest that something was missing or out of place—a balance that had been disturbed.

There was nothing. Just silence, and the small noises made by the automatic fan system on the air-conditioning unit. Kali walked back into the living room where Charlie still sat on the edge of the sofa, exactly where she'd left him.

"Maybe," she said, her voice gentle, "you could just have another look through your sister's room for me after I've gone? Tell me if you think there's anything missing, or anything new that you've never noticed before. I know that sounds strange, but even the smallest diversion from her normal life could be helpful."

He nodded without looking up. She could see that he was rocking slightly, his upper body moving back and forth with tiny, controlled movements. He's trying not to cry again, she thought, and was again swept with the sense that she was an intruder on an intensely private moment. She remembered how others had tried to comfort her when her fiancé and fellow police detective Mike Shirai had been gunned down during a drug raid, how nothing had eased the sense of loss and despair or her fierce, consuming anger. No one, she acknowledged, can truly understand another's grief. Maybe the best thing I can do for Charlie, Kali told herself, is to leave him be.

Pulling a card from her wallet, she scribbled her private cell phone number beneath the number and e-mail for the police station, and left it on the edge of the kitchen counter.

"I left you both of my phone numbers, Charlie. Please feel free to call me anytime. Anytime at all."

Charlie made no move, so she let herself out, walking slowly along the portico that connected Charlie's condo to the others on the same row, leading to the parking area behind the building.

She stepped around a series of puddles, then climbed into the driver's seat of her aging Jeep. She sat there, lost in thought, only stirring when a car pulled into the spot beside her and the driver's blaring music blasted through the car's open windows to jolt her back into alertness. She pulled out slowly, leaving behind the music and the lone figure on the sofa, wrapped in sorrow.

Later, at home, Kali sat at the table and ate her evening meal, assembled from bowls of leftover rice, fish, and grilled papaya sitting in the refrigerator. As she stood at the sink and washed the dish and silverware she'd used, she listened to the sound of Hilo snoring from his cushion, where the massive dog—the result of a brief romantic encounter between a Weimaraner and a Great Dane—lay with his forelegs stretched over the cushion's edge. She watched him for a moment, coming to the conclusion that the dog was on the right track when it came to prioritizing. Outside the window, the light was fading, and she felt drained from the long day. An early night seemed like an excellent idea.

She went outside onto the wide lanai that ran along the front and down one side of her small house, and climbed into the hammock suspended from the ceiling at one end. The screen door opened, followed by the soft padding of dog feet. She felt Hilo's warm head push against the hand she had dangled over the edge of the hammock. Absently, she scratched him behind his ears, listening as the wind picked up and moved through the treetops, stirring the palm fronds and the leaves of the fruit trees that grew across her property. There had been a string of recent storms that had accompanied a distant hurricane, and she could tell from the dampness in the air that another was on the way.

Before she'd eaten, she'd called Walter to tell him about her conversation with Charlie, and to find out about how the soil-gathering expedition at the crime scene had gone. Walter said that no one had been able to detect any new activity at the clearing, and there was no sign that anyone had been there since the last search of the area. He added that the soil samples had been sent off for analysis, with orders that the job be treated as urgent.

She drifted off thinking about the clearing and the tall tree, and was jolted awake from restless dreams about an hour later by a cold blast of wind. She climbed out of the hammock and went back inside, followed by Hilo. She locked the door behind her and closed the windows in the kitchen and living room. She kicked off her shoes and collapsed across her bed, leaving her bedroom window cracked open. Next to her bed, the sound of Hilo settling onto the thick floor rug made a familiar, reassuring sound.

The scent of tropical blooms drifted through from outside. As she stared at the ceiling, she noticed that the paint had begun to peel, and that the constant recent moisture had caused a narrow line of mold to appear along the space between the ceiling trim and the wall. A thin layer of salt clinging to the exterior glass dulled the light filtering through the window. She sighed. Living alone had its advantages, but not when it came to the up-keep of a large piece of property, or the steady list of chores that went along with it. She lay there as the room slowly grew dark, considering that what people so often defined as paradise was, in reality, just an elusive, fleeting dream that we tried to convince ourselves was real.

CHAPTER 6

Unable to stop thinking about Maya Holmes, Kali slept fitfully. By the time the morning light began to edge across the windowsill, she'd given up on the idea of rest. She put on her swimsuit and pulled a towel off the bathroom shelf, making her way across the room to the kitchen and out of the front door. Hilo sat up and stretched, following her at a sleepy pace as she jogged through the damp grass to the path leading down to the beach.

Despite the early hour, the sea was warm. The surface was choppy, reflecting the spate of bad weather, but she waded out and dove into a small incoming wave. She swam strongly until she surfaced past the line of breaking water. For about thirty minutes, she swam parallel to the shore, her long strokes falling into a rhythm that was both meditative and revitalizing. By the time she turned toward the narrow beach and was met by Hilo where he was splashing in the shallow water close to the shore, she felt refreshed and clearheaded.

She toweled off and began the climb back up the long path to her yard, past the slope leading to where Walter's old fishing boat, the Gingerfish, was secured to her private dock. In the distance, she could hear the clanging of a hammer striking metal. She knew that her neighbor Elvar Ellinsson was also an early riser, and was already at his forge working on a knife commission. She hesitated, standing near the edge of the thicket of trees that separated her property from the one Elvar shared with his sister, Birta. The swim had inspired her to think about preparing something substantial for breakfast this morning, and she made up her mind to go next door once she was dressed to see if Elvar was interested in coming over to share a meal.

She wavered as she walked across the lawn toward her house, considering that she was no longer really sure of how her relationship with Elvar should be defined. They'd been neighbors for several years, and had grown to be good friends. But recent events had suggested that there might be something more meaningful developing, so she was uncertain of where the boundaries between them were currently laid.

Hilo raced her up the steps to the lanai. She showered and pulled on a pair of jeans and a short-sleeve T-shirt, lost in thought about Maya's missing car, her computer, and her cell phone.

There was a team working on tracing the calls on the phone number Charlie had supplied, and Walter had put out an alert on the car, but there'd been no sign of it yet. She wondered if and where it would show up, and if its location would reveal anything telling about what Maya's activities had been or whom she might have encountered the day that she'd been killed. Kali hoped that the dead girl's computer might be found in the car, but she wasn't banking on it.

She pulled a carton of eggs and half a melon out of the fridge, then set them on the kitchen counter next to a loaf of raisin bread. She reached into the cabinet and removed two plates. Hesitating, she took two place mats from a kitchen drawer, shaking out the wrinkles. They'd been made by her grandmother, who had embroidered rows of tiny pineapples along the borders of the woven linen cloth. Kali was so afraid of staining and ruining them that they spent most of their time safely folded away, rarely used. Breakfast company was a good reason to take that risk, she felt, and set them on the table beneath the plates.

The sound of Elvar's hammer carried clearly through the morning air, and she smoothed her damp hair, feeling ridiculous. She was a grown woman in her thirties, and if she wanted to invite a neighbor—or a friend, or someone who was possibly becoming more than that—to breakfast, then that's exactly what she'd do.

She sat down on her sofa to slip on her shoes, hoping she wasn't making some tactical error of judgment that other women with more dating experience would have seen as obvious, and was halfway to the door when she heard a car pull into the driveway.

A quick glance out the window showed that it was Walter. Kali went to the door and pushed it open. She stood on the lanai, waiting as he got out.

"Aloha," she said, hoping that whatever had brought him by this early was going to be nothing more than a brief announcement, and that whatever attention it might require could at least wait until she got to the station.

"Aloha yourself," he said, walking up the steps. "What's up?"

"Couple of things," he said. When Kali made no move to sit down on one of the deck chairs or go back inside the house, he looked at her, frowning. "Are you okay? You seem a little tense."

"Me? I'm fine," she said, willing him to leave. "Just went for a quick swim."

"Okay," he said, watching her closely. "Then let's sit down for a minute."

"Sure," she said, moving reluctantly toward a deck chair.

"Inside, if you don't mind," he responded. "I could do with another cup of coffee."

Before she could block his way, he'd pulled open the door and stepped inside. Groaning inwardly, she followed him.

"Well, look at this," he said, glancing at the table and the two plates. "Your intuition and exceptional skills of deduction are at an all-time peak today. How'd you know I missed breakfast?" He looked at her. "Did Nina call and tell you I was on my way over here?"

"She did not," said Kali, feeling cross.

"But you've set the table. Two plates . . ." He suddenly grinned, his eyes crinkling at the corners. "And your fancy place mats? Wait a minute. You weren't expecting me. You were expecting someone else. Let me guess: tall, blond, and carrying a hammer? Possibly a foreign guy with some kind of Thor fixation?"

Kali blushed. "Try not to be an ass, Walter."

"Me?" He slapped his thigh, chuckling. "Nothing could be further from the truth. I'm the guy who can't wait to see you married and settled down with about a dozen kids tugging at your apron strings. Then I'll finally feel like you're safe."

"That's the scariest fate I can imagine," Kali said darkly. "And it was just an idea. I hadn't actually gotten around to asking him to breakfast anyway, thanks to you showing up unannounced."

"Well, I say we make the best of an unfortunate situation," Walter said, surveying the food assembled on the counter. "I'll start the coffee while you get busy with the eggs. I'll take mine scrambled, please."

Kali shook her head, giving up. She pulled a glass bowl out of a cabinet and broke five eggs into it, then added butter to her frying pan and placed it on the stove's gas burner to warm up. Humming, Walter finished the coffee prep and took a knife from a drawer. He began slicing the melon, dividing it up onto the plates Kali had set out.

She watched as he peeled the rind off a small piece of melon and popped it into his mouth. "I have an interview at ten o'clock with Maya's boss," she said. "Hara's coming with me. I assume you have some reason other than a free breakfast for stopping by this morning?"

"I do indeed," he said, carrying the rest of the fruit to the table and turning back to the counter to begin making toast. "We've found the girl's car."

Kali's body tensed. "In a ditch?"

"Nope. Parked in the side lot at the supermarket in Kahului."

"You're kidding," she said in amazement. "That's anywhere from two to five hours from here, depending on traffic."

Walter shrugged. "She might have been making the trip to run a bunch of errands at the bigger stores down there. Isn't that what most of us here on the far coast generally do?"

"It could also have been driven there by someone else and left to cause us a distraction."

"Hard to say at this point. There's CCTV in the parking lot, but the car was parked out of range. It was locked, and there was nothing immediately apparent as being out of the ordinary. Forensics is still going over it, and we'll have it towed up here when they're through, but at least on the surface, there's no sign of a struggle of any kind."

"I'm guessing no phone or computer?"

"Nope. She'd probably have had the phone on her person, right? Or in a purse of some kind. There was nothing like that in the car. A sweater in the back, a map and a pair of sunglasses in the glove box, and an empty water bottle between the driver's seat and the passenger seat that's being checked for fingerprints, but that's about it."

The melted butter in the pan began to sizzle. Kali gave the egg mixture another whisk and poured

it into the pan. She picked up a spatula and turned
to Walter.

"No purchases in the car suggests that she was
there meeting someone," she said. "If she was,
then that person—or persons—may have driven
her back up here, to the forest, or to another site
where she was tortured, and then dragged up
there to do the firewalking ceremony."

Walter poured coffee into two mugs and began
buttering the toast. He watched Kali as she stood
at the stove, her mind clearly not on the details of
cooking.

"You're drying out the eggs," he said. "I like
mine soft, you know." When she made no response, he reached out, taking the spatula from
her hand and stirring the eggs. He smiled know-
ingly. "Hey there. I'm losing you, I think."

"What?" Kali shook her head. "Sorry, it's just
that it doesn't add up. Yes, she must have had
other transport up here to the trail, but I think she
and whoever she was with went straight to the forest. It's unlikely she'd have been able to walk after
being beaten so badly, and someone might have
noticed a woman being forced along a hiking
path." She watched as Walter transferred the eggs
to the plates. Lifting the two coffee mugs, she carried them to the table and sat down across from
him. "That would have been pretty risky."

"Not if it was at night."

"True," she said, her voice conceding to his
point. "Is the ranger station manned during the
night?"

"Not according to Mark Shore."

"Okay, so say she was moved during the early

evening or at night. I still think she'd have been on her own two feet. She was fit, but she was a grown woman. Carrying her that distance—uphill almost all the way from the parking area—would have been difficult and pretty awkward logistically. That also applies to her having been drugged first. So let's say she got up there under her own steam. Maybe even by her own choice. We have to consider that she may have hiked up there willingly without knowing what was going to happen—and also that whatever was going on may have begun as something she was actively participating in."

"As in some crazy game? That's true. Or it could have been at gunpoint," said Walter, around a mouthful of toast. "That would have kept her from calling out for help or attracting attention."

"It would also explain the lack of any signs of struggle where her car was parked." Kali sipped her coffee. "But I think it's likely she knew whomever she was meeting, and that there was some level of trust—enough, at least, to persuade her to get into another vehicle. What happened after that is the question."

"Yeah, one of them, at least," said Walter.

"Maybe I'll get a lead this morning. I'm hopeful that her boss or someone else she worked with might have something useful to say."

"The Something-Something Deep Sea Mining Place, right?"

"Close. The Center for Marine Mining and Research, also known by its acronym, CMMR. The girl's brother gave me the name of her boss, who's also the guy who recommended her for the position. He's the reason she was living on Maui."

"What's his name?"

"Dr. Davos O'Connor. Doctor as in PhD, not the kind that tells you to take your vitamins and get enough sleep."

"I could use some sleep."

"Yeah. Me, too." Kali took a bite of her toast, then reached for a piece of melon. The effects of the swim were wearing off, and she wished she could just crawl back into bed and let go of the weight of what she'd seen in the rainbow tree.

They finished their meal in silence as they each reflected on what they'd so far learned about Maya. It wasn't much. They knew that she'd enjoyed research, and working out, and solving difficult jigsaw puzzles. But mostly, they just knew that she was dead.

CHAPTER 7

By the time Kali had dropped off her Jeep at the station and joined Hara in his cruiser, it was just past nine o'clock in the morning. Ahead of them, a service road curved away from the main one and led toward a modern-looking structure surrounded by a low wall and tall entrance gates. She glanced up from the screen of the car's navigational system, then at Hara, who was driving.

"I think this is the place," she said, "just through those gates. The sign on the lawn up ahead says CMMR. There's some kind of elaborate logo that looks like a submarine with a shovel on the front of it."

Hara eased the car off the main road and drove slowly through a set of tall wrought-iron gates set into stone pillars that adjoined the wall around the building. A paved drive brought them to the side, where another sign identified a parking area for visitors.

They left the cruiser there and went inside, showing their badges to a security guard who was standing just inside the entrance. He pointed toward the reception desk in the wide foyer, and they stepped toward it across a wide expanse of white tiled floor. After identifying themselves as law enforcement to the man behind the desk, they were issued temporary visitor's passes.

As he clipped the white plastic visitor's badge to his pocket, Hara stepped away from the reception desk and looked around the light-filled space with open curiosity. Tall, narrow windows faced a front lawn, and the interior of the building was cool and serene. There was a large color relief map mounted on the main wall, and he walked over to examine it. The map showed a section of sea floor with raised areas identifying underwater mountains and ledges. Kali joined him, peering at the multicolored rills and depressions. As they stood together, studying the fascinating contours, a slender, middle-aged man wearing a rumpled cotton blazer with the sleeves rolled up to the elbows approached the desk area, striding up along a long hallway that led from the building's interior.

"Have you ever been scuba diving?" Hara asked Kali.

The man drew up beside Hara. He'd clearly overheard the question and answered before Kali had a chance to respond. "If you haven't, you should," he said. "The bottom of the sea is one of the most remarkable environments on our planet." He gestured briefly toward the map. "Filled with unsolved mysteries and undiscovered treasures. Every bit as puzzling and unexplored as space, yet most people think oceans are just giant bathtubs with darkness and mud at the bottom."

"And a lot of fish," said Hara.

"Sure," said the man. He grinned. "Plenty of other things, too. The vast majority of the ocean floor remains unexplored. And yet, most people seem to think funds should be directed at Mars, or back at the moon. A shocking lack of imagination, if you ask me. We want to know if there's life on other planets, but we don't seem to care about undiscovered life in our own backyard."

"I've heard that a lot of UFO sightings take place over water," said Hara. "Mysterious things rising from the sea, or diving beneath the surface and disappearing into it."

"Exactly," said the man enthusiastically.

From where she stood on the other side of Hara, Kali listened to the exchange. She looked down at her T-shirt, noticing a new coffee stain just above the hem and realizing too late that she must have dripped coffee onto it while breakfasting with Walter. She did her best to tuck the edge of the shirt into the top of her jeans at the point where the stain was visible.

The man glanced at her, then turned his attention back to Hara.

"Did you know that most estimates say that only about five percent of all the oceans covering Earth have been mapped?"

Hara frowned. "No. I suppose that's not a lot."

The man shrugged. "Well, not if you take into account that seventy percent of the planet's surface is covered by seas and oceans." Abruptly, he thrust out his hand. "I'm Dr. Davos O'Connor, the director of the research laboratory here at CMMR."

"So you pronounce it see-more?" asked Hara.

O'Connor nodded. "I was told there was a police officer requesting my presence, and I'm guessing that might be you." He pretended to look alarmed. "Has someone finally reported that their vintage Aston Martin has gone missing?"

Hara didn't return the smile. "Not that I'm aware of." He looked at Kali, as though unsure of whether he should continue to engage in conversation with O'Connor.

She shook her head, the look almost imperceptible. Unlike Hara, she didn't wear a uniform, and she was trying to decide if Davos O'Connor was ignoring her because he didn't know who she was, or because Hara's sharply pressed dark blue uniform commanded more respect than her jeans and casual shirt—or whether the fact that she was a woman had caused O'Connor to discount her entirely as a possible authority figure.

Hara stepped aside, deferring to Kali. "I'm Officer David Hara. This is Detective Kali Māhoe. It's her you'll need to speak to."

O'Connor swung toward her, startled. His eyes swept over her, taking in her appearance, lingering on her stained shirt. "Oh. You'll have to forgive me. I thought maybe you were here waiting for one of the grad students." He laughed, a short bray of a sound, then dipped his head in acknowledgment. "Please excuse me."

"Of course," she said, her voice mild. She was a

few inches taller than he was, and she sensed that he didn't like the fact that she was looking down at him. Once again, he extended his hand, though with considerably less enthusiasm. She briefly grasped it, trying not to recoil at the softness of his palm. She met his eyes. "Is there someplace where we can speak privately?"

He hesitated, looking at them questioningly. "Why, yes, I suppose so. If it's absolutely necessary."

"I assure you that it is," said Kali. "We'll follow you."

O'Connor shrugged, then turned without saying anything else as he steered them past the desk and into the long hall. A second security guard who stood on the other side of a turnstile gate nodded to them in acknowledgment. After a few feet, O'Connor turned into a second hallway that hadn't been visible from the entrance area of the building. He walked briskly down its length until he was nearly at the end, then thrust open a door that led into a cluttered office. The walls and floor were white, while a long wooden counter ran along one wall at about waist height.

Above the counter and on either side, crowded shelves were crammed with books, periodicals, and paper file folders. There were sea charts on another wall, and a large desk covered with more folders and what looked to Kali like rock samples. More rocks could be seen protruding from a large cardboard box resting on the floor in front of the desk, and an open laptop computer was balanced on a stack of books on one corner. Despite the overall impression of clutter, the space struck Kali as cold and clinical.

O'Connor ushered them inside and closed the door behind them. "So," he said, his voice betraying his interest, "what is it that I can do for you?"

Kali looked around. Other than a swivel chair behind the desk, there was no obvious place to sit. She turned and faced O'Connor directly.

"I'm here to ask you a few questions about one of your employees." She watched him carefully. "Maya Holmes."

He raised his eyebrows in surprise. "Really? Maya? Now, what on earth has she done to get the attention of the police?"

"Can you tell me the last time you saw her?" Kali continued, without answering his question.

"Well, let me see. She's been out collecting samples up off the northeast coast for a few days. Was she trespassing? We have permission, of course, being a respected research facility, to—"

"Was she alone?"

"Yes, she went on her own."

"When is the last time you actually spoke with her?" pressed Kali. She saw a shadow of annoyance register in O'Connor's eyes.

"Maybe . . . well, today is Tuesday, so I suppose it must have been Friday morning." He waited, clearly unsure of what Kali was driving at.

"As you've just said, today is Tuesday. Is it usual for your staff to work from outside of this facility, or to not check in with you after a weekend?" asked Kali. "I'm assuming there's a schedule or some sort of regular working hours."

"Well, yes, more or less—but when one of our team is out in the field and likely to be working over the weekend, I don't necessarily expect to see them on Monday."

"And on Friday, was she actually here, or did you speak to her on the phone?"

"She called me. From her cell phone. She was checking in."

"Would that be a work phone or a private phone?"

His brows drew together. "Private. We don't have separate work phones. Why?"

Hara listened as the exchange continued, his eyes darting from Kali to O'Connor.

"Exactly what time did she phone you?" Kali asked.

O'Connor shook his head. "The exact time? I don't know. Sometime in the morning."

"Check your phone, please."

He pressed his lips together, then reached into his pocket and pulled out his phone. Kali and Hara watched as he scrolled through his list of incoming calls.

"Looks like it was at 10:12 a.m.," he said. "We only spoke briefly. Here, see for yourself."

Kali took the phone and made a note of the number and time. "Did Miss Holmes sound distressed?" she asked, unblinking.

"No, I can't say that she did. Why? What's going on?"

"And how about recently? Has she acted oddly, or expressed any personal concerns?"

O'Connor frowned. "Look, Detective, I'm not the girl's father. She's a junior colleague, and not the kind of person who unloads her personal baggage while she's at work. Before this conversation goes any further, I'd like to know exactly what your questions are all about."

"Miss Holmes was found dead Monday morning. She was deliberately killed, and I am leading the investigation into the circumstances of her death."

O'Connor's mouth opened, then closed. He took a half step backward, bumping into an open box of rocks with one foot. Wordlessly, he turned and walked behind his desk, sinking into his chair. He looked blankly at the wall in front of him, then turned back to Kali and Hara.

"She was . . . she's dead? I don't understand. You mean . . ."

"You'll appreciate that it's very important that you tell us anything you can think of that may be useful. Do you have any knowledge, for instance, of another person, or persons—perhaps a colleague she didn't get along with—who may have wished to cause Miss Holmes harm? Was she at odds with anyone here at work?"

Hara had taken out his notebook and pen and stood, waiting for O'Connor to speak.

"No . . . no. Absolutely not. Maya is . . . was . . . very quiet and focused. Professional. She always seemed to get along well with everyone. But we have a very, very small team in this particular lab. I can't speak for any relationships she may have had beyond here."

"And you've not noticed any odd behavior?" Kali persisted. "Did she seem worried, or preoccupied with her life outside of work?"

O'Connor raised his hands slightly, the palms

turned up in a gesture of uncertainty. "I'm sorry. I wasn't a sounding board. We worked together, but she never confided in me. I don't recall her being worried about anything, but I doubt I'd be someone she'd ever consider sharing her personal concerns with."

"Really?" Kali looked at him, her head tilted slightly to one side. "We've been told by other sources that you were actually very close. According to what we've learned so far, you are the reason that Maya Holmes was working here. You were her course advisor in her university program, weren't you?"

From his chair, O'Connor smiled, but the expression was sad. "Yes, I was her advisor. And yes, I sought her out for this position and encouraged her to take it, and I stand by that decision. She was rather brilliant, and I knew she'd be an asset to our program. But our relationship was purely professional. I'm afraid you'll have to look elsewhere if you want to learn anything about her private life."

Hara shifted his feet, glancing at Kali. She nodded to him, and he turned to address O'Connor.

"Who were her friends here at work? The people she had lunch with, or took her breaks with?"

O'Connor thought for a moment, then shook his head. "I don't think she had any close friends here. I honestly can't recall seeing her socializing with anyone else. I mean, she was always personable, as I've just said, and I think everyone here appreciated her, but she'd been here for just over a year. I can't honestly say that I'm aware of her having formed any particular friendships." He looked at them, apologetic. "I really wish I could be of more help."

Kali thought about Charlie's comments that someone had been contemptuous of her fitness goals. "A source has confided in us that her intention to participate in the Ironman competition was met with some ridicule from a coworker."

O'Connor looked blank. "I'm sorry," he said. "I'm not aware of anything like that."

"Tell me more about her work," said Kali. "What were her responsibilities here?"

"Oh, yes. Of course." He looked at them as though measuring his next words. "I don't suppose you could tell me . . . what happened?"

"No, I can't," said Kali. "But you can show us her work space while you explain what exactly it was that she did on a day-to-day basis."

There was a flash of irritation on his face, but he nodded. "Certainly," he said. "Though I doubt this will be helpful."

"I'll decide that," said Kali.

CHAPTER 8

Rising from his chair, O'Connor walked past Kali and Hara to the door. He led them back out into the hallway, but instead of turning toward the reception area, he walked across the hall to a door with a sign showing the diagram of a staircase. He held it open and they walked through, waiting on the inner landing as he closed the door and headed down a cement staircase. They fell in behind him as he made his way down to a landing one level below his office. From here, they followed him along another hallway that ended at a set of double doors. There was the sound of machinery coming from within.

O'Connor lifted a key card from a lanyard around his neck and held it up against an electronic reader beside the door. A muted buzzing sound indicated the doors had unlocked, and he pushed them open and stepped inside. Kali and Hara were right behind him. They stopped short, taken aback by the difference between the level of activity in this area and the quiet halls on the floor above.

Kali looked around. A group of three people in lab coats were assembled around a low platform that held a long, narrow device that reminded her of a torpedo. Other than one man who glanced up and nodded in acknowledgment to O'Connor, no one else paid any real attention to their presence—they seemed preoccupied with tinkering with the object in front of them.

"Is that some kind of a missile?" asked Hara, his voice tinged with alarm.

"No," said O'Connor. "It's a very sensitive underwater sonar device equipped with precision sensors. It's shaped that way to be streamlined—to help it move smoothly through the water without resistance. This particular unit is one that's carried in a special apparatus beneath our research vessels. Other larger ROV units—remotely operated vehicles—are deployed from the ship's deck. We use most of them to help us identify likely areas to test for mineral deposits."

"And is this what Maya Holmes was working on?"

"Only on the periphery." O'Connor peered at Kali, then looked at Hara, as though weighing something. "I guess this is probably well outside the realm of police training, but do either of you have any exposure to robotic technology?"

Kali stared back at him. "Not this kind, no. But I think we can follow along, if that's what you're worried about." She watched as a scowl formed on his face.

"I'm sure you can," he said.

Judging by his tone, Kali sensed that he didn't think she was capable of finding her own way out of the building. She tried not to smile. "Did Miss Holmes have her own office?" she asked, redirecting the conversation.

"Not as such, no. Like most everyone here, she used one of the workstations over there, against the wall. Part of that long bench."

He made no move to walk toward the area he'd pointed out. Kali watched him, wondering if the news of Maya's death had distracted him to the point of being useless.

"Please show me exactly where," she said.

"Oh, of course." He moved to a section of the station at the very end of the counter. Behind the flat space that was used as a desk was a narrow strip of corkboard. There was a schedule pierced with a colorful pushpin, a small photograph of a tree-fringed lagoon, and several charts and graphs. There was no computer visible, and no discernible drawer or shelf beneath the surface that might have concealed one.

"Did Miss Holmes have a computer that was dedicated to her work?"

"Well, yes—but of course, it wasn't technically her property. All staff members are issued computers that are linked with our internal network."

"And do you know where the computer is?"

O'Connor shook his head. "I'm sure she had it with her. I guess . . . well, I know it isn't here, so maybe it's at her home?"

A woman with long blond hair streaked with gray was standing with the others near the sonar equipment. She watched as Kali and Hara looked through the things on Maya's desk space. As Kali lifted the paper charts to look beneath them, the woman walked over.

"Sorry to intrude," she said, looking nervously from O'Connor to Hara's uniform. "I just wondered if everything is okay."

"Everything's fine, Jody. You can go back to what you were doing," said O'Connor.

"It's just that I've been worried about Maya. Trying to get in touch with her, with no luck." She looked at Hara's uniform, the distress evident in her voice.

"As I said . . ." began O'Connor, but Kali held up her hand, interrupting him.

"Are you a friend of Maya Holmes?" she asked the other woman. She tried not to stare at the woman's face, which was creased with a deep scar that ran from the corner of her left eyebrow to the edge of her upper lip.

Jody nodded. "Yes. Sure. I'm Jody. Jody Phillips. We were supposed to go for a swim over the weekend. She was training for a race, and I was going to time her, but I never heard from her, and she hasn't returned my calls." Her eyes fixed on Hara's badge. "When I saw that you're a policeman, I just got more worried."

"I'm afraid there's bad news," said Kali. "Maybe we could step out into the hallway and chat for a few minutes?"

"Oh, no," said the woman, her voice dropping.

She swayed slightly, and Kali took her by the arm and led her to the door.

Hara reached forward, pulling out the desk chair from the counter. He followed Kali to the doorway and lifted the chair into the hallway, placing it against the wall while using one foot to keep the door propped open. Kali nodded to him, indicating that he should go back into the laboratory.

"Don't let O'Connor or anyone else disturb us," she said, her voice low. "Get a statement from him about his whereabouts from last Friday evening to Sunday afternoon, and find out who those other people are and get their contact information. We'll need statements from them as well."

Nodding, Hara stepped back inside. The door closed behind him.

The woman looked at the chair and sat down, her eyes filled with worry. As her gaze met Kali's, the detective was struck by the same sense of dread she had seen in countless other friends, family, and loved ones connected to the victims of violent crimes. They're all victims, she thought. A killer takes a life and damages the lives of all those left behind, leaving them trying to navigate their way through an aftermath of fear and despair and loss.

And then she had another thought: I know exactly how that feels.

Hara sat behind the wheel of his police cruiser, peering out the windshield at the traffic on the road ahead of him.

"What do you think about what Maya's friend said?" asked Kali.

"The woman with the scar who said she hadn't heard from her all weekend?" Hara frowned. "I think she was telling the truth."

"Yes. Me, too." She looked out the window, watching the lush green scenery slip by, marveling at how such an exquisite landscape could hide so much that was unpleasant. "Everything else she had to say tallies with what Charlie already told us. It's interesting to me that Maya had so few relationships, but I suppose that helps us narrow down possible suspects who had a personal connection to her."

"None of those other people in the lab had much to add," said Hara. "The two men are people who work in the engineering division, and were just there to look at that machine. We've got all their contact info and statements, but from what they said, they didn't seem to really know her. That seems weird—to work in the same space with the same people, but to not really know anything about them."

He looked over at Kali, who had wrapped her arms around her chest. He reached toward the dashboard, adjusting the air conditioner. "I guess the other thing is that I never realized how much time an officer spends interviewing people," he said. He glanced at her, his expression serious. "Especially a detective. Do you ever get tired of it?"

"No," she answered. "I think of it as working out a riddle or a puzzle. You know. One clue or piece at a time, or a few when you get lucky. You spread them all out in your mind, and then you look for the ones that fit together. Eventually a picture reveals itself, and you see the connections."

"Do you see any of those connections yet?"

"No. Not yet."

He was silent as he digested what Kali had said, then turned his head briefly toward her.

"My mother loves puzzles. Sometimes when I visit, I help her with whatever one she's working on. She has a whole system—first, she dumps all the pieces out onto a table she keeps on the back porch. Then she drags all the edge pieces out of the pile. Then she sorts those by color. She winds up with all these little islands of puzzle pieces divided up all over the place, and then she starts reaching for them, pulling them out and putting them together. Seeing what matches up and what doesn't."

Kali nodded. "It's just like that." She laughed, somewhat against her will. "Well, that, plus guns and knives and drugs and motives." She looked out of the window. "And bodies. Always, bodies."

CHAPTER 9

K ali sat up with a start, causing Hilo—who was fast asleep across her lower legs where she lay stretched out on the sofa—to tumble onto the floor. She could see Walter standing in the kitchen doorway, holding a casserole dish in one hand and a paper grocery bag in the other.

"I know you're getting pretty old, but bedtime before seven o'clock? And on the sofa, too. I'm not sure if that's something to worry about, or if it's just plain sad." He walked over to the table.

"Likely a little bit of both," Kali said in agreement, rubbing her eyes with the heel of one hand. She swung her feet to the floor. "I just haven't been sleeping much. To tell you the truth, I haven't been sleeping at all."

"Still dreaming about that girl?" He glanced at

her as he set down the casserole. "It's not like you to let a case get this far under your skin."

"I know. There's just something about it that feels wrong. Or more wrong, I guess, than the usual stuff we see."

She rose slowly and stretched, then sniffed the air and looked at the table. "What's in that dish?"

"Pork roast and sweet potatoes," he said. "Nina sent it over. She made extra for dinner." He pointed to the bag. "There's coconut cake, too. You're lucky it made it all the way over here, you know. Nina wants you to text her to confirm that it all reached you safely, and that I didn't just eat it in the car on the way over."

Hilo followed Kali as she walked to the table, wagging his tail hopefully. She peeled back the edge of the aluminum foil covering the glass baking dish and closed her eyes, breathing in the aroma. "That smells like heaven probably smells," she said. "Is there a special occasion?"

"I felt I owed you for ruining your romantic breakfast. Plus I told Nina there were some things I needed to go over with you, and she seemed relieved. The girls are on a sleepover, and Nina said something about a long bath and a romantic comedy film she's been wanting to watch, preferably without me sitting in the same room offering insightful, ongoing commentary."

Kali laughed. "So Nina gets to enjoy her own version of heaven tonight. As a thank-you to her for dinner, I'll keep you here for a while. I could use some help with the hale wa'a, if you don't mind carrying a ladder for me. All these storms have blown away some of the roof covering the canoe. It needs patching."

Walter's face showed that he was less than thrilled with the prospect. "I don't suppose your Icelandic friend . . ."

"No. This is family business."

"Okay," he said, punctuating the word with a deep sigh. "Anyway, I've got some more news for you." He watched her face closely. "You know we're still monitoring Chad Caesar's Ruler of the News podcast. No luck yet identifying who his inside source is, but he's still getting information he shouldn't have."

Kali did her best not to scowl, but failed completely in the attempt. "Chad." She made the word sound like a curse. "What sort of mischief is he up to now?"

Walter pulled out a chair and sat down. Hilo positioned himself beneath the table, arranging his long body to accommodate Walter's feet.

"Well," Walter said, "he's found out about this new case and how the girl was discovered hanging from the rainbow tree, so he's getting people all stirred up with the idea that there's been a lynching. One listener called in and responded that there's been a witch operating up in the mountains near where the body was found, and a few more people have called in to say they've heard or seen strange things up that way at night—flickering lights, wailing, that kind of thing."

Kali was intrigued. "Leaving aside the idea that Chad has access to restricted information—and that I'm not convinced Chief Pait isn't making sure it's being leaked to him on purpose—are these legitimate sources, or is Chad feeding these ideas to people on purpose and getting them to respond just to sensationalize his reports? I think his podcast sponsors pay him based on how many people tune in."

"Yeah, I thought of that, too."

Kali leaned back against the kitchen counter. Through the window above the sink, the light had shifted toward evening.

"Do you think I might be right about the possibility that Chief Pait is the source?" she asked.

"I don't know, and I know better than to say what I think. But he's a politician to the core, that's for certain."

"It's really kind of amazing how he can turn any horrific event or tragedy into a public relations opportunity," said Kali. "Where did he come from, anyway? I don't think he's from Hawai'i."

"Nope. Sacramento. But he's been here for about thirty years, and the rumor is he's now entertaining visions of a Hawai'i State Senate seat."

"Yeah, I heard something like that, too. Which explains his obsession with putting a spin on everything to make it seem as though nothing bad ever happens here."

There was a brief silence as each of them contemplated a multitude of instances from past cases when it had seemed that Police Chief Leo Pait had been more interested in maintaining the idyllic illusion of Hawai'i as a peaceful paradise instead of addressing its true needs and problems, which weren't much different from any other part of the country.

Walter moved in his chair, breaking the mood. He looked hopefully at the food he'd placed on the table. "Are you going to share this or not?"

Hilo whimpered from beneath the table. Kali considered the similarity between the expressions on Walter's face and the dog's.

"Depends," she said. "Didn't you already eat?"

He looked sheepish. "I left room for seconds," he said.

"Uh-huh. Well, are you going to give me the pleasure of dragging Chad down to the station for questioning?"

"Not yet. I think it could be more useful to let him continue reaching out to his fans and his general podcast community. You know, see if anyone has anything concrete to offer. In the meantime, you get to talk to his viewers—the one who reported the witch, and the people who say they've heard or seen things out of the ordinary. Probably nothing, but you know as well as I do that even the crazy stuff often has a seed of truth in it."

"Okay," she said. "I'll do that first thing in the morning. You have all the contact information for these people?"

"I do indeed." He glanced at the casserole again. "Better to enjoy this before it gets cold, you know."

She smiled and turned around, reaching toward the cabinet where her plates were stacked. "I suppose you're right," she said. "Just don't let the fact that I said so go to your head."

* * *

There was still enough light outside after Kali and Walter had finished washing the dishes and tidying the kitchen to assess the damage to the roof of the hale wa'a, so they crossed the lawn together, walking through the tall grass, enjoying the cool, early evening air and the break in the storms. Beside them, Hilo trotted along, sniffing at the ground.

The hale structure was relatively small. It was open on both ends, topped by a thick covering of palm fronds that had been affixed to a rectangular frame by lengths of thin rope. Within it was an unfinished canoe, resting upon two wooden saw horses and covered by a canvas tarpaulin.

They ducked through the opening on one end. Kali reached out and grasped one edge of the tarp, pulling it gently from the surface of the boat. The canoe's center had been only roughly defined, its core coarsely hewn.

"Mike loved working on this damned thing, didn't he?" Walter said, not really expecting an answer.

"Yeah. He sure did," said Kali. She reached out, picking at the crude, irregular tool marks. "It seems a shame to just leave it here like this, but I feel like I owe it to him to show it some respect."

Walter walked around its tip. "Would have been beautiful." He settled his intense gaze on her. "You know you don't have to keep it. I'm not sure it's healthy. It's a little too much like setting up a shrine. Sometimes you have to let the past fall asleep, and leave it alone."

She looked at him in surprise. "A shrine? That's not what I'm doing."

"Isn't it? When are you going to stop obsessing over what happened? He was killed in the line of duty. We both knew him really well, Kali. You have to accept that he died doing something that he believed in."

She looked around, then nodded deeply. "I know that. And I don't blame myself anymore—though you're right, I did for a long time." She stepped back from the canoe. "Those drugged-up human wastelands that shot him, they're to blame. They thought they were invincible, like they had super-powers. Them and their guns."

"Yes. That's one of the things about methamphetamines that's different, I think, from other drugs. It creates that kind of inflated sense of personal indomitability. We see it all the time—I think both of us have seen it far too often." He hesitated before he said anything else, but her composure reassured him. "We got most of them, Kali. We'll get the last guy, too. It's just a matter of time."

She nodded. "Sure we will. If he's even still in Hawai'i." She smiled at him. "Then maybe I'll find someone to help me finish carving this canoe."

"That would be a real tribute to Mike. I'll help you find a traditional canoe maker. Someone who will do it the way Mike would have done."

"When the time is right."

"Sure," he said. "When the time is right."

Kali pulled the tarp back over the canoe, and they stepped into the open. The tall grass of the sloping lawn reached up against the backs of Kali's bare legs. "Can you get the ladder from the shed? I think we have just enough light to lash those palm fronds back down and add a few new ones before the next storm rolls in. I've already cut a bunch and have them stacked over by the edge of the lanai."

"Sounds like a plan," he said. "You can drag those over here while I go and get the ladder."

Kali nodded, then jogged slowly toward the stack of palm branches she'd collected. Hilo galloped along beside her. As he headed toward the shed, Walter paused, watching the woman and the dog. He began to sing, his voice carrying through the air, reaching her, connecting to her. She heard it and smiled. Despite everything that had happened, she was reminded she wasn't alone in the world.

CHAPTER 10

It was late morning. The sun, momentarily un-hindered by the rain clouds that had hovered over the island for weeks, blasted the roof of the Jeep. Kali slumped in the driver's seat, drumming her fingertips on the steering wheel. The interview with the witness who'd claimed there was a witch in the forest had raised more questions than it answered. Despite the woman's wild claims that a band of witches was flying through the trees and prowling along the beaches each night, Kali felt certain there was a grain of truth in what she had relayed. The woman had seen and heard something; Kali's instincts told her that this much, at least, was true.

Heat waves refracted off the Jeep's metal hood, distorting the air visible through the windscreen.

Kali glanced out the open window of the driver's door and watched as the leaf tips on a flowering roadside bush moved slightly, stirred by a humid, invisible breeze. She sat there, lost in thought about the stories of sorcery she'd learned as a child from her grandmother, trying to recall the details, remembering how some of the tales had frightened her.

The stories had all been part of her education. Her grandmother, Pualani Pali, had been a respected author and historian who had also carried the title of kahuna, a role passed from grandparent to grandchild that had also been conferred to Kali when she was a young child. Learning the lore, legends, and healing traditions of the islands had been integral to the process of preparing her for her own future role as her family's wisdom keeper—a station she still felt completely unprepared for.

Her discussions with her grandmother about practices revolving around dark magic had both fascinated her and made her deeply uneasy. Few stories had directly referenced sorcery, which was rarely practiced openly, but Kali recalled learning how some wicked early Hawaiian priests had performed acts and delivered spells meant to transmit illness, pain, danger, or strife to others. Still other priests could be hired to deliver death to a chosen person through the act of concentrated prayer. The belief that a priest could literally pray another person's life away was one of the darker spells, and sometimes involved specially constructed prayer huts where dark energy could be gathered to fulfill this purpose.

The concept had intrigued her, but largely for the possibility of its counterpart: that it might be possible to pray someone to better circumstances, or happiness, or improvements in their health. As a child, she'd practiced this fervently, passing her silent blessings to those she met—strangers who seemed to be suffering from sadness, or injured birds and creatures she found among the thick brush along the path leading to the beach.

It was the sphere of other, darker applications that she found herself considering as she watched the sky grow menacing in the distance, portending yet another storm. The act of divination by burning had particularly troubled her. A priest known as a kahuna kuni might be contracted to hold a complicated ceremony that culminated with sacrificial burnings. She thought about Maya's charred feet. Historically, firewalking ceremonies had often been practiced to enable warriors or others to demonstrate their bravery and invincibility—to prove allegiance or faith to a leader or an ideal. But that didn't mean that someone hadn't chosen to twist the ceremony to accommodate his or her own perverse needs.

She sat up straight, struck suddenly by another memory. Other ancient rituals involving spell casting had often included a fetcher—a small effigy, often in the form of a carving, which housed a powerful spirit. The fetcher, also called a ki'i, was physical in nature, and was usually small enough to be carried. In many historic cases, the fetcher had been a bone harvested from the corpse of a loved one, or a powerful figure who had died. Nothing like a fetcher had been found in either the clearing beneath the rainbow tree or in the area where the firewalking had taken place, but Kali knew that if it was small or obscure enough, it was possible that the SOC crew might have missed it.

She dialed Walter's number.

"How'd the interview go?" he asked.

"Well enough. At first the witness—an older woman named Mandy—insisted that she's hearing the sounds of witches and torture every night, but we finally narrowed it down to a few specific nights. Unfortunately, she can't be certain that one of them was the night Maya was killed. Mandy lives on the edge of the park and hikes up along the mountain path quite often, sometimes every night. She said she saw some kind of fiery glow moving through the trees, and heard the sounds of screaming several nights in a row. In the morning, after the last time all of this happened, she went outside to discover that the rail along her lanai was covered with evil birds." Kali sighed. "What she described sounds like black-footed albatrosses to me."

Walter snorted. "Yeah, and I'll bet she was cleaning fish or squid on a table nearby. Those birds are pretty opportunistic. They can be aggressive when it comes to dinner."

"I asked her about that. She swears they just appeared, and she took it as an omen. Says she hasn't been back up on the path since. When she heard Chad blabbering on his podcast about a sacrificial murder up on the mountain, she says she put the pieces together and figured it was the screaming she heard, and that it all added up to a witch. She thinks the witch sent the birds to warn her away from the area."

"Very scientific," said Walter, his voice dry. "You know, it's nice to have you around to deal with these particular conversations."

"Because . . . ?"

"Because you can speak that language without rolling your eyes."

"Wow. You just admitted that you think I have a useful skill."

"Now I can hear you rolling your eyes."

"Yeah. Anyway, I didn't call you to trawl for compliments—and if you're being nice because you want something, that isn't going to work either. I've been thinking about what's been historically recorded about occultism in Hawai'i, and I'd like to go back up to the clearing to look around again."

"You think the SOC officers might have missed something?"

"It's possible, particularly if they didn't know what they were looking at." She told Walter about the idea that a fetcher might have been part of a more complex ceremony, and that with everything else occurring at the scene, there was the slim chance that it might have been dropped or lost the night that Maya had been killed.

"Hmm." Walter's voice sounded doubtful. "I don't know. You really think it's worth another trek up there?"

Kali laughed. "Don't worry, I'm not asking you to go."

"Well, you aren't going alone. We don't know what's going on, and it could be dangerous."

She thought about this, and reluctantly agreed he was right. Before she could reassure Walter that she'd be properly armed, he interrupted.

"Why don't you bring your boyfriend? You've said he likes to hike. And he's built like a body-guard."

She wasn't going to admit it to Walter, but the idea of Elvar coming along gave her a profound sense of relief.

"Again—he's not my boyfriend. And it's still a crime scene," she said.

"Well, I'll deputize him for the day."

"Don't be . . ."

"Ridiculous?" he said. "Far from it. When are you thinking of going up there?"

"The sooner the better. It's still early enough today to make it up and back with daylight. I'd like to talk to the ranger again, too. We're all concentrating on the spot where we know the girl was. But what if there's something bigger going on—some group actually practicing some kind of dark magic? There might be signs in other places that would help us figure out what's up."

"Okay. I suppose that makes sense."

An image of the jigsaw puzzle box in the girl's bedroom with the cover displaying the magical knife rose to mind, along with the stack of tarot cards on the bookshelf in the living room of Charlie and Maya's apartment. "If it does look like occultism, we need to determine if that's something Maya Holmes was involved in herself," she said. She didn't want to entertain the idea that the girl may have inadvertently been the instrument of her own murder, but it was too soon to rule it out.

CHAPTER 11

K ali drove home and made a call to Elvar, who confessed that he'd already had a conversation with Walter. He expressed immediate enthusiasm about taking a break from working at his forge to go on a hike, but Kali didn't know how much of this interest had been prompted by what Walter might have said. She decided it was best not to share the more gruesome details of the expedition with him and kept the conversation brief, explaining that she needed to return to a crime scene to have another look around. She advised him to pack a warm, waterproof jacket and a water bottle, and said she'd swing by in the Jeep.

There was no need. By the time she'd collected her own things and made sure that Hilo had plenty of food and water in case she was late or delayed getting back, Elvar had already walked over from his house. Hilo leapt up to greet him, resting his paws on Elvar's shoulders and swinging his tail back and forth.

"Does Hilo realize that he's been replaced today?" he joked as they left the house and climbed into the Jeep. "I feel rather honored."

She smiled, enjoying the cadence of his voice, and the slight accent that betrayed his heritage.

"Hilo's not exactly respectful of evidence," she admitted. "I'll be fired or transferred to a desert somewhere if my dog destroys a crime scene."

Elvar grew serious. "What is it that we're looking for?"

Kali frowned. "I'm not really sure," she admitted. "There's been a report of some odd activity taking place in a remote area of the forest, up toward the summit of a path where there are a couple of clearings." She looked at him, gauging his reaction. "A girl was found there a few days ago. She'd been murdered. We don't know if these recent reports of strange events might be connected."

He scratched his head. "I heard something about that. What should I keep a lookout for?"

"I wish I knew," she said. She grinned, reluctantly. "That would make everything a whole lot easier. But some things to watch for are places that might have been used very recently as a campfire, or anything—words, symbols—that might be carved into tree trunks or drawn on the surface of rocks. And stay on the lookout for small dolls or carvings of figures. They could be very small, maybe just an inch or two, and made from stone or wood, or even cloth."

He looked at her, curious. "You mean like a voo-doo doll?"

She nodded, glancing up from the road to look at him with registered surprise. "Yes, that's actually a pretty good description. Do you know very much about voodoo practices? Is there something like that in Iceland?"

He nodded. "Oh, yes," he said. "In the small village of Hólmavík, we have an entire museum devoted to necromancy. Some of it is quite dark, though tourists seem to find it amusing. And our history has been no kinder to witches than has yours. In the 1600s, people accused of witchcraft were burned at the stake, just like what happened in Salem, Massachusetts."

Kali was intrigued. "Let me guess. Women doling out herbal medicines and botanical cures were accused of casting spells?"

"No, not at all," Elvar said. "In fact, most of the accused witches were men. I believe only one woman was burned at the stake. But many women did engage in acts of sorcery that were kept very quiet. There was one practice that required collecting a human rib from a graveyard on a specific religious holiday in order to create a slithering, doll-like thing. It was called a tilberi, and the witch women would send it out at night on errands, where it would slither and sneak into the barns and fields of other people's farms in order to drain the milk from their cows."

She waited, both repulsed and interested.

"The witches also stole wool from sheep to make this tilberi doll, and they needed to use holy water that was gathered in secret from a church on consecutive Sundays. The witches would go into the church and carry the holy water away in their mouths so that they could spit it into the sheep's wool. The tilberi themselves were terrifying. They were shaped like long, elongated worms or snakes, and could stand up on end and run across the fields where the cows and goats were kept. After they harvested the milk, the tilberi would bring it back so that the witches could use the milk to make butter."

Kali slowed down to accommodate a truck that was turning off the road in front of her. She turned to Elvar. "I'd like to say that all sounds shocking, but it's really not that much worse than some of the things that were done here by so-called holy men who could be hired to get rid of your enemies, or bring harm and misfortune to people you just didn't like. Sort of like freelance mercenary priests."

"Yes. Just like everywhere—there are always people who will take advantage of others, or promise you something if you can pay the right price for it. I suppose most people think magic is about waving a fairy wand and making dreams come true. Birta used to wish for her own horse. I used to wish for a pair of magic skis that would make me fly above the ice and snow."

She looked at him, trying to imagine a younger Elvar who believed in the power of making wishes.

"Did you ever get your skis?"

"Yes, but not magic skis," he said. He smiled. "And Birta finally got a horse. She let me ride him, too."

"I guess," laughed Kali, "magic is a pretty big

topic. You have to start with what your definition of it is."

They drove along for a time in comfortable silence. Kali wondered what she would wish for if she suddenly found herself in possession of a magic wand, but couldn't come up with an answer that satisfied her.

As they pulled into the parking area near the trailhead, Elvar spoke. "When you are involved in a healing ceremony for someone who is ill, do you think it's the same as practicing magic?"

She cut the engine, and they sat there, looking through the windscreen toward the thick canopy of trees rising up the lower slopes of the mountain ahead of them.

"Some people say so," she said. "I think . . . well, I guess I believe there's some kind of energy out there that we can tap into if we can find the right frequency. Something that's not easy to define. Maybe it's not meant to be defined at all. Just believed in." She smiled and opened the door. "If you want the truth, every single day I'm alive— every minute that I grow older—the more I realize that I don't know anything at all."

Elvar opened his own door and climbed out of the Jeep, reaching into the back seat for his jacket. "I know exactly what you mean. Birta's always going on about the meaning of life, especially after she listens to one of her philosophy podcasts. I tell her that I think the meaning of life is to just be engaged enough with our own experience of existence to ask the question."

Kali locked the Jeep's doors, and they set off

along the path. They moved at a good pace, slowing as they reached the section of path just before the summit. The clearing looked different to her. It was later in the day than when she'd first been here, and the shadows fell in different lengths and patterns. And unlike the last time, there was no body swinging from the branch of the eucalyptus tree, no lingering smell of burned flesh or the sounds of conversation from a group of people who'd assembled to deal with the destruction left behind by a killer.

They spent three hours combing through the underbrush leading to the crime scene, as well as just beyond the designated perimeter of where the killing had occurred. They also searched among the stones on the fire path and the surrounding area up to the edge of the precipice, but they found nothing. As far as Kali could tell, no one had been there since the SOC team had finished its own exhaustive search. Discouraged, she sat down on a low rock, watching as Elvar zipped up the front of his jacket and turned to her.

"Do you still think something may have been overlooked?" he asked.

Kali lifted her hands, palms up. "I can't explain it," she said. "But I feel as though there's something here that I'm just not seeing."

"Maybe because it's too obvious?"

"Or maybe because it's actually something that belongs here, but is somehow out of place."

Elvar did a slow turn, peering into the trees and brush beyond the edge of the larger of the two clearings. "What happened here?" he asked.

The shadows underneath the trees seemed to grow murkier. Instead of offering shade, she felt that they had slipped over the surface to hide something . . . or keep it from being exposed.

"I don't know," she said. "But I'm going to find out."

Kali dropped off Elvar at the end of his driveway and continued along the road until she came to George's Island Market. The parking lot was crowded, and she wasn't surprised to see that the interior of the small store was filled with shoppers. George Tsui, the store's proprietor and cashier, looked up and waved when he saw her, then turned his attention back to the young couple who were waiting for their receipt.

As they moved away toward the door, Kali stepped toward the counter. She could see the dramatic headline of the most recent issue of one of the sensationalist tabloids that George favored. There was a poorly manipulated photograph of a two-headed shark leaping through a wave. The headline read: TWO-HEADED SHARK TERRORIZES LOS ANGELES BEACH.

George noticed the direction of her gaze. "Long swim from California, but that's a pretty big shark. You think we have anything to worry about here on Maui?"

"I don't," she said. "If anything, it'll head south to the warmer waters off the coast of Mexico, or maybe even go all the way down to South America. I think the beaches there are more crowded. Better source of food than a lonely swim all the way across the Pacific just to get to us."

"Unless it has a family, and they all travel together. Hawai'i is a very desirable location."

"Do you think sharks are susceptible to the tourist board's advertising campaigns?"

George looked at her, his expression serious. "Who can say? Those ads are pretty compelling. But pretty beaches or not, I know I won't be going swimming anytime soon."

"I'll let you know if I hear anything on the scanner," she said. "But in the meantime, I stopped by to ask you something."

His eyes grew alert.

"Police business?" he asked.

"Yes," she said, knowing that George was a keen observer, and that he overheard things in the store—things that had often proven to be extremely valuable information in past investigations. "This is about a witch. Or witches. Have you heard anything about someone practicing dark magic, maybe up in the forest around the state park?"

He looked around, making sure no customers were close enough to overhear their conversation.

"Yes, I heard about something going on," he said, nodding slowly. "But I didn't pay a whole lot of attention to it. You want me to ask some questions?"

"Nothing direct," she said. "Just let me know if you hear any chatter."

A man with a large shopping basket approached the counter, and Kali stepped back to give him space to unload his groceries.

She smiled at George. "I'll stop by in a couple of days," she said. "Or you can call me if you want to chat."

He nodded solemnly. "Will do. Meanwhile, don't forget about that shark. I think you should stay out of the water."

CHAPTER 12

Later, just as the pale moon had risen above the rain-soaked trees, Kali sat at her kitchen table with a stack of note paper, a pen, a drawing pad, and several magic markers spread out on the surface before her. Her phone was within reach, along with an empty coffee cup. She'd made a rough sketch that showed the rainbow eucalyptus tree and the path leading to the clearing where the firewalking had presumably taken place, and a winding, dotted line that led toward a circle where she'd scrawled the words parking lot.

Outside, the wind was picking up. She could hear the spatter of raindrops striking the window glass. The phone rang, startling her. She looked at the screen and was surprised to see that it was Stitches.

"Aloha," she said.

"Good evening," said Stitches. "I'm sorry to call you this late in the day, but I've just finished the remainder of the autopsy tests ordered on Maya Holmes. Time of death was between seven o'clock and nine o'clock on Saturday evening. You already know about the odd dust and sand, but I thought you'd also like to know as soon as possible that there is no trace of drugs, including methamphetamines or other substances, and no sign of sexual violation of any kind. Also, she was in very good health."

"Until she wasn't," said Kali. The dark statement sat there, filling up the space between them.

Finally, Stitches spoke. "I was able to find tiny pebble and sand fragments in the burn wounds on her feet, which is consistent with your theory of firewalking. There is dirt beneath her fingernails, but no skin. That is disappointing, as I'd hoped to find indication that she'd made contact with her killer, collecting a DNA sample of that person or persons so as to provide a lead. Instead, the fingernails are worn and frayed at the tips, and there are tiny bits of stone in the skin, supporting the idea that the fingertips were scraped on rocks."

There was the rumble of thunder outside, followed by a flash of lightning.

"Was that thunder?" asked Stitches. "The storm is moving in here as well. A lot of wind and drama."

"Yes. Rainy season has settled in, I guess."

"Perhaps it will be accompanied by cooler weather."

"Mudslides, more likely," said Kali.

"True."

For a moment, neither woman said anything more.

"Well, that's all I have to tell you. I wish it was more," said Stitches.

"Yes," said Kali. "So do I."

After the call had ended, Kali sat at the table, mulling over the vivid memory of the girl swinging from the branch. On impulse, she got up and went into the bedroom, running her finger along the book spines arrayed on the shelves along one wall. Her finger stopped when she came to a thick volume with a worn cover that read Lore and Legend of the Hawaiian Archipelago by Pualani Pali, PhD. The author was her grandmother, and the book— which had earned numerous accolades—was widely respected as a seminal work on Hawaiian history and legends.

She carried the book to the table and scanned the index, jotting down page numbers and notes on her pad. She was looking for stories connected to sorcery, and was surprised that there was so little that had been documented on that specific topic. Tales surrounding the rich mythology and ancient beliefs within the islands often had multiple versions, depending upon the sources that had supplied the information. She recalled her grandmother telling her how she'd discovered during her research and interviews that it wasn't uncommon to get a variety of widely differing accounts from people within the same family.

It only took Kali a few minutes to find what she was searching for. It was the story of Pahulu, a powerful sorceress who predated the arrival of the better-known Hawaiian goddess Pele, and whose dominion had spanned the islands of Moloka'i, Lāna'i, and some regions of Maui. Pahulu had not only become associated with nightmares, she also had a strange connection to trees. On her home island of Moloka'i, a forest of hundreds of trees sprang suddenly from the ground, and three of the trees had become possessed by a trio of Pahulu's heirs.

Her education into the legends of Hawai'i had taught Kali that the hierarchy of the island's many deities was convoluted, with stories that often contradicted one another. She knew, too, that even the darkest of magical practitioners was separated by only a fragile, shadowlike veil from more benevolent healers. As had so often proven the case in other parts of the world, practitioners of herb lore were likely to be wrongly associated with the most negative type of witchcraft. In Hawai'i, wise, altruistic healers known as kahuna-lā'au lapa'au were often compassionate priests who held and protected a vast personal knowledge of the medicinal and healing properties of a wide range of botanicals that could be found growing in the wild throughout the island chain.

But it wasn't the altruistic doctors that interested Kali right now. She was looking for tales of the tree-dwelling Kane-i-ka-huila-o-ka-lani, also known as Kane in the Lightning, and Maka-ku-koae, the god who could invoke madness and lunacy—male gods who often chose to manifest their acts through a female sorceress to fulfill their dreadful deeds. The panoply of evil schemers included the kahuna anaana, whose dark skills encompassed the ability to pray another person to death; the kahuna ho'ounauna, who could rob an individual of both their health and sanity while creating a debilitating illness or misfortune for them; and the kahuna kuni, who called upon the power of flames to predict and control the future. These were the malevolent magicians who seemed more likely to be tied to what had taken place in the high forest.

She read well into the night, and fell into a restless sleep, dreaming of a naked girl crying out from a dense thicket of trees. The words of the dream girl were indistinct, but their meaning was clear—she was crying for help, and calling for the sun to rise and show her the way home.

The morning crept toward noon. Before she drove to the station, Kali made a call to the forensics division to find out about progress on the trace on Maya's car to see if a route had been established, and if a more complete list of the calls on her phone had been compiled.

The car news was frustrating. The car hadn't been captured on any of the few traffic camera lights on Maui, making it difficult to determine the route the victim had followed on her way to the supermarket parking lot where the car had been left, or to establish whether it had been left there at some time on Friday or Saturday. No one working at the store during those times had noticed it. It had also been impossible to say whether anyone had been a passenger in the car. Prints from inside the vehicle had been identified as Maya's and Charlie's, and the only prints on the water bottle belonged to Maya.

A comprehensive phone call history to and from Maya's phone was still being compiled, but the calls from Jody over the weekend had been verified—as had the exchange between Maya's phone number and O'Connor's, which showed not one, but two calls on Friday. The first was from Maya to O'Connor in the morning, as he'd said, but the second call was from O'Connor to Maya in the afternoon . . . a call he'd failed to mention. Not, Kali reminded herself, that there was any reason to assume that Maya had been the person to make or receive either of the calls. If she had been taken at that point, and O'Connor was involved, her captor or captors might have used her phone to help O'Connor establish an alibi.

Kali tried to step beyond her dislike of O'Connor long enough to consider the other people she'd so far encountered. She'd gone over and over the statements that had been collected. No one had anything close to a rock-solid alibi. There was nothing to lock onto—except for the feeling that there was far more to the story than had so far been revealed, and that something sinister and cruel had crept out of the deep sea and along the sandy beaches and found its way up a winding forest path to a clearing where it had fully taken shape.

CHAPTER 13

It was just after lunch. The duty officer poked his head around the doorway, looking into the shared area where Kali, Walter, and Hara sat at their desks.

"You've got company, Detective Māhoe," he said. "A woman by the name of Jody Phillips says she wants to talk to you about the Maya Holmes case."

Kali looked up from her computer. She'd been scrolling through the details of the report submitted by Stitches, looking for anything that might give her a new direction to pursue, but there was nothing beyond what she'd already learned during the previous evening's call. She wondered what Jody might want to talk about that couldn't be covered over the phone, but was relieved she'd come to the station all the same. There was nearly always more to be gleaned from a person's body language than just from the words they chose to speak.

"Okay. Please bring her through to the waiting room. I'll be right out."

Walter looked up from his own computer screen, equally curious. "You want some company?"

Kali shook her head. "No, I'll handle it. If it's anything sensitive, she might feel more comfortable talking to another woman. Plus it wouldn't hurt to go over her statement again."

"You think she could be part of this?"

"So far, it seems like she might have been the victim's only friend. She doesn't have any more of an alibi than anyone else, so at this point I just hope she might know something. Even if it's something she doesn't think is connected."

He chewed on his tongue. "Okay. I'll be here if you change your mind. We've finally got the rest of the call traces. I'm going through them now with forensics."

She grabbed a notebook and a voice recorder, then made her way to the small room used for visitors. Jody was standing by the window. She had a hip bag strapped to the belt of her jeans, and she held a thick hardcover book in the crook of her left arm.

"Hi, Jody," said Kali. She smiled reassuringly, hoping her expression didn't betray her intense interest about the motivation for the visit. "Please—sit down. Would you like something to drink?"

"Oh, no . . . that's okay. I won't take up too much

of your time." Jody's eyes darted nervously around the small room, then focused on Kali. "I feel really weird coming here, but I wanted to talk to you without a lot of other people around."

"You mean people at the research center?"

Jody nodded. "Yes. Them for sure. And Charlie, too. I don't want to upset him more than he already is."

"What do you have to tell me that would upset him?" asked Kali. She moved toward two chairs that faced one another and sat down, gesturing for Jody to join her. The woman stepped hesitantly across the room, then sat down slowly, perched stiffly on the edge of the chair's worn cushion. She placed the book she'd been holding across her knees, and Kali could see the title: America Before—The Key to Earth's Lost Civilization.

"It's about Maya," Jody began slowly. "Well, kind of. First, I want to return this." She lifted the book slightly, punctuating her words. "I borrowed it from her, and I'm not sure what to do with it. I should give it to Charlie, but he's having such a hard time, and I don't want to make it worse by showing up at his door with some of Maya's belongings."

"Maybe you should stop by anyway. It might be good for him to have some company." She reached for the book, and Jody handed it to her. It was quite thick, and Kali assumed it had something to do with mining or geology. She looked at the author's name. It appeared vaguely familiar. "Graham Hancock," she said aloud. "Geologist? Marine scientist?"

Jody shook her head. "Neither, actually. He's an author and journalist with an interest in early civilizations who's posited some fascinating theories about some of the oldest structures on the planet. The Egyptian pyramids, the ruins of Göbekli Tepe in Turkey, and plenty of other places, including North America."

"Is he an archaeologist?"

Again, Jody shook her head. "He's not. And even though he's done more legitimate research than a lot of actual archaeologists working today, his ideas and well-supported theories are derided by the university-trained crowd because he's a journalist by profession without an advanced degree in the sciences—and because they didn't bother to do the legwork to come up with these theories before he did. So they ridicule him and dismiss his work, even though some of it has been proven." She looked disgusted. "It's just like in so many areas of academia. People love to scorn the work of those they feel to be educationally inferior, or even from people whom they consider to have come from the 'wrong' school—but the naysayers are always pretty quick to turn around and claim the ideas as their own once they've become indisputable. It makes me sick."

Kali looked down at the book again, studying the cover art. Jody reached over and tapped the book. "Anyway, that's a lot like what Maya was facing, and she enjoyed this book so much that I asked her if I could borrow it for a while."

"What do you mean it was like what Maya was facing?"

Jody hesitated, weighing her response. "Well, she only had a bachelor's degree, though she was working on her master's. A lot of the people on our research team are close to having doctorates, already have doctorates, or have multiple degrees. They were always condescending to her, but the truth is she had a brilliant mind that could leap past them in both thought and conversation. They didn't like that. Instead of listening to her or giving her the respect she deserved as a colleague, they were more inclined to rephrase her theories and present them as their own, especially at meetings that involved other departments at the lab." Jody let out a labored breath. "It was maddening. O'Connor was the worst. It was as though he felt that because she worked for him, he could claim her work as his own."

"What about you?" asked Kali. She passed the book back to Jody. "What is your education?"

Jody seemed embarrassed. "Engineering doctorate. I was the peculiar neighborhood kid who wanted to build spaceships and robotic sea serpents instead of playing with dolls."

"There's nothing weird about that. Too many girls think they have to conform to how culture has decided they should act, or what they should want to do with their lives. Good for you."

"Yeah, no argument here. But I still get the occasional patronizing look or flippant remark from some guy who wants to brag about how many car engines he rebuilt in high school." She smiled. "Maybe you know what I mean. I've never actually met a woman detective before."

Kali could see that Jody was relaxing.

"I nearly went into academia myself," Kali said. "I've also seen that sort of thing happen. My grandmother was a well-known historian who earned a PhD, but because of her gender and the time period when she was in school, she faced a lot of mockery from her male peers. And even from some of her professors. When her research gained a lot of positive attention—and her books were added to teaching curriculums at universities around the world—a lot of those cynics were pretty quick to jump into the spotlight to say how much they admired her, or even to claim that they'd been personally invaluable to her work."

"That's awful. It must have been infuriating."

"Maybe," said Kali, thinking back to the past. "She never complained about it. She was always gracious and forgiving."

"So was Maya, at least on the surface. But I think it bugged her. Even though she didn't have an advanced degree, she'd already received a lot of attention in her field. I'm sure that's why Dr. O'Connor wanted her to come here to Maui—so he could brag about how his team had all the brightest and best. But enough about that—the other reason I came here was to tell you that one of Maya's friends who was interning at the research lab—a guy named Trey—seems to have gone missing."

Kali's focus immediately sharpened. "So he's not actually a colleague?"

"No, he's technically a student working on his degree in robotics and artificial intelligence. In addition to her job, I think Maya had some private project she was working on in her spare time, and I think that Trey was helping her with it. But he's kind of squirrely—you know, undependable. Doesn't always show up when he says he will. Now it's been three days since he's been to the lab, and with everything that's happened . . . well, with him being Maya's friend and all, I thought maybe you might want to know about it."

Kali was on her feet. "No one's mentioned him as a friend. What's his full name? And do you know how close they were?"

"His name is Trey Carter, and they weren't really close at all. Maya was just trying to be nice to him, I think."

"Do you know anything about him, like an address or contact information?"

Jody looked uneasy. She reached up and touched her scar, then abruptly pulled her hand away. "He has a university e-mail address, but as far as a living address—well, I kind of suspect he might have been camping out in the lab. I remember Maya saying he'd had a falling-out with his roommate and didn't want to go back to the place they were sharing. He hasn't answered my e-mails. And I found a pillow and deflated air mattress in one of the storage rooms at the lab. I didn't say anything to anyone, but I've seen Trey going in and out of there, and just assumed those were his things." She looked down at the floor. "I don't want to get anyone into trouble. Trey's a nice enough guy. But . . ."

"But what?"

"I think he's into drugs." She looked at Kali, her

eyes pleading. "Honestly, I'm not trying to snitch. I just really want to know that he's okay. Especially since . . . well, you know."

"You did the right thing telling me, Jody. We'll see if we can find him. Let's go and make a report, and you can give me what information you have."

CHAPTER 14

Kali sat next to Walter in his patrol car, watching the stream of slow-moving traffic as it made its way along the Hana Highway. It appeared that every third car was a convertible with the top down.

"Where do you think all these convertibles come from?" asked Walter, peering intently at the passing cars. "Statistically, it seems impossible that the rental agencies have that many available."

"Improbable, not impossible," Kali said. She watched for a moment. "It also seems like there's a preponderance of red convertibles."

"Not my favorite color."

"Mine, either. Something aggressive about it." Kali was silent for a moment. "I just saw a study on the color of car least likely to be involved in a crash—the researchers said yellow came in at about twelve percent lower overall, followed closely by white cars, then beige. Maya's car was yellow."

Walter looked at her sideways from the driver's seat. "Are you going to tell me that drivers of yellow cars are less likely to be in a crash, but more likely to be found hanging from a tree branch?"

"I was not. I was thinking more along the lines of how cheerful yellow is, and how everything we've learned about Maya suggests a nice person. Liked animals, had a happy-colored car, was tidy and responsible, championed the environment, was dedicated to her work . . . I suppose I'm struggling to come up with any obvious reason that would make her the victim of such a particularly horrific crime."

There was a break in the line of cars moving past, and Walter eased into the near lane behind a delivery van with a large magnetic sign on the side that was advertising floral displays.

"Nice people often get pushed around, are bullied, or are persecuted by people who feel threatened by them," he said. "But you know all this. Also, people who seem nice aren't necessarily nice at all." He raised an eyebrow. "Seems like it's you always lecturing me about the yin-yang of the universe, or pointing out how the dynamics of good and evil—or light and dark, or whatever it is you call it—are always in flux."

"Striving for balance. Yeah, that's one of my favorite speeches, for sure." She laughed, the sound low and somehow unhappy. "I guess it's just that sometimes, being confronted with just the dark part of the equation gets to me."

"That's good," he said. "It's when it becomes ordinary and you start to grow immune that there's a problem." He waited before adding, "But I'm a little worried that you're letting this case get too far under your skin."

She shrugged. "Maybe. I don't know."

"Just don't lose perspective. Trust me. You get too close, you lose sight of the bigger picture."

She thought about this as they drove along, heading for the duplex that was listed in the university database as Trey Carter's current address, one he shared with fellow student Barry Wells. The building was an older duplex divided into two separate apartments, and Trey and Barry's was the top floor unit. As Walter pulled into the driveway and parked, Kali surveyed the surroundings. The building was shabby but not decrepit, with wood siding and a large wrap-around deck on the upper level. She could see a bicycle leaning against the upstairs rail, and laundry hanging over its edge. Sliding glass doors faced the street, and a wide staircase on one side led from the parking area to the top floor apartment.

As they approached the base of the stairs, they both saw movement in the small backyard. A tall boy with short blond hair and glasses looked up from where he was scraping a portable outdoor grill mounted on wheels. He glanced toward them as they appeared near the bottom of the stairs, his hand reaching to push his glasses up. The gesture left a small smudge of blackened soot on the bridge of his nose.

"Aloha," called Kali. "Are you Barry Wells?"

He nodded, looking with open curiosity at Walter's uniform. "Whatever it is," he said, his voice wry, "I didn't do it, I swear."

Walter grunted. "Yeah, I've heard that before."

Kali smiled. "We're actually looking for your roommate, Trey Carter. Have you by any chance seen him?"

"No, and I don't have any reason to expect that I will," said Barry. "Unless he plans to show up with his share of the rent—which, for the record, he owes me for the past three months."

"We were hoping you might have some information on where to find him," Walter said. "He's been reported missing. He hasn't shown up at his job for several days."

Barry made a small, dismissive sound. "That's hardly newsworthy. Most likely you'll find him behind a building somewhere, stoned out of his mind."

"Oh?" said Kali. "Care to expand on that a bit?"

Barry put down the tool he was holding and placed it on the edge of the grill. Kali and Walter could see that the steel wool on the end of the tool's handle was frayed and peeling away from the flat piece of plastic to which it had once been securely adhered.

"Well, okay," said Barry. He walked over to the steps and sat down on the edge of one, looking at them. "Trey's a tweaker. At least, I guess that's the name for it. He got mixed up in some stuff at school. Some people fooling around with meth. Crystal meth, you know? It really messed him up. Can't say I'm surprised he hasn't been coming in to work. Just a matter of time before he gets banned from campus and has his internship canceled, if you ask me."

"And you have no idea where he might be staying?" asked Kali, watching him closely.

"Zero idea, zero interest," said Barry, his voice flat. "And he'd better not come back here."

"Has he removed his belongings?"

Barry looked away for a second, then turned to them and shrugged. "In a manner of speaking, I suppose. He came back here whacked out of his head and started busting the place up. So I kicked him out. And then I took all his stuff and tossed it over the deck rail down into the parking area in front of the house. Not that he had much to throw. The place came furnished, and the television and speakers are mine. He had a few books and some clothes, and some personal stuff." His expression was defiant. "I told him not to come back, and he hasn't."

"Sounds like a classic breakup," said Walter. "What does he drive?"

"He sold his car a few months ago. It wasn't much of anything—an old beater. Since then he's been getting around on his bicycle," said Barry. "That's how he left—all his things stuffed into his backpack."

"What color was it? Anything special about it?" asked Walter.

"Nah—not really. It was an older ten-speed. Silver, but the paint was pretty dinged up. It had some rust on it, but it seemed to get him where he needed to go."

"What about the people he was hanging around? Do you know who was supplying him with drugs?"

"I don't know a whole lot about that. Not that you're interested, but I had a family member who got hooked on pain pills, and I just don't have any room for that kind of thing in my life anymore. I know he never brought anyone here. Not even any girls. Trey and I weren't the kind of friends who talked to one another about our lives or anything like that. At the beginning of the fall semester, I posted that I was looking for a roommate, and he was the first person who answered the ad who had an actual serious-sounding job. And at the time, if he was using drugs, he must not have been doing it very often, because I didn't pick up on it at all. He was pretty quiet, gave me a couple of months' rent in advance, and ate most of his meals somewhere else. Pretty low-key."

"Was there a clear point when you began to notice his behavior changing?" asked Kali.

Barry wrinkled his nose, thinking about her question. "I guess I'd say he was acting a little weird by the time the holidays rolled around. I thought maybe it was some kind of personal thing that had him out of sorts. You know, like he wanted to go home to be with family but couldn't afford it. He didn't volunteer anything, and I didn't ask. Like I said, we didn't really know each other very well, and I didn't feel like it was any of my business."

"And his conduct got worse after that?"

Barry scowled. "I'll say. He'd bang doors and swear and shout for no apparent reason. Not at me, not directly. More like he was yelling at himself. And he started to get messy. He'd bring takeout home, and leave food and trash all over the place. Barbecue sauce all over the sofa and carpet that I had to clean up. Filthy bathroom. That kind of stuff. And," he went on, leaning in, "I can't prove he did this, or I would have reported it, but some cash disappeared from my desk drawer."

"How much?" asked Walter.

"Two hundred bucks. My mom sent me a big birthday check. I'd just cashed it and stashed some of it in my desk, underneath some school papers. I went straight to Trey about it as soon as I saw him, but he denied taking it. That was it as far as I was concerned. That's when I kicked him out."

"And you're absolutely positive you don't know anything at all about the people he was buying drugs from?" asked Kali.

Barry looked thoughtful. "Well, I never saw any of them, or like an actual transaction, but I guess I got the feeling that they were local, or maybe even other students." He shrugged again. "There was one time, not long before he flipped out, that I said something about how he needed to clean up his life and quit the drug thing, or his life was going to be hard. He got all bent out of shape, and asked me what I knew about things being hard—that he'd always been one step away from losing everything. He didn't seem to think he had any responsibility about that."

"You're certain there's nothing belonging to him that got left behind?" asked Kali.

Barry shook his head. "No. Like I said, he didn't

have much to start with." He gestured toward the
door at the top of the deck. "Feel free to look
around if you like. His room is the one with
nothing in it except a bed and a floor lamp."

Kali left Walter to finish up with any questions
he had, and walked up the stairs to the upper
apartment. The sliding doors were open, and she
stepped through into a single main space where a
short peninsula extended from wall cabinets that
separated the kitchen space from a living room.
That side of the space was fitted with a worn beige
sectional sofa and a wall-mounted television. There
was a low coffee table with books stacked on its
surface. A short hall led between the kitchen and
living room area to the door of a single bathroom.
The door was open, and she could see a combination bathtub-shower on the back wall. A shower
curtain covered with a sailboat pattern hung from
a rod. The curtain was pulled back all the way,
exposing white wall tiles separated by gray grout.

Just before the bathroom, bedrooms opened off
either side of the hall. One of the two rooms was
clearly well lived-in. She could see clothes strewn
across a rumpled bed, and a long desk against one
wall with a lamp on one side. The closet door was
open, revealing a row of shirts and a stack of shoes
on the floor. The wall beside the bed had a chest
of drawers, and a jumble of personal items on its
surface.

Kali turned toward the second bedroom. It was
identically furnished, but barren of any belongings. The bed had been stripped, and there were
no personal items or clothing in sight. She went

into the room and pulled out the dresser drawers and the single drawer in the desk, but they were empty. She pulled the dresser and nightstand away from the wall, then checked beneath them and under the bed. She pulled the mattress up on its side to look beneath it, but found nothing.

In the closet, a row of empty plastic hangers hung from a metal bar. Several of them had fallen to the floor, as though the hangers had been discarded when whatever clothing they had once held had been pulled off. There were a few coins lying on the carpet on the closet floor, and a small piece of paper. She picked it up, curious. It was a store receipt for a milkshake, burger, and fries from a local fast food restaurant. On the back, the words Wela Wela Cave had been scrawled, followed by the words Call first. There was no phone number.

Kali looked around the room once more, but could find nothing else that might be linked to its former occupant. She pulled a plastic evidence bag from her back pocket and dropped the receipt into it. Holding the bag, she walked back down the stairs to where Barry was still seated. He stood up as she approached, looking at her expectantly.

"Well?" he asked. "I don't suppose you found my missing cash?"

"No," she said. "Sorry about that." She glanced at the receipt, then held it out so he could see it. "Is this yours?"

He took it and looked carefully at the name of the restaurant, then shook his head, mildly disgusted. "Definitely not mine," he said, handing it back to her without turning it over. "I never eat the crap from those places. It's all filled with chemicals and made out of animals that died some horrible death in a factory warehouse."

"What about Trey? Does he eat at this kind of place?" Kali asked.

"Yeah, all the time. Why?"

"Do you know what the Wela Wela Cave is, or where it's located?"

He looked confused. "The what cave?"

"Wela Wela," she repeated.

"Sorry, never heard of it. Some kind of halfway house for druggies?"

"I don't know." She looked at him. Her instincts said he was telling her the truth, and she nodded to Walter, satisfied.

He straightened up, looking down at Barry. "Guess we'll let you get back to your grill scraping," he said. "But make sure you let us know if you hear anything from Trey, or about him. This is officially a missing persons case."

Barry stood up and nodded. "Sure," he said. "Sorry I can't be more helpful, but I'm happy to do whatever. As long as I don't have to take him back in."

"You don't," said Kali. She handed him her card. "It's best if you just give me a call. I'll deal with it. I'm pretty used to drug addicts."

As she and Walter walked back to the car, Walter turned to her. "I think I know that place. The Hot Hot Cave, right?"

"That's what wela means. Hot."

"Yeah. I'm pretty sure it's a fairly new strip club on O'ahu."

She looked at him in surprise. "Something you want to bribe me from not telling your wife?"

He grunted. "Hardly. I'll check with the Vice division to see if they've got it under surveillance, or if they've heard of any possible drug trafficking."

Kali felt herself tense up. "Okay. In the meantime, I'll check to see if any of the shelters have taken in anyone matching Trey Carter's description. Probably a good idea to check the homeless areas, too. I doubt this kid went all the way to O'ahu just to get a fix."

CHAPTER 15

By the next morning, no one that fit the description of Trey Carter had been seen at any of Maui's shelters, nor was there any record of him having been arrested, admitted to a hospital or clinic, or discovered dead or incapacitated.

Armed with a photograph of Trey taken from his driver's license, Kali left her house early. She drove toward the larger homeless encampments near the southeast and eastern central beaches, working outward in an ever-widening radius from the area closest to the lab. By noon, her inquiries had met with nothing more than shrugs of disinterest, occasional hostility, and multiple requests for money.

Dressed in her habitual jeans and a particularly worn T-shirt splashed with bleach stains, which she'd chosen in the hope of not being immedi-

ately identifiable as a police officer, she'd walked
among the micro units that had recently been
erected by a community project, designed to provide a greater degree of shelter than the makeshift
blanket tents and large boxes that served as the majority of temporary homes among the displaced. By
one-thirty, she estimated she'd talked to several hundred people, and she was both tired and hungry.

Heightened by a sense of frustration, she felt
her mood take a dark turn. She stood on the edge
of the coastal road, gazing out across the sea of
tents, wondering about the multitude of paths that
had led these particular people to be here, now, in
this place, without any apparent options. She knew
that there were at least as many stories as there
were people, and that many of those she'd spoken
with today, or could see now as she looked at the
encampment, had found themselves in an esca-
lating downward spiral of financial hardship or
mental health issues, or had been fleeing from
something even less palatable than living in the
open without a permanent address. Whatever the
reason, the sight of the bedlam made her uncom-
fortably aware of how easily circumstances could
change.

She shook her head to clear it. Turning away
from the water, she walked through the groups of
people sitting in the shade of the palms or beneath the many awnings that had been created
from blankets and tarpaulins, and found her way
back to the place where she'd left her Jeep. She
wanted some privacy while she checked in with
Walter.

She pulled her phone from her pocket and dialed his number. He answered on the second ring.

"Please tell me you've got some good news," he said. "Or that you're bringing me a fish sandwich."

"No, sorry. Neither one. And you need to stop obsessing about food. I'm just touching base. I haven't had any luck—seems like no one's seen this kid . . . or if they have, they aren't saying."

"Well, so far today at least, his body hasn't shown up. Of course, it's still pretty early."

"You're such an optimist."

There was a moment of foreboding silence before Walter responded. "I have to say, Kali, that this kid's disappearance so close to the girl's murder suggests that A, he was involved or knows something, or B, that he's also become a victim. The link of them both working at the lab and being on friendly terms with one another is too much of a coincidence."

"I agree—but I'm leaning toward him hiding out because he knows about Maya and is scared. Something tells me he's still alive and breathing."

"That's because you want him to be."

"Maybe," she said, her voice trailing off. "Anyway, I'm going to make one more pass through this area and then head back to the station. If he's hiding, it's because he's got information. What's Hara doing later today? Any chance I can borrow him to help me this afternoon?"

"I've got him on traffic right now. And don't knock yourself out. Someone will have seen Trey Carter. We've got his photo going out on the news and on social media today." He hesitated. "But if you do find him, and he doesn't volunteer to come in, bring him in anyway. Let me know if he looks like trouble."

She ended the call and sat in the Jeep, staring out at the road, until Walter's mention of a fish sandwich and her own growing hunger got the better of her. She drove back along the coast, stopping at a parking lot where a number of food trucks were gathered. She bought herself a banana and mango smoothie and went back to sit in the Jeep, going over in her mind all of the places where someone without a car might be camped within reasonable distance of fresh water. If Trey was trying to score drugs, he'd most likely be in one of the larger encampments. If, on the other hand, he was trying to avoid being found, he'd likely choose a more remote location with fewer people around.

There was a map in her glove box, and she marked the location of the research lab. There was a stretch of beach about three miles from there, and Kali knew that the area was less frequented by tourists because of the steepness of the access path and the amount of lava rock protruding from the sand. There were cleared stretches, however, and she'd seen people camping there in the past. The area that seemed most attractive was on the opposite side of the road from the sea, where thick vegetation gave way to several small meadows a short distance off the main path. More importantly, it was within walking distance of a natural spring. The area wasn't regularly patrolled, and though camping wasn't allowed, that fact hadn't stopped it from being occasionally used.

Kali drove there and parked off the road where

the Jeep wouldn't be immediately obvious to anyone in the wooded area. She snapped the holster
for her stun gun onto her belt, and made her way
along the moist ground of the footpath, which
climbed gradually toward a line of low hills. The
first clearing was empty, but the amount of litter
on the ground indicated that others had recently
been there.

She stayed on the main path, which began to
narrow as it climbed. About sixty yards in, she
caught a glimpse of something artificially blue
peeking through the underbrush to her left. She
could tell from the faint sound of moving water
and the scent of damp earth that the spring head
wasn't far away. As the path made a wide turn, taking a course that ran along the base of the slope,
she saw a deep glade where a small, beat-up blue
tent had been erected toward the back of a grassy
patch of ground. The front end of a silver bicycle
was visible, leaning on a tree behind the tent.

There was no reaction to her approach, and no
one in sight. She moved slowly toward the tent for
a better view, and could see the edge of a small
plastic cooler set beside the entrance. The tent's
front flap was pulled back, and two feet protruded
from the interior. The feet were large, bony, and
bare. She noted that they were rough and cal-
loused, with ragged nails. They looked to her like
a man's feet. One foot twitched as she drew closer,
flicking away a buzzing insect. Whomever the foot
belonged to appeared to be conscious.

Kali stopped where she was and called out.
"Anybody home? Maui Police Department here."

She placed one hand on her belt, not knowing what to expect.

In response to her voice, both feet jerked in surprise, then withdrew as the person inside prepared to crawl out. A second later, a man's head appeared. Kali mentally compared it to the photograph she'd been showing all morning. It was definitely the same face, but she was startled by how much older it appeared than the twenty-three-year-old missing man's photo.

"Trey Carter?" she asked, despite immediately recognizing him. "My name is Detective Kali Māhoe. I need to speak with you. Please come all the way out of the tent. Slowly. Let me see your hands."

The man's face fell. Reluctantly, he extracted himself completely from the inside of the tent and stood in front of her, his bare arms hanging by his sides. He wore nothing but a pair of baggy swim shorts, which exposed his bony ribcage and spindly arms and legs. Kali saw that despite his shaved head and minimalist clothing, he looked somehow unkempt and disheveled.

"What do you want?" he asked. He sounded scared.

"You've been reported missing, Mr. Carter."

"Missing? I'm right here."

"Yes, I can see that. However, you haven't shown up for work for over three days, and a missing persons report has been filed."

Trey lifted his arms and wrapped them around his torso in a protective gesture. She saw him rocking back and forth, recognizing the arm wrapping and repetitive movement as the familiar self-comforting

behaviors often exhibited by habitual methamphetamine users.

"Who made the report?" he asked.

"I'm afraid I'm not at liberty to say. Right now, I
need you to gather your belongings and come
with me. There are some questions that need to be
answered, and this isn't the place for that."

He looked at her, sizing her up. "And if I don't
want to come?"

She tapped her stun gun, not bothering to
point out that his physical condition made him
less of a threat than he might be imagining. He
followed the movement with his eyes, recognizing
the stun device.

"We can do this the aloha way, or we can do it
the other way," she said calmly. "Your choice."

He weighed the options, but only briefly. His
shoulders drooped. "Am I under arrest?"

"No, you're not. But I should tell you that one
of your colleagues has been found dead, and you
are a person of interest."

His eyes widened, and he shook his head, as if
maybe he hadn't heard her correctly. He stopped
rocking and stepped forward slightly, his body
tense. "What are you talking about?"

"Maya Holmes has been discovered dead."

His pale face turned gray. Kali had expected
shock or distress, but not this look. This look said
that the news was bad, but it wasn't unexpected.

CHAPTER 16

The air conditioner mounted to the wall made a rattling sound. Kali, seated next to Walter, glanced at it briefly, then stared across the metal table of the police station's interview room, where Trey Carter sat. So far the dialogue had yielded nothing in the way of useful information, other than a confirmation that Trey was heavily involved in the use of methamphetamines. He was steadfastly vague about his sources, claiming that his drug purchases were motivated purely by need and opportunity and never involved the same dealers.

"People are coming and going everywhere on this island," he said, shifting nervously in his seat. "You can't expect me to know everyone's name. And it's not like the same people are always out there selling, you know?"

"A smart guy like you would recognize photos, though, wouldn't you?" Beneath Walter's look of skepticism was a layer of disgust at Trey's uncreative lie.

Kali tried to keep her impatience in check. "According to your former roommate, your drug use has escalated over the past few months. Which means you're buying more, which means you're likely relying on a familiar source or sources. It's time for you to share some names."

"I swear," said Trey, growing more agitated, "I don't know any names. And even if I did, I'd be crazy to tell the police."

"Was Maya Holmes using drugs?" asked Walter. "Did she get them from you, or supply them to you?"

Trey shook his head. "No way. Maya was trying to get me to stop. She was pretty serious about it, so I can't imagine she'd get involved herself. She was way into healthy things, like working out and eating the right kinds of foods and taking vitamins. She didn't even drink, not even beer." He looked off into the distance, then down at the table where his hands rested, his fingers entwined. He clenched them together, the gesture brief. Then he looked up at Kali and Walter. "She was really, like, pretty awesome," he said in a soft voice.

"You didn't seem too surprised to hear that she'd been killed." Kali was direct, watching him closely as he twisted again in his seat.

He lifted his shoulders slightly, then dropped them. "That's the thing about people who are always trying to help. Other people might see them as nosy."

"You mean the meth dealers saw her as a threat?" asked Walter.

Trey squirmed, uncomfortable. "I don't know what to tell you. Maybe she said some things that other people overheard and didn't like. Who knows? Word gets around, right?"

"You need to be a little more specific," said Kali. "Do you mean people at the laboratory?"

"No," said Trey. "I mean just in general. Like, we'd go for a walk and she'd be talking about how exercise was a better thing to focus on, that you could even get high if you worked out hard enough." His nervousness grew. "Those science people at the lab—they were all pretty self-involved, you know? Thinking about their careers, and getting book deals, and being on television as experts. Lots of big egos there. Maya was different, even though she was smarter than all of them."

Kali felt herself losing her patience. She looked away from the man across the table, staring at the gray cement wall behind his head. She saw images there: people running, police officers crouching, three young men with handguns, a lone figure being propelled backward as blood sprayed from his neck. In her mind, she heard things, too—the sound of shouting, of gunfire, of herself running onto the scene too late to be of any help to Mike . . . too late to do anything but hold him as his life slipped away.

There was another image, too. This one was of another young person whose life was being destroyed by drugs: Makena Shirai, Mike's daughter, who had been unable to separate her dependence on drugs from their connection to her father's death. Kali took a deep breath, then another. When she turned back to Trey, she focused on him as an individual—a troubled kid who had no real idea of the kind of cold and violent world he'd allowed himself to be drawn into.

Walter's phone beeped. He glanced at the screen and passed the phone to Kali. She read the text from Hara: Phone records show girl received call from Trey Carter number morning of estimated death.

Kali looked back at Trey. "When is the last time you spoke with Maya Holmes, Mr. Carter?"

Again, Trey shrugged. "A couple of days ago? I'm not sure," he said.

"Think harder," said Walter, his voice devoid of humor.

Kali stared at him, and she felt him flinch beneath the intensity of her gaze. "Did you take her to the Wela Wela Cave?" she asked.

He jerked in his seat. He looked at her with widened eyes. "How do you know about that place?"

"Wrong answer," she said. "You tell me about how you know about it."

"It's just, you know . . ." he stammered. "I've never been there. It's on O'ahu. Someone told me about it."

"Who told you, and what did they say?" asked Walter.

"That it was a place to go if you wanted to score really high-grade crystal."

"Who told you that?" Walter persisted.

"I can't remember," said Trey. He stared at the table. "I think . . . I think it was someone on the street that I bought some stuff from. I said I was seriously considering leaving Maui and going to O'ahu to look for work. This guy I was buying from said if I went there, to check this place out."

"And that you should call first?" asked Kali.

"Yeah," he said. "I was supposed to call the main number, and then when someone answered, say I belonged to the Geology Club."

"What's that?" asked Walter.

"You know—crystal, rock, geology. It was kind of a password. If I said that, I'd be connected to someone else."

"Did you ever call?" asked Kali.

"No, why would I? I'm here, not there. I was going to check it out if I actually moved, but so far I haven't found a way to do that."

"If you're short of money, why aren't you going in to work?"

"Work?" Trey laughed. "Have you ever been an intern? I don't get paid. It's just for my résumé, to help get a job in the future. I was going to get paid by Maya, maybe, if her plans worked out."

Kali tried not to show her surprise.

"Her plans to branch out with her own research?" she asked, taking a wild stab.

"No," said Trey. "I don't know anything about that. I mean her plans for the future. She said she was working on something, and if it came together there might be some way I could help." As he looked at them, Kali could see there was genuine sadness in his eyes. "She promised. And Maya was one of those people who always keep their promises."

*   *   *

Kali leafed through her interview notes. Trey Carter had been taken to a local shelter, but she knew it was unlikely he'd be there by morning. She thought about Mike's daughter, Makena. Kali had taken her to more than one shelter, as well as to plenty of counseling sessions in the past, and nothing had ever made the slightest bit of difference. Trying to help a person who didn't want help, she'd concluded, was roughly the same as trying to force a truck that was ten feet wide through a tunnel that was only six just because you really wanted it to fit; the tunnel was highly unlikely to accommodate you just because you thought it should.

She read through the statement made by Davos O'Connor, looking for something that seemed out of place beyond the unreported phone call. There was no mention at all of Trey Carter, or of him having been a friend of Maya's. The question of drug use among all the members of the research team hadn't been addressed, and Kali felt that the new information they'd gathered warranted another conversation with O'Connor and the others at CMMR who had worked with Maya. O'Connor had had ample time to let the police know about the afternoon phone call that he'd not mentioned during the initial interview at the lab. Kali reached for her phone, intending to call the office at CMMR to set up a time to come by, then reconsidered. This time, she'd drop in unannounced.

CHAPTER 17

Kali stood in front of the reception desk at CMMR, waiting for the young clerk behind the desk to issue her a temporary visitor's badge. She had come on her own. She adjusted the jacket she'd worn and tugged at the collar of the blouse beneath it. She wasn't in any mood to endure O'Connor's barely concealed sneers at random coffee stains on T-shirts today.

The same young man who had been at the desk when Kali had come with Hara had recognized her. When she explained why she was there, he seemed jumpy about letting her into the interior space beyond the entrance lobby without an official escort. She made it clear that obstructing a police investigation was not in the best interests of the clerk or anyone else connected to the facility, and was finally ushered through in the company of the lobby area security guard without further argument.

As she passed the desk clerk on her way through the security gate, she saw him fumble with the keypad on the desk phone. She didn't bother to wait to hear what he had to say to whomever he was calling.

The guard noticed, too. "Don't take it personally," he said. "That guy is wound so tight I keep expecting his head to pop off and hit the ceiling."

"Any particular reason you're aware of?" she asked.

"No—he's been that way since I've been here, which has only been a few weeks. Weird place. Always too quiet."

She understood what he meant. The halls, as during her first visit, were completely empty. There was no ambient music softening the atmosphere, and the effect was vaguely unsettling. Retracing her steps to the door of O'Connor's office, she wasn't surprised to find that he wasn't at his desk. As she made her way beside the security guard along the tiled hall, she heard the clatter of footsteps as the clerk hurried to catch up with them.

"I've just checked," he said. "Dr. O'Connor isn't available right now, so if you'd like to schedule . . ." She ignored him, opening the stairwell door and stepping onto the landing.

"It's all under control," the guard said to the clerk, who stood looking at them with a frown. The clerk retreated, his worried expression clearly signaling that he expected Kali's expedition to cost him his job before the end of the day.

The guard followed her down the steps into the windowless space of the floor below. She walked along the lower corridor until she reached the laboratory where Maya had worked. Kali turned to the guard.

"Have you ever caught a whiff of anyone here being involved in drugs—or anything to do with the occult?"

He looked surprised. "Nothing like that," he said. "But as I mentioned, I haven't been here that long. I don't have much of a sense yet who the different people are." He frowned. "Though I will say that there's one scrawny guy with all kinds of crazy tattoos who seems like a pretty strange character."

"I'll keep my eye out for him," she said. She gestured toward the laboratory doors. "Do you have an access key to this room?"

"No," he said. "I wasn't issued keys or passes to any of the individual rooms, workshops, or lab spaces. I only have a set of keys for the front doors, rear emergency exit, and the loading bay behind the building. We'll just use the buzzer until someone lets you in."

Outside of the closed doors that separated the hall from the working lab, Kali stood to one side. The guard activated an intercom mounted by the door, asking if Dr. O'Connor was available to meet with a visitor. Kali leaned toward the speaker. "Police visitor," she emphasized.

There was no sound of footsteps, but the door was abruptly pulled open, and O'Connor stood in the frame. He nodded briskly to the guard, dismissing him. His expression revealed his displeasure as he regarded Kali.

"Detective," he said, his voice curt. "I wasn't aware that we had an appointment."

"We don't." She stepped past him, into the larger space. The bright overhead lights glared against the white surfaces.

There was the sound of someone humming. In the back of the room, a man wearing a white lab coat stood in front of a large platform that was mounted to the floor, which could be raised or lowered as needed. The ROV from her previous visit was no longer in sight, but the surface of the platform was covered with mechanical equipment. The man in the lab coat paused in his examination of a small device in front of him as Kali came through the door. He stopped humming and regarded her with undisguised curiosity.

"I thought you might prefer speaking to me here," she said to O'Connor, "but if you'd rather come down to the police station to make a statement, that's also an option."

O'Connor scowled. "Really, I can't imagine what else you might need from me." He gestured toward the man in the back of the room. "As you can see, I'm quite busy."

"Doing what?" she asked, walking toward the platform.

"Sorry about this, Byron," said O'Connor to the other man, following Kali. "It's about Maya, I suppose."

The man looked more interested. "Oh," he said. "What a mess, right? Poor kid."

Kali looked at him closely. She guessed him to be in his late thirties. He was tall and soft looking, with a round face.

"Did you know Maya Holmes?" she asked him.

He shrugged, then brushed back a lock of thin, sandy-colored hair that had fallen partially across one eye. "Sure. As much as anyone, I guess."

"Who are you, and what do you do here?"

He smiled. "Byron Coolidge. And I don't do anything here, really. I'm in the chemistry division. Davos—Dr. O'Connor—had a question about a possible alternative fuel source for his new toy, and asked me if I could take a look and offer an opinion."

"Byron is a PhD candidate who comes in for a few hours each week," said O'Connor.

"I see. And do you have an office here as well?" asked Kali.

Byron laughed. "Hardly. But the lab where my coffee cup is and where I'm mostly working is down at the end of the hall. That's as close to an office as I'm likely to get for a while."

"That's convenient," said Kali. She pulled her badge out from beneath her jacket. "I'm Detective Kali Māhoe. You can wait for me there, and I'll stop by after I've finished speaking with Dr. O'-Connor."

He said nothing, but shot a questioning look at O'Connor before leaving through the wide double doors leading to the corridor.

"Was that really necessary?" asked O'Connor as the doors swung shut. His frown had coalesced into a row of deep furrows along his forehead. "Honestly. Do you get some pleasure out of bullying people?"

Kali met his eyes. "You're terribly defensive. Is there a particular reason for that? Maybe there's something you haven't told me, like the fact that the day before she was killed, Maya Holmes received a call from a phone number that's been identified as yours? The second call was made just after three in the afternoon."

"As you already know, she was working in the field at that unfortunate time. I always check in with staff who are not actually in the lab."

"Why would you use her personal number?"

"Because she doesn't have a work phone, as I've already told you," said O'Connor sharply. "Don't your colleagues ever contact you on your personal phone?"

She ignored his question. "Did she answer your later call?"

"She did not."

"And that didn't concern you?"

O'Connor looked away. "I wasn't her babysitter. I assumed she would get my messages and check in when she had an opportunity to do so."

"And her work computer still hasn't turned up?"

"I would have contacted you if it had."

"Where were you this past weekend, Dr. O'Connor? From Saturday morning until Sunday afternoon?"

He looked at her, surprised. "Why on earth are you asking me that? I gave that information to the other officer. The one dressed in an actual uniform. Are you suggesting that I need an attorney?"

Kali shrugged. "That's for you to determine, I suppose. I'm simply asking you to tell me where you were. As part of an official investigation, just so we're clear."

"Here, mostly," he said. "Until late on Friday,

and then back here again Saturday morning. The sign-in logs at the front desk will bear that out."

"And security cameras?"

"Sure," he said. "You must have noticed them in the lobby. They're all over the place."

"And what about Saturday afternoon and evening, and through Sunday afternoon?"

"At home, catching up on life. Sorry I can't produce surveillance tapes to prove that, but I expect my neighbors saw me working on the lawn and moving around. My car was parked in the driveway."

"Were you alone?"

He glanced away briefly. "I've been divorced for the past ten years."

"That doesn't answer my question."

"Yes, I was alone. I'm still taking applications for the next Mrs. O'Connor."

She closed her notepad. "Well, good luck with that. I'll let you know if I have any more questions."

"I'm sure you will. Perhaps next time you could make an appointment with the desk instead of barging in here and embarrassing me in front of my colleagues as though I've done something to be ashamed of."

"Perhaps next time, I'll just have you escorted to the police station and we can chat there." Kali turned toward the exit. "Which way to Mr. Coolidge's work space?"

O'Connor walked away from her, back toward the platform where the bits and pieces of his project were laid out.

"End of the hall on the left," he said, without

looking at her. "There's a big clue on the door that says Lab B-4. I'm sure you can find it—that's what detectives are good at, isn't it?"

Kali tried not to smile as she left the room. She was glad she'd gotten under his skin, but she didn't necessarily need him to see her looking satisfied.

At the door marked B-4, she pressed the buzzer mounted on the wall and waited. A moment later, it was pulled open, and she stepped into a space that was even more sterile-looking than O'Connor's lab. This room was larger, and had several rows of long tables. Byron Coolidge was measuring a clear liquid into a glass beaker, with two younger people, whom Kali assumed might be students, carefully observing him. One was a plump, studious-looking girl with short red hair who was wearing a white lab coat similar to the one worn by Coolidge; the other was a slightly built young man wearing a tight black T-shirt, also under a lab coat. The cuffs of his long, loose sleeves were rolled back, exposing his lower arms, revealing many tattoos. The front of the coat was unbuttoned and open enough to show that his T-shirt advertised INXS, a popular rock band from the 1970s and '80s. His long and oily hair was pulled back into a ponytail that revealed both ears, pierced in multiple places.

The two younger people watched Kali as she walked in. The man in the black T-shirt reached up and smoothed back his hair. The movement was sinuous, and she felt herself recoil. He regarded her unblinkingly, his dark eyes glittering.

"Detective Kali Māhoe," she said, identifying herself. She lifted her badge from where it hung on a thin chain around her neck. "I'd like to speak with you alone, Mr. Coolidge."

"Wow. That's a real detective's shield," said the man in the black T-shirt. "Right?" He stared at her, then moved his gaze to her badge, transfixed.

Kali looked at him. She noted how his thick eyelids drooped. "That's right. And your name is?"

"I'm Vance Sousa," he said. He glanced briefly at Coolidge. "Chief assistant to the alchemist here." He turned and backed up against the table, hoisting himself onto the edge, his feet dangling.

Byron Coolidge looked uncomfortable.

Kali raised her brow. "Alchemy. How interesting." She focused on Coolidge. "So you're a master of transmutation?"

Vance grinned, his lips drawing back and revealing stained, uneven teeth. He slapped his thighs with both hands. "You get it! Cool."

The girl made a small, derisive sound as she pulled off her gloves. "I'm Gloria, not that you asked," she said, sounding bored. "That's Gloria as in Gloria Marsh. And assuming that this little visit is about Maya Holmes, I didn't know her. Except I always saw her sprinting up and down the roads around here. Always looked to me like she was running away from something." When Kali made no reply, the girl tossed her gloves into a trash bin near the table. "So if nobody needs me, which I'm sure they don't, I'm going to go get something to eat." She looked pointedly at Kali. "The level of testosterone in this room is more than I can handle on an empty stomach."

"What do you do here?" asked Kali, ignoring the girl's deliberate slight.

"I work in materials sciences," she said. "And I probably fulfill some legal requirement for how many women are part of the research program." She glanced at Byron and Vance. "Right, boys?"

"Leave me your contact information," Kali said.

"Really? I said I didn't know the running girl."

"Leave it anyway."

The girl rolled her eyes, then walked over to a counter in the corner and found a piece of paper and a pen. She scribbled something on it and left it there.

"Name, address, phone number. That all you need?" she asked.

Kali nodded. The girl left. The door made a soft, sucking sound as it closed behind her. Kali stared at it, fully aware that Gloria Marsh was the one who was running away.

CHAPTER 18

There was a momentary silence. Byron turned to Kali, shrugging.

"My apologies, Detective," he said. "I guess we're all a little testy. First the incident with Maya, and now we've been warned by our patrons that if there's any delay publishing our paper on this project, our next round of funding may be in jeopardy. It's all very distressing."

Kali stared at him, wondering how he could compare what had happened to Maya Holmes with the loss of institutional funding.

"I can see why you're all so distraught," she said, her tone dry.

"So you're here about Maya," said Vance. "We've all been talking about it, you know. It's not like it's some big secret. You aren't a big secret, either."

"And what is that supposed to mean?" Kali asked, surprised by his statement.

"It means that after you were here the first time, Dr. O'Connor looked you up," said Vance. "He found a couple of articles about how you're not just an ordinary, boring, villain-chasing cop. You're some kind of a Hawaiian kahuna priestess, and you have a degree of your own, in cultural anthropology."

"My professional background isn't the topic of today's discussion," she said, trying to keep her impatience in check. She watched Vance, looking more closely at his tattoos. "You also knew Maya Holmes?"

"Knew her? Well, that's a big question, isn't it?" he asked. "I mean, philosophically, who really and truly knows anyone else—their deepest hopes and dreams? Their existential fears and desires?" He laughed, and Kali flinched at the sharp, loud sound. "I'd say we would immediately recognize one another across the room at a party, but neither one of us would have been interested enough to waste the energy of pretending to have a conversation."

Kali couldn't help but be fascinated by the man's unapologetic combination of sarcasm and arrogance. She glanced at Byron. So far he hadn't had a chance to say much of anything. Vance was like an out-of-control freight train, running over the room's energy like a wild current. As she watched him, moving her eyes over the artwork on his arms, he pounded his thighs again, then grinned at Byron.

"She likes my tattoos, I think. See?" He flexed one arm, displaying the intricate designs inked into his flesh. "Which one's your favorite? Flowers? Symbols?"

"I'm afraid I don't have a favorite," she said.

"But I know you have one, too, on your arm. Tribal band with a spear, right? It was in the picture they used in that newspaper story. It said you got it the traditional way, with an animal bone that was tapped by hand. I'm going to get one, too. Mine's going to be a volcano, with Pele standing on top of it."

"You'll have to forgive me, Mr. Sousa—I'm afraid I'm not here to chat with you about body art. Perhaps some other time. You can leave your contact information for me before you go."

Again, the short, piercing laugh. He turned his head sideways, staring at her. "Aw, come on . . . you must have a favorite. Maybe it's my kaleidoscopic dolphin?" he pressed. "Check this out." He lifted his forearm, revealing a cartoonish dolphin figure that was vaguely ominous. The swirl of blue and green patterns that formed the dolphin's elongated, standing figure were sharply outlined beneath protruding yellow lips that were entirely out of proportion with the rest of the body. Enormous, gaping eyes had been drawn above the lips, the pupils replaced by flames.

Kali found the image slightly unsettling, but she gave no indication. Instead she turned to Byron and addressed him directly. "Again, I'd like to speak with you privately."

From his table perch, Vance slid to the floor. He

pulled a pen and piece of paper out of his pocket and wrote his name and phone number on it. He stood in front of Byron, rocking from side to side.

"Anything I can do to help, boss? Take care of some errands? Make some coffee? Order some lunch?"

Byron looked steadily at Vance. "Why don't you just take a break for a while? Maybe gallop around the grounds a few times and burn off some of that excess energy?"

Vance went around behind the table, reaching for something on the floor. He emerged holding a small backpack, which he slid over one shoulder, holding onto the strap with one hand. Grinning, he handed Kali the piece of paper he was holding. As he left, he gave another of his brief bark-like laughs and waved, then disappeared into the hallway.

Turning to her, Byron sighed. "I'm sorry," he said. "I realize it's exhausting, but what can you do? He's just . . . well . . . one of those people with a constant surplus of energy."

"Is he a student?"

"Yes, a graduate student. Gloria as well."

"Aren't you technically a graduate student yourself?"

"Doctoral candidate." His voice was mild, and the contrast with Vance's nervous energy was stark. "Free labor, really. Along with our own degree work, we have teaching responsibilities, and we help out with the research. I'm the leader on this particular research team. We're woefully behind on our work. Which is what we were occupied with prior to your arrival."

"Please tell me how well you knew Maya Holmes."

"Well," he said, making an effort to rack his brain. "I wouldn't say we were friends, but I suppose we were friendly. We worked together on the periphery of compatible research. She was directly involved with Dr. O'Connor's part, not with my own. I guess it would be accurate to say we were both working on different ends of the same project."

"Please be more specific."

"Dr. O'Connor and I have been developing an innovative new mapping system that may very well revolutionize the way mineral deposits are located on the ocean floor. And more importantly, how they're mined. We've all been trying to sort out some of the mechanics of the new system, but it's very involved. It's taking far longer than expected."

She was intrigued. "Can you give me an example?"

"Well, the idea is to eliminate random drilling. Suffice it to say, there would be no more need to search for needles in underwater haystacks."

"Was Maya Holmes working on that aspect of the research?"

He smiled, but the gesture was condescending. "Hardly. She was working on some of the hardware for Dr. O'Connor, but . . . well, I'm not sure if you realize that Maya wasn't really an engineer yet. Comparatively to other members of the team, her education was . . . minimal."

She did her best to keep her voice even, despite an immediate and strongly negative reaction to Byron's words—and the look of superiority on his face.

"Let me see if I understand you correctly. Are you saying that because she hadn't earned an advanced degree that she couldn't possibly have been intelligent enough to have a larger role in the development of this technology?"

Byron shrugged. "Isn't that a reasonable assumption?"

She stared at him, puzzled by his response. He didn't seem the least bit uncomfortable with his statement.

"I hardly think so," she said, watching him carefully. "What about intelligent people with economic restrictions that keep them from becoming PhDs?"

"That's what scholarships and loans are for," he said, his voice dismissive. "If someone has a drive or capacity for higher learning, I think it's safe to assume that they will have the necessary creativity to find a way."

Kali took a deep breath. There were already enough people in her life with overinflated egos that shared Byron's opinion for her to bother pointing out the obvious flaws in this viewpoint. She looked at him, taking note of his messy hair, his disheveled button-down shirt and his lab coat, noticing the missing button and the frayed collar. She was unlikely to change his opinion, and she wasn't interested in trying.

"Lucky for me you're so smart," she said. She folded back her notebook to a fresh page. "You won't have any trouble telling me everything you know about Maya Holmes, and giving me a minute-by-minute description of where you were last weekend. Just for fun, let's start with last Friday, and take it from there."

She saw his face fall. The sight was intensely gratifying.

Kali left the lab and walked to the side of the building, where she'd parked in the visitor's lot. She was halfway to her Jeep when she saw Vance jump down from where he'd been seated on the low cement wall that bordered the line of parking spaces, separating them from the entrance road. As he made his way toward her, she was aware that he'd been watching for her.

It had rained again while she was inside, and she stood on the hot, wet pavement and waited as he approached.

"You really are a kahuna, right?" he said. "That's crazy! I want to be one, too. I'm just curious about how you'd define it—is that more like being a minister, or like being a magic doctor?"

"I guess you'll have to look it up," she said, turning and stepping away. "That should be easy for someone who works in research." She kept walking.

"No, wait," he said, falling into step beside her. "I'm really interested. Hawai'i is so primeval and mystical. All those crazy stories and legends, you know?"

She slowed, looking at him. He smelled of perspiration and cheap bodywash. "I see. So you're also a scholar of world legends?"

He failed to pick up on her tone.

"I wouldn't say scholar," he said. "Just really interested."

"Why is that?"

Again he smiled, and she felt a chill when she saw his dark eyes narrow so easily into slits. "The world is such a mysterious place, don't you think? Since I came here to Hawai'i, I've learned about some of the stories. But I've never met a woman priest before."

"You still haven't," she said. "Where were you last weekend?"

He grinned. "I was here for a while on Saturday, then I went surfing that night and on Sunday morning. The night surfing was better. It was like riding the moonlight! I like getting in touch with the planet, you know? Immersing myself in the power of Mother Nature, drinking her in."

"So you fell off your surfboard?"

He laughed. The harsh sound startled a row of birds sitting on the power line connected to the laboratory building. Vance watched them fly away, flapping his arms at them. Kali stood perfectly still, waiting. Finally, Vance turned his attention back to her.

"Do you believe that there really are separate forces of light and dark out there—that that kind of thing is real?" he asked. "Do you think you'd know if you actually stood face-to-face with evil?"

She watched him closely, nodding. "I always have," she said calmly.

"Even if it's invisible? You must know the world is filled with powerful things you can't see. Like gravity, and dark matter, and promises. Like things that wait for you to turn your back, and then climb inside?"

"Like a Sitting God, Vance? Is that what you mean?"

He flapped his arms again. "The Sitting God! I know that one—I know that one! You don't know he's coming, then he slips in and takes you over, and then you're a god, too."

"Something like that," she said. "Now, if you don't mind—unless, of course, there's something you want to share with me about Maya Holmes or anything you may have heard about what happened to her, I need to be on my way. You can call me this afternoon and give me the names of the people you were surfing with. Plus the where and the when. Got it?"

He dropped back, still grinning. From the corner of her eye, she could see him jogging in place. She climbed into the driver's seat and started the engine, glancing in her rearview mirror as she began to back out slowly. Vance was no longer there. She looked around, bewildered, running her eyes along the service road, scanning the front of the building. He seemed to have evaporated into thin air.

CHAPTER 19

"Let's bring him in right away, along with the other people who were on the girl's research team," said Walter, waiting until Kali had finished describing her encounter with Vance. "This guy is giving me the creeps, and I haven't even had the pleasure of meeting him."

Kali stood by the coffeemaker, breathing in the scent of the fresh bag of Kona roast she'd just opened. "I would say he's unstable. And from what I observed of his erratic movements, he's using drugs. My guess would be cocaine. Stimulants are always popular with students. And the girl, Gloria Marsh, couldn't wait to get away from me."

Hara looked up from his desk. "I'm available to go and get them if you want," he said.

Walter nodded. "Okay. We've talked to everyone else who knew or worked with Maya, which is a surprisingly small number of people. Except for this weird guy and the unfriendly girl, the scant information we have has been verified or corroborated to the extent that it can be. Not that people aren't bald-faced liars, of course. And while it's still a possibility that unknown persons outside her circle targeted her as a victim, it's more likely that the killers were people she knew."

"Clearly, more than one person was involved," said Kali, pouring water into the coffeemaker, "but there's no clear motive or opportunity, and I still don't feel like the clues are suggesting some kind of scenario like an organized gang. As for this group of people at the laboratory, I don't think they could sign a birthday card together without some kind of drama."

"Granted," said Walter, "though we've seen people who don't get along rally before in order to commit a crime. I guess the good news is that when more than one individual is involved, there's a better chance of someone slipping up, or running their mouth to brag, or saying something out of a sudden sense of guilt."

"Or a sudden desire to point the finger away from themselves in an attempt to create distance from the crime."

Walter stood up and looked at Kali. "Okay. Just for grins, let's bring in Dr. O'Connor, the Coolidge guy, your buddy Vance, and the two girls working with all of them. Jody what's-her-name and the girl you met today."

Hara rose to his feet.

"Do we need warrants on anyone?" asked Hara.

"We may," said Kali, "but for now, let's see if we

can get them to agree to talk to us just to be helpful."

"Right," said Walter. "Let's start making house
calls, and getting them here today if possible. It's
likely not everyone is going to volunteer their assistance."

By the end of the day, everyone except for
Vance had agreed to another interview, having arrived separately and under their own steam. Each
had taken a turn in the interview room. Vance
hadn't answered his phone or responded to the
messages left for him, and Hara, who'd been dis-
patched to Vance's address, reported that there
was no one there—but that there were several surf-
boards leaning against the wall of the garage in
the place where he lived, and music playing inside
the apartment.

O'Connor's outrage at the additional interview
at a police station was monumental, but he had
nothing new to say—nor did Jody Phillips or
Byron Coolidge, who seemed more intrigued by
the interview room and process than annoyed at
having to be there to answer more questions.

Kali had found Gloria Marsh to be the most unusual of the group. She was surly and uncoopera-
tive. Since she'd made her lack of respect for
detectives abundantly clear before she'd left the
lab, Kali asked Walter to take the lead on the interview.

Across from them, Gloria sat in the stiff metal
chair with her legs spread apart and her hands in

her lap. Walter advised her of her right to an attor-
ney, which she declined with the roll of her eyes.
She looked at them and yawned, then turned to
Kali.

"How come you get to dress like you're heading
to the farmer's market for your organic broccoli
sprouts, but he has to wear a uniform?" she asked.

"Are you interested in the way people dress?"
asked Walter. Kali said nothing, only watched the
girl's studied indifference. It struck her as practiced, a response to authority that she'd found to
be successful in the past.

"Not especially. Just saying, you know? You look
hot as hell in those uniform clothes. Uncomfortable." She nodded to Kali. "But she gets to pull a
T-shirt off the bedpost and put on her favorite
jeans and come to work. Seems a little unfair, if
you ask me."

"No one did," said Walter. The firmness in his
voice got her attention. She went momentarily
silent. "I want you to tell me about Maya Holmes,
who was murdered, and I want you to skip the
made-up stuff about how you didn't know her."

"Does this mean I'm a suspect?" Gloria asked.
She was clearly making an effort to maintain an air
of churlishness, but her voice had lost some of its
earlier confidence.

"Just answer my questions."

Gloria sat up slightly in the chair. "Listen," she
said. "I worked in the same room with her some of
the time. We said things to one another like
'Please pass the duct tape,' but that's about it. She
wasn't really my type. Gorgeous, sure, but I don't

go in for the sporty gals. I like women who are a little more . . . feminine. Softer to the touch than all those hard muscles."

"So you asked her out and got turned down." Walter leaned forward a little, putting his forearms on the table. "That must have been embarrassing. Did word get around?"

"I didn't ask her out," said Gloria. She reached up and pulled at one of her earrings. Kali could see that her skin was flushed. "I was involved with someone else, but I'm not anymore."

"But you were attracted to her, and she knew it, and gave you the signal not to bother trying," he pressed. "That's just as bad, isn't it?"

"You should know. I bet you've got a whole bunch of rejection memories under your belt."

"It must have been pretty tough to see her every day and know you couldn't have her," said Walter. "Was it so bad that you preferred to have her dead?"

"How did she die?" asked Gloria, leaning forward, gaze fixed on Walter. "Tell me—was it slow and painful? Did the pretty girl have it bad?"

"You tell me. You were there, weren't you?"

Gloria swung her gaze back toward Kali. Her eyes glittered with anger. "Whose show is this, anyway? Are you going to let him badger me? I didn't kill her."

Kali said nothing.

"But you know who did," said Walter. "And you know why. Was it drugs? Who is the person supplying drugs to people at the research center? Is it Vance Sousa?"

Gloria looked at him in astonishment. "You can't be serious. Vance the Vampire? The guy's an idiot. Sure, he's most likely using—or he's on some kind of prescription meds that make him act like a rabid monkey—but no one there is a dealer. You've got a real screw loose if that's what you think."

"Well, here's your big chance to set me straight," said Walter. "There's something dishonest going on there, and you can help us sort it out, or you can go down for being part of it."

She stared back at him, unblinking.

"Guess this is where I tell you our conversation is at an impasse," she said. "And that it will remain in that state until I have legal representation."

"Duly noted," said Walter. He sat back in his chair, smiling. "I guess if you need to lawyer up, there's a whole lot you don't want to say."

Gloria looked away, but she didn't say another word. Kali thought she'd said plenty.

CHAPTER 20

Hilo leapt from his seat in the Jeep and raced across the short stretch of lawn between the driveway and the house. He thundered up the front steps, and Kali shook her head, wishing—not for the first time—that she had a fraction of the big dog's energy. She shifted the cloth grocery bag she was carrying to her other shoulder and followed Hilo up the creaking porch steps, wanting nothing more than to kick off her shoes and make dinner.

She reached out to fit her key into the door lock, pushing against the wood as she gripped the bottom of the small bag of groceries to keep it from swinging against the door. Hilo bounded inside just ahead of her, then came to an abrupt halt in the middle of the kitchen, legs splayed, head lowered. A low, fierce growl escaped his throat, and Kali could see a ridge of stiff hair running the length of his spine, standing on end.

She stood absolutely still, listening. Her eyes swept the space within her immediate view. There was no sign or sound of anyone else moving in the rooms opening off the kitchen and living room, but she had an overwhelming sense that something was out of order. She lowered the bag slowly to the floor, making no sound. Her hand slipped into her messenger bag, and she removed her gun. Reaching out with her left hand, she tapped Hilo lightly on his hips. He sat immediately, but Kali could see that his lips were parted, and his mouth was slightly open, revealing his teeth. Drool ran from his lower lip. His entire body was tense.

Holding the gun with both hands extended in front of her, she moved past the table, still covered with her papers and research on sorcery, and stepped carefully along one wall, making a quick search of the spaces behind the sofa and kitchen counter. Her heart was pounding as she went into the small guest bedroom that opened off one wall of the living room. It was empty. She moved into the bathroom, seeing nothing lurking behind the opaque glass of the shower door.

The only room left was her own bedroom. She stepped in, sweeping the room for any sign of an intruder. There was no one there, but her bedroom window was raised. The glass was intact, but she could see that the latch had been pried open. The rim of the wooden frame was splintered, and small chunks of wood littered the sill and floor beneath it.

She whistled, and Hilo sprang into the room,

making a beeline for the window. He sniffed it, then followed a scent around the room and into the living room. She walked behind him as he made his way through the house, retracing the steps of whoever it was that had forced his or her way inside. The hair on his back was still standing on end, and she realized that she was experiencing a similar sensation—the skin on the back of her own neck seemed to tingle with the tension of the moment.

His investigation complete, Hilo returned to Kali's side, pressing his body close against her upper leg. Still gripping the gun with her right hand, she pulled her cell phone from her bag with her free hand and called Walter.

"Hey," she said in answer to his hello. "I don't want to sound overly paranoid, but someone broke into my house and I'm not sure whether they might still be on the property somewhere. Can you . . ."

She could hear the sound of a door slamming, and Walter's voice came in grunts that signaled he was running.

"On my way," he said. "I'll radio from the car and get someone over there. Stay on the line with me, and do not go outside. Do you hear me? Do not go outside."

In the background, she could hear the noise of the engine turning over. Seconds later, she overheard Walter talking to dispatch on the car's radio.

"Okay," he said to her directly, when he was through, "give me any details you can."

"There's not much. Bedroom window was jimmied open, but the glass wasn't broken. I haven't checked everything yet to see what might have been taken, but there's nothing obvious missing, like the television." She felt her heart lurch as she hurried back toward her bedroom. "I haven't looked through my jewelry."

"I'm halfway to your house right now. Hara should be there before me."

"Okay," she said, standing in front of her chest of drawers. On the surface, the small ceramic bowl—the one with the raised hibiscus flower in the bottom that she used to hold her few pieces of jewelry—was where she'd left it. A sudden sense of anxiety overwhelmed her as she pulled up the edge of her shirt and covered her hand to tip the bowl over. The contents spilled onto the surface of the wood. She scanned the few items, counting the rings and earrings and necklaces. There was her grandmother's gold wedding band, and the sapphire earrings that had been a gift from Mike. Nothing was missing. Her heart slowed in relief.

On the floor beneath the bookshelf next to the dresser, several books lay scattered. She knelt in front of them, making a quick assessment of the titles.

"None of my jewelry was taken," she said, "but some books are knocked over onto the floor. It looks like they were pulled out. Maybe someone was looking for something more valuable that they thought I might have hidden out of sight."

"Well, you know the drill. Leave everything where it is until we've checked for prints."

In the distance, the wail of sirens could be heard.

"Is that the cavalry that I hear?" asked Kali, listening. "Maybe you should kill the sirens. I think someone might have been here when I got home, and I scared them out of the house. If they're still on the property, we might have a chance of tracking them. Hilo picked up a scent right away. I'll set him loose as soon as you get here."

"Hara's nearly there. I'm another ten minutes away," said Walter. "But stay on the phone until he's inside with you."

"Right," she said. A sense of uneasiness flooded through her. She looked around the small room, watching as a breeze moved through the open window and made the curtain flutter. She'd never felt uncomfortable living alone, especially with a dog as large as Hilo keeping her company, but she hated the feeling that someone had entered her private space uninvited. She wondered who it had been and what they'd been hoping to accomplish.

It seemed like only a few minutes had passed before she heard Hara's footsteps hurrying across her lanai. She met him at the door, and was moved by the level of concern on his face. Hilo, already agitated, sniffed suspiciously at Hara's leg. Kali gripped the dog's collar firmly.

"Are you okay?" Hara asked.

"I'm fine," she said. "Now that you're here I'll have a better look around inside for anything that might be missing, but I think we should let Hilo out first to see if he can pick up the intruder's scent. Let's walk around to the side of the house—whoever it was left through the same window they entered through. I'm going to bring Hilo around to that spot."

Hara nodded and turned back toward the door.

Behind him, Kali led Hilo to the side of the house where the bedroom window had been forced open. Holding tight to his collar, she avoided the softer ground beneath the window that might have prints, and let him go.

"Fetch, boy," she said. He leapt across the grass and bolted past Hara, darting into the thick shrubbery that crept toward the edge of the lawn. There was no path running among the bushes and trees there, so Hilo wove through the foliage, following a twisting line that circled back to the end of the driveway.

Hara was already at the end of the drive by the time Kali had jogged from the house to the lawn. She whistled sharply for Hilo, and he turned and ran back to her side.

"Did you notice a car pulling away from the road near your driveway once you got home?" Hara asked. "Maybe someone was waiting for whoever was in your house, or that person or persons may have left a car parked close by, just out of sight."

"No," said Kali. "Though honestly, I wasn't paying that much attention. I was pretty focused on getting groceries inside."

Hara pulled a powerful flashlight off his duty belt and began to examine the soft ground at the end of the driveway, moving along the verge of the road just beyond the junction of pavement and dirt drive.

"Motorcycle tracks," he said, his voice sure. Kali joined him, examining the clear set of tracks revealed by the flashlight's beam.

Walter's cruiser pulled in behind Hara's car. He climbed out and hurried toward them.

"The dog tracked a scent to this spot, sir," said Hara. "No sign of anyone, but these motorcycle tracks are fresh."

"Okay," said Walter. "Mark off this spot. Ren Santos is sending someone over to collect prints and any other evidence we can find. I'm going to go through the house with Detective Māhoe."

They left Hara there and walked across the soft grass and up the steps of the lanai, Hilo beside them.

"We're probably making too big a deal about this," said Kali. "It was probably some kid who thought they'd get lucky and find some cash lying around."

Walter looked at her quizzically. "You get bumped on the head? You said your jewelry was sitting right there, in plain sight."

She considered his point. "Yeah. They'd moved around the house for sure. Hilo was worked up from the moment we went inside. I'm just trying to make this seem less weird than it might be."

Walter snorted. "Don't waste your time. There's zero chance you're going to convince me that this was some random event."

Together they walked through the house, paying attention to details. Back in her bedroom, Kali pointed to the pile of books on the floor. "They looked through my books."

"Anything significant about that? First editions or something like that?"

"No," she said slowly, looking at the titles that could be seen easily without picking them up.

"Nothing valuable, except . . ." She halted, suddenly concerned.

"Except what?"

"My grandmother's book," she said slowly, looking more closely at the pile.

"The one she won all those awards for? About the Hawaiian legends?"

"Yes," said Kali. "I kept it right here, on the top shelf, but I had it out to do some research for this case. I hadn't put it back yet . . . it was on the kitchen table." She turned suddenly and went back into the other room to look through the papers on the table, but quickly returned. The book wasn't there. She stood in the doorway of the bedroom.

"Everything okay?" he asked.

"It's gone," she said, doing her best to keep her distress contained.

"But it's not the only copy, right?"

"It was the first copy," she said. "When the book was printed, she was over the moon with happiness. She kept the very first book she lifted out of the box when they arrived from the publisher, and she left it to me."

"Damn. I'm sorry, Kali."

She nodded, taking a deep breath. Distracted, her gaze roamed around the bedroom, then stopped when she saw a small corner of blue silky material sticking out from the upper drawer of a narrow bureau on one wall. A tiny bit of lace could be seen. The drawer itself was slightly askew. Kali walked closer, staring closely at the material.

"What's that?" asked Walter, following her.

She bit her lip, appearing somewhere between

horrified and mortified. "That drawer," she said, "is where I keep my undergarments. Panties, bras, et cetera."

"And it wasn't like that this morning when you left?"

"It was not," she said. "I know, because I took some clean things out of the laundry basket instead of pulling open that drawer, which sticks. All this rain has made the wood swell, and it was jammed pretty tight. I didn't want to fool around with it." She looked at Walter. "I was going to empty it out and plane down the edges so it would open and close more smoothly, but I just haven't gotten around to it." She eyed the drawer and the small corner of exposed lace, and gave an involuntary shudder. "You don't think someone looked through there, do you?"

"Guess we'll know in a few minutes," he said.

Walter and Kali both turned toward the bedroom door. The sound of people entering through the front door could be heard, and Kali recognized the voices of Ren, Hara, and several of Ren's team. She filled them in on the new details she and Walter had discovered, and stood out of the way as Ren dusted the windowsill, window frame, dresser, and books with fingerprint powder. He moved methodically throughout the room, assisted by Walter.

"Sorry about all this, Kali," Ren said to her. "I'm afraid we're making a mess all over your house."

"Don't worry about it," she said. She looked at the dresser drawer, feeling awkward.

"I'm not getting any prints at all, except for what's likely yours," Ren said. "Feel free to make a more thorough search if you think you're missing any belongings."

"Okay," she said. She looked at Walter with imploring eyes. "Maybe you could start some coffee for everyone while I look around a bit more?" She glanced meaningfully at the dresser.

"Good idea," he said. He looked at Ren. "Hara can show you where those motorcycle tire prints are. Now that we've got more people here, more lights, we can go through the path the intruder seems to have taken through the trees, check the ground more thoroughly. Hara said he could see prints outside, just beneath the window."

Ren nodded and left the room, speaking to Hara in the kitchen. Walter turned to Kali. "You need some help getting that drawer open?"

She shook her head, grasping the small glass knobs screwed into the wooden surface, and gently rocked the drawer back and forth until it pulled open. Inside, everything had been jumbled into a pile on one side. Kali felt a wave of nausea sweep through her stomach. She felt as though she might retch. Her neat stacks of panties and bras were a snarl of lace, silk, and satin. It was quite clear that someone had been through them, and had seemingly made a point of letting her know where their hands had been.

After Ren and his team had gone, Kali left Hara in the kitchen, where he'd volunteered to gather up and wash the coffee cups that had been used. She and Walter stepped out onto the lanai.

"I don't want you staying here alone. You and

Hilo pack up and follow me back to the house. I'll call Nina and ask her to put Beth and Suki in Lara's room. You can have their room till we figure this out."

Kali shook her head. "No. I'm not going to let some pervert run me out of my own home. If he— and I'm pretty sure it's a he at this point—comes back, I'll make sure he's sorry he did."

Walter scowled. "I'm not calling your Hawaiian warrior goddess powers into question, Kali. But someone was here and they clearly want to mess with your head. Your grandmother's book is the only thing that's missing, and your most personal clothing items were rifled with. That says a number of things: Someone has a good idea of what's important to you; they left your jewelry and took a book; and they made sure you'd see they man-handled your intimate belongings. It wasn't your jeans that got tossed around. They wanted to alarm you. I don't want them to feel as though they need to escalate their behavior because you're sitting here ignoring all of this."

"I'm not ignoring it," she said. "And I appreciate your concern. But this is my home, and I'm not leaving." She glanced toward the end of the lanai, where Hilo sat staring out into the yard. "Besides, I have Hilo here with me. He's good protection."

"Not if someone throws a poison steak into the yard or shoots him in order to get to you."

"Someone's just trying to scare me."

"Well, they've definitely scared me," he said.

She gazed out over the yard toward the ocean, where the moon was visible above the water. "You think this has something to do with the Holmes case? Somebody who wants to scare women?"

"In my experience, people who want to scare women are almost always afraid of them," said Walter. "But yes, it seems like this might be related, and I don't like it one little bit."

Hara stood in the doorway, hesitating to interrupt them. "Detective, if you have a hammer, I can close up that window for the night. I can't fix the frame, but I can make sure it doesn't come open."

Walter nodded. "Good idea." He turned to Kali. "You go find the tools he needs. I'll be back shortly."

"Where are you going?"

He didn't answer. Kali only watched as he strode down the lanai steps. She went into the house and into the spare bedroom to retrieve a toolbox from the floor of the room's small closet. She and Hara were busy securing the window when she heard Walter come back inside. He was engaged in conversation with someone, so she excused herself from Hara to find out who it was. When she stepped into the living room, she was surprised to see Elvar standing beside Walter. He was holding a rolled-up sleeping bag in one hand, a sword in the other. There was a large hunting knife in a leather sheath affixed to his belt.

"What's going on?" she asked, directing her question to both men.

Elvar gazed at her, his face deadpan. "I've been assigned bodyguard duties," he said. He reached down with the hand holding the sleeping bag and patted the sheath. With the other, he waggled the sword.

Walter looked at Kali, daring her to disagree. "That's right," he said. "He's still deputized, so he doesn't have a choice."

"Now wait just a minute," Kali stuttered. "I don't need . . ."

"Yes, you do. You either come home with me right now, or you've got a twenty-four-seven body-guard. My call as police captain. Understood?"

Kali looked at Elvar, and felt her face flush.

"Just for tonight," she said.

"We'll start with that," said Elvar. "Hilo can stand guard with you in the bedroom. I'll be out here on the sofa." He lifted the sword, which glinted in the glow of the ceiling light. "Walter gave me permission to stab anyone who tries to get inside this house without your express invitation."

Kali glared at Walter, who glared back at her.

"Any questions?" Walter asked, crossing his arms over his chest.

"Not at this exact moment," she said, her eyes narrowed. She turned away from Walter. Her voice softened. "And thank you, Elvar. This is very generous of you."

Hara joined them, the toolbox in one hand. Kali looked around at the faces of the three men. She felt a deep sense of gratitude that there were this many people in her life who cared about her well-being.

"I appreciate this, everyone," she said. She turned back to Walter, who was staring at her as though challenging her to argue. "Especially you, Uncle Walter," she said. "Stop by in the morning, and I'll make coconut pancakes for breakfast."

Walter's face relaxed, and a wide smile spread into his cheeks.

"Deal," he said, then turned and headed for the door, gesturing for Hara to follow.

Elvar looked at her, also smiling. "Any chance you could loan me a pillow?" he asked. "I forgot to bring mine."

CHAPTER 21

There were no disturbances in the night, and Kali woke to the scent of coffee. In the kitchen, Elvar was singing softly. The song was Icelandic, and though she couldn't understand the words, the tune was soothing. She lay in bed, not moving, but watching tiny dust particles hover along the beam of sunlight flooding through the window. An unfamiliar sense of contentment washed over her.

Her door was slightly open, and she realized that Hilo wasn't in the room. She sat up and swung her feet to the floor, then stood and stretched. She reached for the light cotton robe hanging from a hook inside her closet door and slipped it on. She glanced into the mirror over the bureau and regarded her tangled hair. It had been a long time since anyone had seen her this early in the day before she'd showered and dressed, and as she listened to Elvar's song, she suddenly felt awkward.

In the kitchen, Hilo was stretched out on the floor. He glanced up as she walked in, his tail thumping against the worn wooden boards, but he didn't bother to get up. Kali saw that his food bowl had been filled, and that Elvar's sleeping bag had been neatly rolled up and was resting beside the sofa.

Elvar turned away from the counter where he was setting out silverware and smiled at her. She was struck by how natural it seemed to see him there, even though she couldn't remember a time that he'd ever been here this early, or had prepared coffee for her in her own kitchen. She saw the way the morning light glinted on the highlights in his blond hair, and how the light picked up the flecks of gold around the center of his sea-green eyes. The corners of his eyes crinkled as he smiled at her, and memories rose, unbidden, of all the mornings she'd seen Mike standing in that very spot, fussing over his glass coffee press, clearing up the random grounds that always managed to find their way to the countertop.

"Good morning," he said. "Coffee's ready. Would you like a cup?"

She smiled at him in return. "I would love a cup."

"Then sit down and I'll bring it to you."

She pulled out a chair from the table and sat down. Elvar filled two coffee mugs and brought them over, setting hers down carefully in front of her. The gesture was intimate, familiar, and she breathed in the steam rising from the cup, closing her eyes for a moment. For the briefest of seconds, she was transported to the past. When she opened her eyes, Elvar was settling into the chair beside her, holding his own cup. Kali looked at him. Their eyes met. She took a sip of coffee, relishing this fleeting moment when everything seemed to be in a state of perfect equilibrium, before the reality of the day seeped in.

It was over before she wanted it to be. The sound of Walter's cruiser pulling in caused both Kali and Elvar to turn toward the windows overlooking the lanai and the front yard. Kali sighed.

"Guess I'd better get busy with pancakes," she said. "Walter never forgets a promise like that."

Elvar grinned. "I'll be your sous-chef," he said. "Where do you keep the macadamia nuts?"

Kali sat beside Walter in the cruiser, wishing she'd eaten one less pancake. The carbohydrates, combined with the sugar in the coconut syrup, had caused a drowsy reaction. She would have given a lot to just crawl back into bed for another hour instead of heading to the station.

After breakfast, Elvar had offered to wash the dishes. While he was clearing up, Kali and Walter had installed the motion-sensitive cameras he'd brought with him, positioning them at several points around the perimeter of the house. She admitted to herself that while she felt reassured by their presence, she wouldn't mind if Walter insisted that Elvar continue with his nocturnal body-guard duties.

Now she sat quietly in the cruiser as Walter steered around a palm branch lying in the road-way. Though she had decided to not bring up the topic of bodyguards, he seemed to read her train of thought.

"Big guy like that, rattling around your castle armed to the teeth with swords and knives. Must have made you feel like a princess being guarded by the kingdom's best warrior." Grinning, he turned toward her, waiting for a reaction.

"Have I ever told you that you're an interfering old busybody?" she asked.

"More times than I can remember."

"So I don't need to make the speech all over again?"

"Can if you want to. But it won't do any good."

"That's what I thought."

Kali turned away, looking out the window, but Walter wasn't finished.

"It's just that in the grand scheme of things . . ."

His phone rang, interrupting his lecture. Both he and Kali glanced at the phone mount and the display screen. Walter grunted.

"Good morning, Dr. Stitchard," he said.

"A good morning to you as well, Captain. Are you able to talk?"

"I've got you on speaker right now. I'm en route to the station with Detective Māhoe."

"I'll be brief. We've had two bodies delivered. Both methamphetamine casualties, both identified as local university students. Sudden heart failure."

"Damn," swore Walter.

"Sending you details via e-mail. I don't know if there's a connection, but thought you might want to know. It's a very potent concoction."

"Thanks," said Walter. He ended the call, staring ahead at the back of the Toyota minivan in front of him. He was no longer smiling.

"Given the amount of drugs circulating on this island, it's not necessarily related, but I'm going to bet it is," said Kali. "Students again. That doesn't feel random either."

"No, it doesn't." Walter turned off the road into the parking area of the station, pulling the cruiser into his reserved spot. They climbed out and went inside, where the air-conditioning system was working overtime despite the damp weather and cooler air.

"The kids who shot Mike," said Kali. "Most of them were college-aged, but none of them were in school or had any connection to the university."

"No, but whoever is running this new ring might actually be a student. We've got plenty of people watching, and there doesn't seem to be anyone showing up on campus who's out of place."

"What about a teacher or someone else who works there?" asked Kali. "Food services, maintenance . . ."

Walter pondered her question. "We did background checks on all of the employees, but I don't see why it couldn't be someone who appears clean on the surface."

"It's usually the same people selling and cooking it up, though," said Kali. "So, that means someone who has a place to set up a workshop and the means to do it without being caught. A mini-factory."

"Exactly. You've seen those places and the stuff they use—vats of scary chemicals, which, as we've all learned, can be highly explosive if they get mixed up."

Kali thought about the meth production facilities she'd encountered in the past in her capacity as a detective. They'd ranged from garages attached to private homes in affluent suburbs to garden sheds or whole apartments, and—in one case—the basement of a dealer's grandfather's small house, where the elderly man who lived upstairs had no idea of what his grandson and his cohorts were doing in the space just beneath him until the whole structure exploded in flames. Kali remembered that the man had arrived home from an outing with his friends to discover that his home was a collapsed pile of smoldering rubble, and the houses on either side seriously damaged. The would-be drug entrepreneurs in the basement had all perished in the explosion.

"Let's get a warrant to search CMMR," she said. "We've got all those scientists and all that quiet laboratory space, as well as a connection to the university via the grad students working with O'Connor."

"Agreed," said Walter.

"Can you expedite it?"

"Chief Pait will get it pushed through. He's anxious for this case to be wrapped up."

"Okay," said Kali. "There's a lot of space in that building, and it's a little weird that the security guards don't have access to the majority of rooms. Let's go see what's in them."

CHAPTER 22

By the afternoon, the rain had returned, and was growing in intensity. Kali had borrowed Walter's car to run out for a late lunch. She returned the car to its parking spot, then made a dash for the building's entrance. Her head was down, and she failed to see the man who'd just stepped through the door on his way out. As they collided, the man reached out with both hands and placed them on her shoulders to steady her. The momentum caused both of them to fall to the wet ground.

Kali sat up, her knees bent. The man rolled over on his side and groaned, then sat up and faced her. It was Chad Caesar, a local actor who'd gained considerable fame for his role as an investigative journalist on *Lights Out Maui*, a canceled criminal drama series that had been shot on location locally. Since then, he'd parlayed his celebrity status into his current occupation as a podcast host and blogger. Like the television show, his podcast enjoyed a huge following. Kali was not a fan of his sensationalist pseudo-reporting, or his podcast—which he'd dubbed Chad Caesar, Ruler of the News—and had long suspected that someone within the island's police department was feeding inside news to Chad. He'd been able, on multiple occasions, to include pieces of information in his broadcasts that hadn't yet been released to the public.

"You again," said Kali. She stood up, peeling wet leaves from the back of her jeans.

Chad stood up as well, quickly recovering his composure. He smiled brightly, slicking back his damp golden hair with one hand. He reached out toward her with the other.

"Here, let me help you tidy up," he said, leaning closer. He flashed another wide, bright smile in her direction, but she drew back, immune to his charms and cover-boy looks.

"Hands to yourself, Chad," she said, moving away from him and closer to the door. "Please feel free to carry on with your day, and whatever that involves."

He fell in behind her, reaching forward to grasp the door handle and pull it open before she had a chance to do it herself. She walked through, ignoring him.

"I actually came here to see you, Detective," he said, hurrying up beside her.

She halted, turning toward him and doing her best to keep her expression neutral. "And what on earth have I done to deserve such an honor?"

"I did another show last night about the witches up in the mountains," he said, oblivious to the undertone of mockery. He pulled his cell phone from his pocket. "And then this morning, I got this text."

He opened his screen and found the message he was looking for, then passed the phone to Kali. She peered at the screen, reading the words displayed there: GIVE THE PACKAGE TO THE HOLY COP. The sender was identified only as Kane.

She looked at Chad. "What package?"

"I brought it here from the studio," he said.

"You mean your house."

Chad frowned. "The studio space is actually separate . . ."

"Whatever, Chad," she said, continuing across the lobby. She looked around, concerned. "Where is this package?"

"Well, you weren't here, and neither was Captain Alaka'i, so I left it at the counter with the police officer who was there, to give to you when you got back." He smiled again. "And here you are."

"Here I am," she said, trying to keep her voice level. She hurried toward the desk. The duty officer watched her approach, and hid a smile when he saw that she was accompanied by Chad. "You stay here," she said to Chad, and made her way into the restricted area of the station.

"The package that guy brought in has been

checked out," the duty officer told her. "Sniffer dogs went over it. There was some kind of chemical residue. They didn't like it, so it was scanned and opened. No fingerprints. We've still got the packaging, of course, which is a jumble of prints."

"What's inside?" she asked.

"It's with the captain." His voice was guarded. There was a look of distaste on his face. "He didn't like it any more than the dogs did, and neither will you." He glanced at Chad. "Good thing Mr. Movie Star came back with you so we don't have to call him in. We're going to need his fingerprints, even if it's just for elimination. I'll keep him here so you can talk to him after you've had a look."

Apprehension engulfed her. She walked into the space she shared with Walter and Hara. Walter was standing at his desk. He had gloves on, and was examining something in a small cardboard box sitting on the desk's surface. As she walked toward him, she could see thin blue tissue paper sticking out between the cardboard flaps.

"What's going on?" she asked.

Walter moved, blocking her view of the desk.

"Before I show you, I want to remind you that this is some kind of a sick prank, probably connected to whoever the jerk is that got into your house. So there's no sense in getting worked up over it. Understand?" His voice was gruff. "Someone wants to rattle your cage. Don't let them do it. And put these on."

Walter tossed her a pair of thin latex gloves that he'd clearly had waiting for her, then turned and lifted the box and held it out. She gazed inside and saw a skeleton hand, its thin, jointed bones resting on the tissue paper. On one finger was a ring bearing the insignia of a police shield.

"What in the hell is this supposed to be? Is that an actual hand?"

"No—it looks real, but it's plastic, and is probably one of those Halloween decorations," said Walter. "The ring's not real either. It's also plastic, and someone used a magic marker to write the letters on it."

She looked more closely at the ring, then pulled back in shock. In addition to the letters spelling out Police Dept., there were two large letters, clearly meant to be initials.

"MS," she said, barely breathing. "Mike. Mike Shirai." She looked at Walter as her entire body pulsated with the searing heat of raw anger—pure, unadulterated rage.

"Yeah," said Walter. "That's what I thought, too."

"Who in the hell would do something like this?" she asked. "I mean seriously, what could they possibly hope to achieve?" She sat down at her desk, troubled.

"That, for starters," said Walter, pulling his chair over to face her. "Shook you up, right? Somebody wants you to feel as though your power has been taken away from you."

She thought about this for a moment, then shook her head. "That's just part of it," she said. "I'm pretty sure this is meant to be a fetcher, or a poor representation of one." She got up and walked back to where the box sat open on Walter's desk. Slowly, she lifted the plastic hand, turning it over and checking for anything that might be underneath it. There was nothing beyond the wrapping paper.

"One of the ways a kahuna with evil intentions achieved domination over others was to take a bone from a corpse. But the context here is all mixed up. Someone wanted to signal to me that they know these legends, and to imply they'd captured Mike's mana, or his spiritual energy, and now have control over it. But they've got it all wrong—they've used the ring correctly as a sort of identification symbol, but by sending it to me, they've lost control of its power."

"Sounds disturbing. And complicated."

"It's both of those things," agreed Kali. "This is one of the stories I was looking at in my grandmother's book. She wrote a section on sorcery, and I was hoping to find something that might be relevant to the Holmes case. Remember I said the book was on the kitchen table? It may have still been open to that chapter." Her eyes grew dark. "It's the same person, Walter—I know it is. Whoever broke in is also the sender of this little gift."

Walter nodded, turning her words over in his mind.

"Okay—but what about Mike's initials on the ring? Who would know that?"

"Mike's connection to me is the kind of information that's probably pretty easy to locate, especially if someone wanted to find the name of a person I'd been close to whom I'd also lost. Or . . ." She looked toward the door leading to the front of the station. "Put this horrible box somewhere out of sight, and let's find out from my buddy Chad exactly what he was talking about on his podcast last night."

They found Chad sitting in the reception area, chatting to an older woman who'd come in to report that her mail had been stolen. The woman had recognized him, and was clearly charmed to be sitting beside him. Chad was animated, regaling her with stories connected to the set of the television series. Her eyes were wide as she listened to him.

Kali and Walter walked in, interrupting the performance.

"Come with me, Chad," said Kali.

The woman looked up. "Oh dear." She turned to Chad. "Are you in trouble? Is there anything I can do to help?"

"No trouble," he said, with an air of somber self-importance. "I'm assisting with an important investigation."

Kali bit her lip. She supposed that technically, there was enough truth in what he'd said to let it go.

The woman beamed in approval. "The police are so lucky to have you living in the area, Mr. Caesar."

"Call me Chad, please," he said, standing up. "Would you like to get a picture with me before I go?"

She looked elated. Reaching into her handbag, she pulled out her phone and handed it to Kali.

"Would you mind terribly, dear? I'm sure you could take a better photo than I could."

There was a soft chuckle, and Kali turned to

Walter, eyebrows raised. "Not a single word from you," she said. She took the woman's phone and waited until Chad had placed one arm around the woman's shoulders and turned to the camera. He changed his pose several times, and Kali took several photographs before handing the phone back to its owner.

"Thank you, Mr . . . Chad," said the lady, shyly. "I can't wait to show this to my friends!"

Chad grinned at her, then turned to Kali and Walter. He clapped his hands together. "Now," he said, "down to business, right? What can I do to help you today?"

"Why don't we all go back to your office, Mr. Caesar?" asked Walter. He winked at Chad, who looked momentarily confused, then winked back.

"Great idea," he said. "Let's do that."

Chad sat next to Walter's desk, one long leg crossed casually over the other.

"No," he said, looking at Kali and Walter. "There were no call-ins last night. I did the show without a guest, because I wanted to delve into the witch issue a little more deeply."

"Is that the only thing you talked about?"

He looked at Kali, uneasy. "Pretty much, yes."

"You realize," she said, "that your show is archived, and we can pull it up and listen to the whole thing. You could save us some time if you give us a breakdown of the topics you covered, and if you discussed the case of the girl in the tree."

"Well," Chad began slowly, "I also read out some

statistics about the drug problem on Maui. Crystal meth. I may have mentioned that users of this particular drug can be beset with hallucinations, and that maybe the weird reports were from someone who was having a drug-induced experience and imagined seeing or hearing things in the mountains." He looked over at Walter's desk, reaching out to fiddle with the edge of a piece of paper.

"And?" asked Kali, knowing there was more.

"Well, um, I may have made a few personal references to things that have happened to people I know. Bad things, connected to drugs."

"Be more specific."

Chad sighed. "I'm sorry if I was out of line, Detective, but I think—no, I'm pretty sure—that I may have said that a friend of mine had suffered a terrible loss when her boyfriend was killed during a drug raid."

Kali sat back in her chair. She clenched her teeth together to keep from saying what was on her mind.

Walter watched her. He gave a tiny shake of his head, and addressed Chad. "Did you mention the name of the person who was killed, or what he did for a living?"

Chad looked at Kali, then quickly turned to Walter. He looked a little scared, and very much embarrassed. "I believe so, yes."

"And were the initials of that person by any chance MS?"

Chad nodded. "They were, yes," he said, his voice unnaturally quiet.

Kali got up and walked toward the coffeemaker sitting on the countertop along one wall. She reached up to take a mug off the shelf above the counter. Her hand was shaking.

Behind her, Chad was standing. His bravado had evaporated.

Walter reached out and shook his hand.

"Thanks for your help, Chad," he said. "I'll show you out."

Kali stood quietly at the counter, counting her breaths and fighting to regain her composure. As Walter and Chad reached the door, Chad turned his head, shooting a look of remorse in her direction. She said nothing, waiting for the sound of fading footsteps that would tell her he was gone.

A few moments later, Walter returned. He joined her at the counter, reaching for another mug and pouring coffee for both of them. Holding his cup, he turned around, leaning against the edge of the counter.

"I know you're angry," he said. "But I really think you should look at the bright side."

"Oh, really?" she said. "And what exactly would that be?"

"He told all his listeners that you were his friend," said Walter, grinning. "You know, if we hurry, we could catch him in the parking lot. I can get a couple of photos for you on your phone like you did for that lady. His arm over your shoulder. Your arm over his shoulder. We'll get a bunch of different angles."

"Or," she said, her jaw tight, "I could get a job

on a cruise ship and leave you here alone while I explore places that are really far away."

"Like where?"

"Like anywhere," she said. "Right now, Antarctica sounds appealing. Lots of penguins, and no witches or ongoing tropical storms. And no Chad Caesar."

CHAPTER 23

The interior of George's Island Market was cool and dry. Kali stood just inside the automatic glass doors, wiping the rain from her face. From where he sat behind the counter next to a cash register, George glanced up briefly, then back down at the newspaper in his hands.

"According to the reporter who worked on this front page story, the Bigfoot that's been sighted up in the high country was probably brought here from Montana when it was still a little Bigfoot."

Kali considered the unlikeliness of this theory. "Seems like someone would have noticed, don't you think?"

George looked at her, his expression serious. "Could have been smuggled onto a sailboat in disguise. Or maybe brought here on a private plane when it was tiny and less noticeable."

"Only one? That would be an awfully lonely existence. New forest, new terrain. Learning to live off fruit."

"Kids love fruit. Maybe little Bigfoots like sweets, too."

"Maybe," she said, smiling at George. Clutching her shopping bag in one hand, she wiped her feet vigorously on the doormat. The drops of rain that clung to her waterproof jacket sprayed outward, onto the already wet, mud-streaked floor. She considered that there was nothing sweet on her grocery list, which was limited to eggs, coffee, fish, and tea. Lifting a hand basket from a stack near the entrance, she made her way along the store's aisles, passing other shoppers as she gathered the items she'd come for.

When she reached the bakery display, she hesitated. Many of the available treats on display had been locally produced, and she saw a loaf of mango bread that had been made with macadamia nuts and coconut. She thought about the pineapple cake that one of the police officers had brought in to the police station earlier that week. It had been devoured—largely by Walter—by the afternoon of its arrival, and she'd never sampled it. On impulse, she decided to buy the bread and bring it to the station when she went in the next morning. She liked the idea of arriving at work with something normal and sweet, and grasped at the possibility that it might help dispel the darkness that had descended in the wake of the delivery of the ghoulish package.

At the checkout counter, George put down his newspaper and considered her selections.

"These are good eggs," he said. "Big and speckled. That nice couple that have been fixing up the old farm near the crossroads have been supplying most of them. Bring them in fresh every morning."

"Have you gone up to the farm to meet their chickens?" she asked. She slid the bread onto the countertop. "I know you like to know where things come from."

"No," he said, thoughtfully. "I haven't been up there yet, but I'll go pretty soon. I heard they have a child—a daughter—who was hurt in a crash a while ago, before they came here to Maui. Motorcycle, I think. Maybe I can bring a basket of things by for them. Make them feel welcome."

Kali nodded as she handed him her credit card. She'd known George all her life, and knew that he never hesitated to go out of his way to be kind, or to help someone in need if it was within his power.

He returned her credit card along with her receipt, watching her carefully.

"I don't have any news for you about that thing you asked," he said. "But speaking of daughters . . . I was just wondering about Makena. Haven't seen her around in quite a while now. I heard something about her leaving the island. That true?"

Imperceptibly, Kali winced. Mike had lost his young wife to illness when Makena was only two. Makena's current path toward self-destruction belied the sweet, curious toddler she'd once been.

"It might be," admitted Kali. "I haven't heard from her in a while either. I guess you know she's not likely to confide in me."

George reached for the damp bag that Kali had

laid on the counter. Slowly, he placed some of her items inside, putting the eggs carefully on the top of the flat plastic cover of the mango bread.

"What I heard isn't good," he said. He pushed the bag toward her. "My friend who lives in Honolulu has a son. Not a good kid. Gets into a lot of trouble. Drug trouble. Anyway, when my friend went to see his son to check in on him, there was a girl there. Passed out. My friend said his son claims she was his new girlfriend from Maui. Bragged that she was the daughter of a cop. I asked him if he knew the girl's name, and he said he heard his son call the girl Makena."

Kali digested this unwelcome bit of information.

"It's not that uncommon a name," she said slowly. "But the daughter of a cop . . . I guess that's probably not just a coincidence." She shook her head. "I don't know what to do about her, George. I want so much to help her, but it seems pretty clear that she's not interested in being helped."

"I always wonder what goes wrong," he said. "You see these nice children, happy and laughing. And then you run into them when they're all grown up, and they're a mess. I remember Makena when she was about ten or eleven. Always singing."

"I remember that, too."

George looked up at her and met her eyes. He smiled, a wide one filled with conviction.

"You, though. You turned out good. Your grandmother would be proud of you."

Kali laughed. "Not if she saw me buying bread instead of baking it myself. She'd tell me that the act of creating bread should be approached with reverence, and with gratitude to the flour and the fruit and the nuts."

George laughed with her. "And she'd be right. But this bread is pretty good. You go home and enjoy it, and don't let that dog eat it all."

"I'll do my best," she said.

Another customer approached the cash register, and Kali picked up her bag and turned toward the door.

"You take care, George," she said.

"You do the same, Kali. You be sure to do the same."

The light coming in the window over Kali's desk was murky. All morning, thunder had rumbled in the distance. She looked at the bleak view, which did nothing to reflect the general air of sparkle and sunshine that the glossy travel magazines and highly trafficked destination honeymoon websites preferred to portray.

Her phone buzzed, and she lifted it from her desk, noting with dismay the identity of the caller.

"Good morning, Detective Māhoe," said a deep, familiar voice.

"Chief Pait," said Kali. Her shoulders sagged.

"I'm calling about this girl-in-the-tree business," he said.

"Yes, sir. And thanks for getting the search warrant for the research center cleared. We've got a team moving in this afternoon. We're doing our best to wrap up the investigation as quickly as possible."

"Not as quickly as the public would like," he

said. His tone betrayed a level of disappointment that Kali felt was somehow directed at her personally. "I've got flash flooding and car crashes all over the island, and I don't think I should have to tell you that all this nonsense about witches on Maui is unacceptable."

"Understood, sir."

"Although, now that I think about it, it's really all about the kind of witches and sorcery, isn't it?" His voice grew curious. "Now, if we had a Harry Potter type of situation, it wouldn't be so difficult to manage. Might even be a boon to tourism. The Magic of Maui, or something like that."

Kali stifled an urge to throw the phone.

"A young woman has been murdered, sir," she said. "Brutally. This isn't happy magic that we're dealing with."

"No, no, of course not. Wasn't implying anything of the sort. Still, you catch my drift, don't you? How a more benign kind of magic . . ."

"Yes, sir, I understand. Is there anything else I can help you with today?"

"Just checking in," he said. "Moral support, letting you know I'm here to help."

"Thank you, sir," she said. "I appreciate that."

Pait rang off. Kali sat in the dim light, tapping her fingers restlessly along the edge of her desk, wondering where the line stood between good magic and the kind that left a young woman's feet burned, and her lungs filled with deadly, suffocating dust.

CHAPTER 24

Kali and Walter stood in the lobby of CMMR. The search team had dispersed throughout the building, and the staff, researchers, and assistants were gathered together, standing in small groups near the reception desk or huddled together outside the front doors beneath the roof overhang. Kali could see Gloria Marsh standing among the people there. Water dripped in a steady stream from the edge of the roof, forming puddles on the cement surface below.

She turned to Walter. "I can't believe we got nothing from her after her lawyer friend showed up—just the usual warning that if we weren't going to charge her with something, we'd do well to leave her alone."

"I believe his threat was police harassment."

"That's what it was." She watched as Gloria

reached out to the man standing beside her, laughing as though the search of the building was of no interest. "I didn't like her much before, and I don't like her at all now."

"I don't like this building," said Walter, looking around at the stark spaces. "Feels cold and unfriendly."

On the other side of the lobby, O'Connor and Byron Coolidge were standing together. Kali and Walter turned to watch them. When the search warrant had been presented and O'Connor was summoned to the desk, he'd bellowed about injustice and interruptions, but appeared—at least for the moment—to be entirely out of steam. He kept his back to Kali, and she could see that his hands were shoved into the pockets of his lab coat. Byron seemed far less distressed as he stood quietly, watching the activity around him with interest.

"You recognize most of these people?" asked Walter.

Kali nodded. "We've talked to all of them, concentrating on the ones connected to O'Connor and his team." She did a quick head count. "There are only thirty people here, almost all of whom know nothing about Maya Holmes."

"That doesn't seem like much of a staff for a place this size. I would have expected a couple hundred, at least."

"I wonder," said Kali. She pulled out her phone and called Hara. "Can you check something for me?" she asked. "See if you can find out if CMMR is in any kind of financial trouble—if people have been let go, laid off, anything like that."

Walter waited until she ended the call. "Didn't

you say that one of these people complained that their funding was in question?" he asked.

"Yes. That was Byron Coolidge. He seemed more concerned about that than the fact that a woman he worked with had been tortured and killed."

She looked over at him. His appearance was as untidy as when she'd last encountered him. He seemed to feel her stare, and suddenly looked toward her. Meeting her eyes, he smiled briefly and raised his hand in a half wave. There was an immediate reaction from O'Connor, who said something critical. The words were indistinguishable, but the meaning was clear. Chastised, Byron immediately turned away and gazed out of the window.

"That O'Connor guy's a real jerk," said Walter, who had seen the exchange.

"They both are, in my opinion," said Kali. "Self-involved. But I'd bet anything that if you asked either one, they'd claim that their work is for the benefit of the entire human species."

From the corridor on the far side of the security turnstile, Kali could see several uniformed officers approaching, followed by a number of other people, some of whom were dressed in hazmat suits.

"They sent a big search team up here from Wailuku," said Walter. "You think they've found anything?"

"I think we're about to find out. Why don't you go and talk to them while I keep an eye on these people?"

He left, walking toward the turnstile, where he was met by an officer. Their conversation was brief, and Walter returned a minute later. Kali only needed to see the expression on his face to know that nothing had turned up during the search.

"Nada," he said. "Not even anything that looked remotely like a code violation." He looked around the room. "We can go ahead and let these people back in."

After the last of the search team filed out of the building, Kali signaled to the guard that he could allow the CMMR employees to reenter the secure areas. She watched as they made their way through the gate, chattering excitedly. Byron went through on his own, but O'Connor came striding angrily across the lobby, halting in front of Kali.

"Are you finally satisfied?" he asked. His face was distorted with fury. "As soon as word of this gets out, I'm done. Finished. No one will touch us. My lab will be the laughingstock of the entire scientific community, and I have you to thank for that. You can be certain I'll take this to the highest possible office. I hope you lose your job. You certainly aren't very good at it."

He spun on his heel and headed toward his office. They were watching him stomp away, and didn't notice Gloria trailing in behind the last of the people who had been waiting outside. She stopped next to Kali.

"Nicely done," said Gloria. She waved her arms around. "As far as disruption goes, I've really got to hand it to you. This was a monumentally effective way to piss off O'Connor and make sure nothing gets done for however many days it takes for people to stop talking about it."

"Am I supposed to say you're welcome?" asked Kali.

"Unnecessary," said Gloria. "Let's say I've already inferred it from your posture." She smirked. "Sucks to be wrong, doesn't it?"

"Interesting that you take such pleasure in the failure of others," said Kali, her voice mild.

"Yeah, I've had more than one therapist tell me the same thing." She turned away to follow the others. "See ya," she said. She winked at Kali. "Let me know when this is all over if you want to grab lunch or have a drink."

"Look at you," said Walter when Gloria was out of earshot. "You've got offers for dates all over the place. I think Icelandic Thor is a better fit, though. Plus he's a hell of a lot easier to get along with. That little redhead is cute, but she's also kind of scary."

"Scary enough to be involved with murder?"

"If I was a betting man, which you know I'm not, my answer would be a great big yes."

Hara was waiting for Kali at the station.

"This is kind of interesting," he said. He held out several printed pages to her, then looked down at his notebook. "The actual building where CMMR is housed is owned by a conglomerate. The board of directors is made up of people in various science fields, but Davos O'Connor is listed as the director, and has been from the very beginning."

"Where do they get their money?"

"It looks like direct funding for specific projects.

Wealthy patrons of the sciences, mostly. A few who have part-time homes on Maui, but a lot of people in New York, California, Asia, and Europe. Several of them have big media connections, and there are a lot of newspaper articles and magazine features that focus on these people and provide them with an outlet to tell everyone about how the things they're developing will have a great impact on the environment."

"Any political ties?"

Hara frowned. "No, ma'am. Not that I've been able to tell, but a lot of prominent people like to keep that kind of thing to themselves, don't they?"

"They do. Makes it easier to play whatever side of an issue is most convenient or beneficial at any given moment."

"I was able to get through to someone who was listed as a former member of the board, but stepped down last year. A lady named Helena Freher who inherited a bunch of money from her family. They were in the boating industry. Big container boats."

"And? Did she have anything interesting to say?"

Hara nodded. "Well, she seems to really hate Dr. O'Connor." He looked down at his notes. "What she said exactly is that he 'wastes money, has no respect for deadlines, and has atrocious table manners.' "

Kali smiled. "Did she say they've been able to monetize any of the research coming out of CMMR?"

"No, she wouldn't say. But she made it clear she wasn't impressed with any of their work so far, and that she wasn't the only one of the board who held that opinion."

"Okay. Thank you—that's all helpful. Seems like O'Connor may be under some pressure to come up with something clever to appease the board, or to inspire the benefactors to keep writing checks."

"Is that motive, ma'am?"

"Yes," she said. "That's exactly what it is."

CHAPTER 25

It had been a long and difficult day. Beneath the scanty shelter of the soaked fronds of a towering coconut palm in the station parking lot, Kali sat in the Jeep and watched the wind and rain beat against the windscreen. In her mind, she kept replaying her encounter at the lab with Vance and Byron, knowing that there was something amiss with the story she'd been fed.

She slipped the Jeep into gear and was just preparing to back out when she saw Walter bolt through the front door of the station, holding his phone aloft in one hand while being followed closely by Hara and several other officers. Her phone buzzed at nearly the same time as she saw them exit the building, and she glanced at the screen, tensing as Walter's number came up.

Hara dashed toward his cruiser. She watched,

apprehensive, as Walter made a beeline for the Jeep, calling to her against the wind.

"Kali! Wait up!"

She rolled down her window as he ran up. He stood there, his hands grasping the edge of the glass.

"Island Market," he gasped. "Leave the Jeep here and come with me. We need sirens." He pulled at her door, agitated. "Come on! It's George. A customer just made an emergency call—said someone's tried to blow up the store with George inside."

She was already out of the Jeep and on the ground, running beside Walter as they moved toward his car. Hara's siren wailed in warning as he passed them and pulled onto the main road. They reached the cruiser and climbed in, following Hara. The two cars raced toward the store. Kali could already hear the corresponding fire and ambulance sirens converging in the same direction. She was enveloped by a sense of dread.

"What did the caller say?" she asked, snapping her seat belt into place as the police car sped around a line of traffic halted on the road.

"Said something that sounded like bomb," Walter responded, his voice terse. "Then there was a blast, and we lost the connection."

They drove in anxious silence, listening to the scanner for more details of what had taken place. The road was slick with rain, and leaves blown onto the asphalt surface made their high speed more dangerous. The dispatcher was relaying the few available details: mixed reports of fire and a possible explosive device. As they drew closer, they could see black smoke billowing through the rain, fusing with the dark, low sky.

The first two fire engines, tasked with fire suppression, had already arrived by the time Walter and Kali pulled in. They could see that the fire truck transporting the crew had also reached the scene. The hydrant at the edge of the parking area had been tapped, and the fire officer in charge of the incident was setting up a command post. As the firefighters were pulling on their protective gear, Kali recognized many of the names displayed along the bottom edge of the backs of their black bunker gear. The protective uniforms were trimmed with reflective, fluorescent yellow-green bands that had once stood out against the darker clothing when they were new, but had become worn and dulled by repeated exposure to soot. She felt her heart race at the thought of the danger they faced— danger they were all too well aware of, but had nevertheless chosen to confront, regardless of the risk to themselves.

Walter swung the car into the parking lot next to an ambulance and left to find the fire chief while Kali joined Hara, who was directing traffic and creating an access lane for the emergency vehicles. Despite the weather, a crowd of onlookers was already gathering. Kali instructed Hara to carry on with traffic while she did her best to deal with the spectators.

Behind her, she heard the clamor of activity, and tried to concentrate on keeping people back from the scene while she searched for a glimpse of George. She was unable to spot him among the increasing number of people congregated along the

roadway and in the parking area. Her worry
turned to panic.

A ladder had been set up along the front section of the roof, near a space where smoke was
rolling from a broken window. As Kali stood with
her back to the growing crowd, arms outstretched,
she watched as members of the fire crew made
their way into the front of the store near the
checkout area, while others began to ascend the
ladder at the end of the store, past the window.
One of them, a man she knew by name, was carrying a chainsaw, and as soon as the crew had
reached their position on the roof, the sound of
the saw's engine roared to life. The firefighter who
wielded it began to cut a hole in the roof above the
space where the smoke was seeping out. She knew
they were attempting to provide a larger vent to
give the flames an egress that would help prevent
them from moving into the duct space between
the ceiling and the roof.

A sudden cry erupted from below, near where
the store's glass doors had once stood, and Kali's
heart lurched as she saw two firefighters, their
faces obscured by respirators, jog from the space
with an inert figure carried between them. The
ambulance crew was waiting nearby, and the figure
was transferred quickly to a stretcher and wheeled
rapidly toward the open rear doors of the ambulance. From where Kali stood, she could clearly see
the white helmet of the fire chief and Walter
standing next to him. As the stretcher was taken
from the building, Walter followed, striding along
in its wake. Kali watched as the stretcher was

hooked on and lifted into the ambulance. When the vehicle failed to immediately activate its siren and pull out of the parking area, she felt a new, far more intense sense of alarm descend upon her.

Through the melee, she kept Walter in her sights. He was leaning against the rear of the ambulance, engaged in conversation with one of the paramedics. As she watched, he seemed to relax. A few moments later, she saw him nod to the paramedic. He turned away from the ambulance as it began to pull out and walked toward her, wiping the rain from his face with the back of his hand. As he passed the crowd, an elderly woman who had been standing on one side, alone and away from the other people watching, dashed away from the throng and ran toward him. She grasped him by the arm and began to gesture wildly, pointing at the store, then back to the ambulance. Walter listened, then turned and pointed at Kali. She saw the woman nod in acknowledgment, and a moment later, both the woman and Walter had joined her.

"George is stable," Walter said. "Hurt, and he has some burns, but word is he'll be fine. I'll fill you in on the details in a minute, but first, this is Mrs. Bailey. She was here when the fire broke out. I want you to hear what she has to say."

"Yes," said the woman, clearly agitated. "George had just closed up early. I had checked out and was almost at my car with my groceries when I saw a motorcycle come careening up to the front of the store. A man jumped off and smashed the window glass with something, then I saw him throw an object inside and jump back onto the motorcycle. A few seconds went by, and then I heard an explosion. I didn't see the fire right away, but when I ran around to the doors, there were flames all along the aisle where all the cleaning supplies are. I tried to get back inside, but I couldn't get close because it was so hot. I knew George was in there, but I couldn't see him. When I left with my groceries, he was sitting at the counter, closing up his till." She had tears streaming down her face. "I couldn't do anything to help! Oh, I do hope he'll be okay. I can't bear the thought of anything happening to him."

Kali looked at the woman, estimating her to be in her late seventies or early eighties. Her disheveled hair was mostly white, pulled away from her lined face. Kali could see that her blouse was singed, and that the backs of her hands were red and irritated. She was soaked from the rain.

"You called 911, which was exactly the right thing to do," Kali said in a kind, grateful voice.

"No," said the woman, her distress overwhelming her. "George is my friend. I should have searched inside to find him. I should have saved him."

"He's being looked after right now," said Walter. Gently, he put his hand on the woman's shoulder. "You'll be able to talk to him soon. I know how grateful he'll be that you were here and were able to help. If not for you, it might have been some time before anyone noticed the fire and called to report it. By then, things might have been much, much worse. You did a good thing today."

This didn't seem to mollify the woman. She hung her head, as if ashamed. "I always wondered what I would do if I was in a situation where it was up to me to save someone. I always imagined that I would become a superhero and save the day."

"I think that's exactly what you did," said Kali. She looked around. The crowd had become larger, despite the downpour. She heard Hara, his voice carrying above the din, instructing a group of people with their cell phone cameras pointed at the fire to back away from the scene and give the rescue teams the space they needed. His voice carried an authority she hadn't heard in it before, and even in the midst of the turmoil unfolding around her, she felt a surge of pride.

"We need to have your hands looked at. But first, if you can, I'd like you to tell Detective Māhoe everything you just told me—everything you can remember, from the moment you became aware of the motorcycle pulling up at the store. Anything at all—what color it was, who you saw. Any little detail."

The woman looked up at Kali. "It was a black motorcycle. A sporty kind, but not new, I don't think. It looked shiny, but it was wet from the rain. I was between the front door and the parking area, and I don't think the driver even saw me. Maybe he just didn't care that there was a pedestrian there, but he was driving way too fast and not staying in the parking lane, and I jumped back because I was afraid he might hit me."

Kali listened, imaging the scene in her mind.

"What happened next?" she asked.

The woman turned back toward the store, where the fire crew was doing its best to dampen the flames still issuing from within.

"Then it slammed to a stop, and the driver put

his kickstand down and jumped off. It was definitely a man. He had something in his hand, and he smashed the glass of the front window on the far corner of the store, there, where all the smoke is. I saw him throw something inside, then he got back on his motorcycle. I thought he must have thrown a bomb. I just couldn't process it. Then I heard what sounded like an explosion coming from inside, and the smoke just poured out through the broken part of the glass."

"And the man on the motorcycle? What did he do?"

"He roared away. He nearly hit that tall lamppost over there near the entrance to the parking lot on his way out."

Kali waited, letting the woman gather her thoughts.

"And the driver?" she finally asked. "Can you tell me anything at all about him? Did you see his face?"

"No . . ." she said slowly, conjuring the scene in her own mind. "I saw that he had dark hair. I don't think he was an older person. And he was wearing a short-sleeved shirt."

"You're sure of this description? And that his shirt had short sleeves?" asked Kali.

"Oh yes. I'm absolutely positive," said Mrs. Bailey. "All the parking lot lights were on, and the lights around the store. That's why I could see all the tattoos on his arm when he threw the bomb." She looked at Kali with widening eyes. "I thought it was very strange that someone who liked cartoons would try to blow up a building."

Kali held her breath. "Cartoons?"

"Yes," said the woman. She shuddered. "It looked like there was a big tattoo of a dolphin on his arm. Not a beautiful dolphin—it was a scary cartoon one. I know it sounds strange, but I'm sure of it." She looked up at Kali. "You know, I used to love dolphins. Until tonight."

CHAPTER 26

B ased on Mrs. Bailey's description of the dark-haired man with the strange tattoo on the motorcycle, and the gift sent to Kali, an immediate all-points bulletin was broadcast in an effort to locate Vance Sousa. A visit to the apartment listed as his residence failed to yield him or a motorcycle, but a search inside—borne out by photos sent from the officers who were at his address—revealed an apparent obsession with Hawaiian lore. His walls were covered with posters and drawings of gods and goddesses from various legends, and numerous carved tiki statues were displayed throughout the rooms of the apartment.

As the level of activity at the fire scene wound down, Kali sat in Walter's cruiser, scrolling through the images. Whoever Vance's unfortunate landlord happened to be, reflected Kali, he or she was unlikely to be pleased about the colorful drawings and lettering scrawled across the walls. A large, carved tiki stood on a table beside one end of the sofa. On the wall behind the sofa, someone had painted an enormous volcano in the act of erupting. Lava poured down the sides toward the figure of a tiki man with bared teeth, rising from tall, spiky grass in the foreground.

She paused on the image of the carved tiki on the table, enlarging it to study it more closely. Though it had appeared at first glance to be just another of the same carvings in Vance's collection, she realized that the figure on the table was female. It had the same gaping, toothed grin, long arms reaching toward the ground, and carved headdress, but the trunk of the figure had elongated breasts. It was Pahulu, the sorceress who often delivered her dark magic in the form of nightmares.

Walter came back to the car and slipped into his seat, leaning his head back against the headrest.

"What are you looking at?" he asked.

"All the evidence we need to pin this witch business on Vance Sousa," she said, and showed him the photos taken at his apartment.

"You think he's the head witch—or whatever you would call the person pulling the strings? I'm sure there's some kind of meaningful title."

"It seems as though he might be," she said. "The person who sent that text to Chad called themself 'Kane' like the dark priest, and I'm sure he's given himself some crazy title out of a cult movie . . . Master Necromancer or something like that. But I still don't think he's got the organizational skills to pull off the firewalking ceremony or clean up a murder scene. And if the others are involved, I can't see the all-powerful Dr. O'Connor—or any of those other researchers—letting someone as unpredictable and volatile as Vance call the shots. Can you?"

He shook his head. "It seems equally unlikely that if it is one of them, that they'd put up with Vance drawing all this crazy attention to them."

She looked out into the dark sky. A ripple of thunder moved through, accompanied by a distant arc of lightning. She watched as the ladder truck and the second ambulance left, moving at a far slower speed than had heralded their arrival.

"It's hard to get crazy under control after it's already been set loose. Maybe," she said slowly, "they aren't letting him draw attention to them, but away from them."

"Meaning?"

"I'm not sure yet." The frustration was evident in her voice. "I need to think about it."

By the time Walter had driven her home, it was nearly two o'clock in the morning. She looked through the security camera footage, finding nothing of concern. She was exhausted. The investigation, combined with the endless days and nights of rain and wind, was taking a toll. She felt as though she could sleep for months, or for however long it took for the sun to return and the world to right itself.

She leaned against the wall of her shower, letting the warm, soothing spray soak her. Her head ached, and she rubbed her temples, trying to re-

lieve the tension that had settled there. After ten
minutes had passed, she stepped out of the shower
and dried off, then slipped on the loose cotton
pants and old T-shirt that she slept in. When she
came out of the bathroom, Hilo was standing at
the window looking out over the lanai. The rain
had settled into a light mist. Outside, the half-
revealed moon cast a pale light across the front
yard, glinting on the wet surfaces. The wind, blowing through the damp branches and palm fronds,
formed shapes among the moving shadows.

Hilo's ears twitched. Kali heard the dog's low
growl, and watched as his long body trembled. She
stepped out of the light cast by the table lamp set
beside the end of the sofa, and edged into the
open door of her bedroom, reaching for the gun
resting on the tall chest of drawers just inside.
Carefully, she moved toward the back door.

"Stay, boy," she said softly. In response, Hilo
whimpered, swinging his head toward her. As she
reached out with her left hand and grasped the
door handle, there was a loud whooshing sound,
and a burst of light outside in the yard. She flung
open the door and rushed down the steps. The
sound of a motorcycle roaring away could be
heard on the main road, but her attention was immediately focused on the hale wa'a housing the
canoe, which was engulfed in flames.

Her weariness forgotten, she raced across the
lawn toward the hale. Flames shot through the
roof as the palm fronds that formed it crackled
and were consumed. She could smell the unmistakable odor of gasoline. Through the flames, the
canoe was visible, wreathed in fire, the outline of

the long, slender chunk of wood providing a core of fuel.

Even as a cry of rage escaped her lips, she saw movement on the path dividing the trees on the edge of the property, and the figures of Elvar and Birta running toward her.

"Kali! Are you all right?" Elvar shouted. Beside him, Birta held up her arm, attempting to shield her face from the heat of the flames.

"I'll get the hose!" yelled Birta, looking wildly toward the side of the house where the exterior water spigot protruded from the siding, a long green hose coiled on the ground beside it.

"No!" shouted Kali. "No water! Grab the fire extinguisher from the kitchen! Use the back door!"

Even as she looked from the hale to the house, Kali was filled with a sense of dismay. She'd heard a motorcycle, but had no guarantee that the perpetrator—or perpetrators—had left. For all she knew, someone could be hiding in the trees, or could have doused other areas of her property with gasoline. She thought of Hilo inside, and of Birta heading into the house for the fire extinguisher. If whoever had started the fire was watching, they might have taken the opportunity to get inside while she was distracted on the lawn.

"Elvar! Call for help," she yelled as she spun around and bolted toward the house behind Birta. Even as she reached the clear patch of ground leading to the bottom step, Birta was on her way out of the house, the fire extinguisher in one hand. Hilo rushed past her and launched himself from the door landing to the ground in a single leap. He made a beeline for Kali's side, barking in distress.

Kali saw Birta point the fire extinguisher at the base of the flames, releasing the foam spray and swinging the nozzle from side to side with controlled movements. Birta began to circle the hale, and Kali took off at a sprint, making her way around the perimeter of the house. The thick, wet grass clung to her legs, soaking the fabric of her thin pants. She could feel the cool wetness between her toes, and was faintly aware of a damp breeze moving the branches of the trees, releasing the rain gathered on the surface of their leaves.

Hilo moved beside her, sniffing the ground. He followed a scent for a short distance between the hale and the house, then turned and galloped toward the driveway, his nose close to the ground. Kali adjusted the grip on her gun and followed him, staying in the deeper shadows along the driveway's edge. When the dog reached the spot just beyond the driveway where it met the paved road as it curved away, he halted and sat, gazing at Kali.

"Good boy," she said, looking to the left and right. There were no street lights on this stretch of road, and she could see very little. She jogged back to the house. The hale was smoking, but the flames were confined to a few spots on the ground just beneath the line where the roof had fallen in. Elvar and Birta were still there. Elvar was stomping the ground, doing his best to smother the spots that were still smoldering.

Kali stopped, gun hanging by her side, and

looked at what remained of the small structure that had protected the canoe. Birta was shaking the fire extinguisher, which was nearly spent. Kali watched as she sprayed the last of the foaming agent onto the ground.

Elvar turned to Kali and caught her eye. "Help's on the way," he said. He looked briefly at the hale, then walked closer to her. He didn't reach out; he just stood there, beside her. "I'm so sorry, Kali," he said.

She nodded. "Yeah," she said. "Thanks."

Sitting on the lanai, still wet, Kali and Walter watched as the responding fire crew and officers inspected the hale ruins and did a thorough search of the grounds, checking to be certain that nothing else had been treated with gasoline or another substance that might ignite. Birta and Elvar had gone home, though both had done their best to convince Kali to bring Hilo and spend the night in their spare room. She had declined, and Walter had been displeased.

"Two fires in one night? That's not a coincidence, and you're not staying here," he said after Elvar and Birta had left.

"Yes, I am," Kali said firmly. "I've already told you I'm not letting some degenerate scare me away from my home."

"It's not safe, Kali. I'd bet my best ukulele that Vance Sousa was behind this drama as well as burning down George's store. Clearly he's still in the area, and until we find him, you're in danger."

"I'm not going to wind up in a tree, if that's what you're worried about."

"That's exactly what I'm worried about," he said. He looked toward the wreckage of the hale.

"If this Vance character—and someone else—is trying to scare me, they haven't thought things through," she said. "They aren't just targeting me, they've threatened people I care about. Whoever it is must know they're just really pissing me off, and that it's going to make me more determined to find out who they are."

"I see," said Walter. He wasn't smiling. "You're crediting some psychopath with reasoning powers they're unlikely to have. And we don't know where he's hiding right now. His apartment's being watched, but he hasn't gone back there." He looked around. "Your house is surrounded by a couple zillion acres of thick forest and wild land. He could be anywhere. He could be watching us right now, planning some new mischief."

"Maybe," she said. "I don't know. I do know this has gotten pretty personal, and I'm seriously angry."

"If you won't come with me, I'm leaving an officer here tonight to keep an eye on things. Tomorrow I'm going to put up an alarm system with an alert, and you're going to have someone here on the grounds until this is wrapped up."

"Okay," she said. "We can do that, not that the cameras have done any good. Someone's being pretty careful."

The scent of burned wood hung in the air.

"Mike's canoe . . ." began Walter, but Kali shook her head.

"Don't," she said. "It's gone. That's all there is to it. Talking about it isn't going to bring it back."

"Maybe not, but . . ."

"It was just a boat," she said in a flat voice. "Not even a boat, really. More like a promise. I remember the day when Mike cut the tree. He asked permission first, promising the tree and its spirit that it wasn't being taken for some trivial reason, but that he'd selected it for its beauty and strength—that it would be honored and tended well. He said he would take the tree on a journey across the water, and that it would be powerful and free."

They sat quietly for a few minutes.

"Maybe it's for the best," she finally said. "Just like you said before."

Walter looked down at the floor of the lanai, only dimly visible in the moonlight. "This isn't what I meant," he said. He shook his head. "This, what happened tonight, is wrong."

She stood up. She swayed from fatigue, and reached out to grasp one of the columns supporting the roof of the lanai. The night air felt cold. Beneath the sounds of the officers and firefighters going about their jobs, she could hear the pounding of the surf as the tide came in and crashed against the lava rocks along the shore.

"Here's the thing," she said. "The only truth any of us can be absolutely certain of is that we will all—every one of us—eventually lose everything that matters to us. Nothing is constant. Nothing exists in stasis. Tonight, it was George's turn to lose his store, and my turn to lose an almost boat. I still have my memories."

Walter watched her, seeing her stern profile outlined in the pale light. She stood, tall and very still, gazing intently toward the sea. Then she closed her eyes. He waited, seeing her breath slow, the tenseness in her shoulders begin to dissipate. She opened her eyes and turned to him.

"Thank you for caring about me, Uncle. You make the world a better place. Now come inside and help me make some coffee." She gestured toward the people moving about in the yard. "They could probably use some caffeine. I know I could." She looked down at the soaked legs of her sleeping pants. "And I guess I should put on some actual clothes."

CHAPTER 27

In the morning, Kali woke to the scent of fire still hanging in the wet air, and to something else: warm dog breath. It was late, and Hilo had taken up a position on the floor beside her bed, his nose resting on the sheet directly in front of her face.

"Sorry, fella," she said, sitting up and dropping her feet to the floor. "You must be starving."

She filled his bowl and cleaned his water dish, refilling it and setting it on the small woven floor mat beside the refrigerator. She watched him eat and spill water onto the floor planks, but she had no appetite of her own. From the kitchen window, the sad mass of charred palm leaves and wood resting on the singed ground was clearly visible. Again, she was engulfed by a feeling of profound weariness she knew had nothing to do with how many hours she had slept, and everything to do with frustration and fear.

The knowledge that someone had entered her private space again without her being aware—and had caused damage to something she deeply valued—had left her feeling exposed and vulnerable. She got up and wandered around, straightening the pillows on the sofa and wiping down the table and counter. There were empty coffee mugs stacked in the sink. She hadn't had the energy to deal with them the night before, nor could she bear having anyone help her clean up.

The hot water ran into the sink, and Kali thrust her hands into the suds. This she could do: tidy her kitchen and clean up her yard and throw away all of her undergarments and buy new ones. She could add more locks to her doors and place even more security cameras around the house. It might take longer than she'd like, but she'd find the person who had violated her space and make them accountable. What she couldn't do was shake off the feeling that the whole world was spinning out of her control.

As she was putting away the clean dishes, she heard a car pull up. A few moments later, the kitchen door opened and Walter's head appeared around the edge.

"Hey, you," he said. "I told everyone to leave you alone this morning so you could get some sleep. Thought I'd stop by instead of calling."

She waited, knowing instinctively that there was more bad news.

"There's no sign of Vance Sousa. And that kid,

Trey Carter, has done a runner. Hara and I went to pick him up at the shelter to see what he might know about what's going on, but he was gone and someone there said he'd talked to Trey, who said he went off yesterday to hitch a ride for the ferry at Kahului."

"When was this?"

"The person at the shelter said he took off mid-morning."

Kali sighed. "That means he's already in Honolulu, or somewhere else on Oʻahu. But at least we know he was gone before the fire started." She thought about the timing. "It's a little worrisome that both Carter and Sousa are missing."

"We've got someone checking CCTV footage to see if we can catch Trey leaving the port area in Honolulu."

"He doesn't have any money, and if he took his tent and his drug habit with him, chances are good he didn't go any further than the homeless community there."

"Exactly what I'm thinking." He looked at her. "I also think it might be good for you to have a change of scenery."

"Paris? London?"

He grinned. "You wish. I want you out of here, yes—but I'm afraid it's only going to be as far as Oʻahu. You've already talked to this kid and might be able to find him without spooking him. I want to get him back to Maui where we can track his movements more easily. And while you're over there, see what kind of vibes you can pick up at the Wela Wela Cave."

She nodded. "Okay. You want me to see if Larry

Mahuka's planning on taking his Cessna over to
O'ahu so I can catch a ride with him?"

"No need," he said. "I know you aren't crazy
about flying, and since you've already been trau-
matized enough for one week, you're expected on
the afternoon ferry. And there's a room reserved
for you in Honolulu. You're booked for two nights,
but you can extend if necessary. I'll have an officer
stationed here during the day, and I'm going to
spend the nights here on the boat while you're
gone."

"Hilo will be thrilled."

"He'll have to sleep on the boat with me. I want
it to look like your place is empty."

"You just want to make sure no one takes a torch
to your old tub."

"True dat," he said, glancing fondly toward the
slope leading to where the Gingerfish rested in
the water. "I already talked to your neighbors, and
they're going to let me keep my car—not the
cruiser—parked over there at their house. With
your Jeep gone, anyone wanting to cause you
more grief might feel like they've got opportunity
and an open invitation."

A chill ran down her spine, thinking of the possibility of arriving home to find nothing left. The
house was old, and small, and in need of multiple
repairs, but every square inch of it held some precious memory, and she couldn't bear the thought
of losing it.

Walter seemed to intuit her thoughts.

"Don't worry," he said. "Between me, Hilo, and
your Icelandic strongman, we've got this under control."

*   *   *

Kali made her way off the ferry at Honolulu Harbor's Pier 19 and up toward the taxis that were queued along Kukahi Street. Walter had made her reservation at the Beach Gem Hotel close to the Diamond Head area, which had become the epi-center of the island's growing homeless commu-nity. It was late in the day, so she unpacked the few belongings she'd brought, and went out to find something for dinner.

There was a small café open a few blocks from the hotel, and she went in and found a booth near the front windows. She'd lived in Honolulu for sev-eral years with Mike while they were both working on the municipal police force, but the city had never felt as comfortable to her as the greener, quieter landscape offered by Maui. She wanted to hear birdsong, not traffic. When her grandmother had left her the small house close to Hana, the move had seemed like the right one.

The café menu wasn't extensive, but she or-dered a grilled fish sandwich with macaroni salad and a glass of pineapple iced tea. Walter called while she was waiting for her food.

"I'm on the boat," he said. "Your dog is sleeping on my bunk."

"That's because you don't have a sofa onboard."

"If you ever have kids, they're going to be spoiled rotten."

"I'm just going to have more dogs."

Walter grunted. "How's the hotel?"

"It's fine. A little worn around the edges, but close to Diamond Head."

"Are things as gnarly over there as I've heard?"

"I haven't been over there yet. But I thought the Department of Land and Natural Resources did a big sweep about a year ago and cleared out most of the tents and cleaned up the debris."

"They did. And it stayed clear for a couple of months—then the tents started popping up again. It's a problem. There aren't adequate facilities nearby to provide bathrooms and sanitary resources, so you can imagine the living conditions. If a virus or disease pops up in that kind of densely populated situation, keeping it under control is going to be impossible."

"Well, if some of the population has been dispersed, it might make it easier to find Trey Carter."

"Here's hoping," said Walter. "You've got a ride up there tomorrow. Officer Jennifer Kama from Vice is going to pick you up in the morning at the hotel and go up there with you."

"I know her," said Kali.

"She's part of the team monitoring the meth network within the homeless communities."

"How are the people there financing purchases?" asked Kali. "They can't afford food, but there's money for drugs?"

"Seems to be how it works. Think about the physical condition of confirmed, frequent users. Food is no longer a priority, let alone nutritious food."

Across the line, Kali heard sudden barking in the background. She tensed. "What's going on?" she asked.

"Your dog," said Walter.

"I hear him. What's he barking at?"

"Bird. Some kind of petrel, I think. Hilo just dove off the side of the boat to see if he could catch it."

She groaned inwardly, picturing the soaking wet dog shaking water all over the interior of Walter's small cabin space.

"And did he?"

"Nah. Bird flew away. I think I heard it laughing."

CHAPTER 20

Officer Jennifer Kama was standing by the hotel registration desk, chatting with one of the morning staff when Kali got off the elevator. Like Kali, she was dressed in worn jeans and an old shirt. Kali knew from the loose, oversized shirt that Jennifer was carrying a gun.

As Kali walked across the lobby and approached her, Jennifer turned away from the desk, meeting Kali in the middle of the lobby's seating area.

"Good to see you, Kali," she said.

"Same here."

"I assume you're up for a hike?" Jennifer looked down at Kali's shoes, and nodded in approval. "Those should do. We're heading up to Kapena Falls first. Some of the footing will be slick."

"So much rain," said Kali.

"Which means mudslides, of course."

"And that means blocked roads, and traffic jams, and rental cars upside-down in ditches. Or worse."

"Yeah," said Jennifer. "You still driving that wreck of a Jeep with the giant dog riding shotgun?"

"I refuse to part with either one of them."

"Well, you should have brought the Jeep with you."

Jennifer had left her own vehicle, a small four-wheel-drive truck, parked under the hotel's entrance portico. They set off on the road leading to the access point for the trail to the falls. Jennifer explained that she'd been brought up to speed on the situation on Maui, and that a description and photograph of Trey Carter had already been circulated. He'd been spotted on the CCTV camera at the passenger terminal wearing a large backpack and headed toward Nimitz Highway, presumably to hitch a ride. From that point, he'd disappeared.

Their route took them past the Foster Botanical Garden and Punchbowl Crater. They turned off the main road onto the Pali Highway. To their right was Pu'u 'Ualaka'a State Park. A few miles along, Jennifer pulled over, and they struck out on the trail leading west across the Nu'uanu Stream. By the time they'd been hiking for ten minutes or so, both were covered with mud spatters, and their hair had tangled in the wind.

Soon they saw encampments, and trash accumulated among the shrubs and trees. Just above the pool at the base of the falls, Kali could see four separate campsites. As they drew closer, a man and two women came into view, resting on sleeping bags spread out on a flat, rocky area. The women were talking, but fell silent as they caught sight of Kali and Jennifer.

One of them sat up.

"Hi," said Kali. "We're trying to find our friend's campsite. Trey Carter—maybe you've seen him?"

"Don't recognize the name," said the woman, clearly suspicious.

"Well, this is what he looks like," said Jennifer, pulling a sheet of paper out of the pocket of her jeans. It was folded, and she opened it up and held it in front of the woman and her companions.

"Nope," said the woman who had already spoken.

The man watched them.

"What are you after?" he asked.

"Just Trey," said Jennifer. "He promised us some star-gazing."

The other woman snorted. "I bet," she said. "What are you really after?"

"A dry place to sleep," said Kali. "I guess we'll keep looking."

"Yeah," said Jennifer, her tone suggesting that she'd expected a little more camaraderie. "Thanks anyway."

"So much for blending in," muttered Jennifer. "Sometimes I think there's a neon sign over my head that's constantly blinking COP."

They turned and followed the path to the falls that fed into Alapena Pool at its base. There was another campsite here, set into a small, clear area close to the edge of the rocky ledge above the cascading water. They could see an older man sitting on the rocks, his legs and feet dangling over the pool.

Jennifer pointed. "So this is a big part of the problem—why we have to keep clearing out these camps. A lot of these people are using the water to bathe in, and the whole area—including the pool below the falls—as a toilet. We've got big reservoirs up here, and the waters are becoming increasingly contaminated. A lot of experts are concerned about bacteria and viruses."

"It's not just here," said Kali, gazing up at the man on the rocks. "It's everywhere. Friends in California tell me stories about Los Angeles and San Francisco. And we've got a huge problem on Maui, too."

They followed the path along the stream, heading south from the falls. There were several other campsites, but no one admitted to knowing anything about Trey Carter.

"I think we need better social programs," said Jennifer, "but maybe trying a different approach from what we've done so far. Give people a better shelter—develop some of these countless empty retail spaces into living spaces."

"Yes, but maybe the key is to also give people work. Something purposeful to do to help restore their sense of meaning and dignity. There are plenty of countries that offer paid work in exchange for simple, valuable labor, like keeping streets clean."

Jennifer looked thoughtful. "I know. I don't understand why communities aren't trying that. I think it might actually work here."

They'd gone for some way without seeing any more campsites, and Jennifer suggested that they head for the next location on Sand Island, which had a much larger population of displaced people. They made their way back to the truck. Retracing their route, they eventually turned southwest to find the access road to the island that skirted Ke'ehi Harbor and led to Sand Island Recreation Area.

"These camps were cleared, too," said Jennifer. She sighed. "Camping here was—and still is—illegal, but as you can see, we just don't have the manpower to keep up with it."

Again, they parked and headed toward the beach, where rows of ramshackle tents could be seen. The area was chaos: Bicycles, furniture, cooking equipment, and piles of trash were interspersed with makeshift tents, as well as tents that looked as though they'd come straight from a high-end camping outfitter.

They walked among groups of people who were gathered together, as well as numerous single individuals sitting, standing, or lying among the confusion. No one had seen Trey or remembered seeing anyone like him. Finally, they stopped in front of a woman with a small boy of five or so who was sitting beneath a tarp that had been stretched across a bent tent frame. The woman glared at them, muttering to them to go away and leave her alone, but the little boy reached out and took the printout of Trey's picture from Jennifer's outstretched hand. He studied it solemnly, then turned and pointed to the thick shrubs set back from the main beach.

"Sleeping man," he said, his soft voice blurring the edges of the words.

"Thank you," said Kali, smiling at him. She glanced at the woman, who looked away.

The boy stepped out from the shade of the tarp and watched as Kali and Jennifer navigated the crowded area, moving between a cooler and a collection of suitcases. They walked in the direction the child had indicated.

Kali could see the tip of a blue tent behind a clump of bushes. It looked like the same tent she'd seen on Maui. She stepped forward carefully, not wanting to scare Trey away if he was there.

Like before, she could see his long feet protruding from the opening of the tent, his body too tall to fit comfortably inside. And like before, the feet were bare and splayed apart, resting on the ground.

This time, however, there was no twitching. Kali moved closer and looked inside, then stepped back. She turned to Jennifer.

"It's definitely him," she said. "But he isn't sleeping."

CHAPTER 29

By the time Kali and Jennifer had made their way back to the parking area where they'd left the truck, Trey's remains had been relegated to the care of Honolulu's chief medical examiner.

A heavily foliaged area about twenty feet from the blue tent had revealed several large garbage bags containing a variety of paraphernalia that suggested someone had recently disposed of multiple items commonly used in the production of crystal meth. A hazardous materials response team was called in, confirming that the trash bags were filled with exactly that: used coffee filters, cat litter, funnels, salt, rubber gloves, and empty boxes of cold medication tablets.

There were also several empty gasoline cans, and because of the associated hazards, the area was cleared of people. As Kali and Jennifer were leaving, a large group of angry people had been assembled to be organized for transfer to a city shelter.

Kali saw the little boy standing next to his mother, who was arguing with a police official. The boy stood quietly, then turned to Kali and lifted one hand, waving shyly.

"Let's talk to the mother and child before they leave," said Kali. "The boy was close to the tent and saw Trey at some point, which is why he told us he was sleeping. He may have seen other people going in or out."

"You go ahead. I need to get this area confined so that it's not contaminated any more than it already has been." She gazed around. "Lot of people here. Either someone knows that somebody was cooking meth, or they saw this debris being dumped here, possibly without realizing how dangerous it is. Our camera shots of Carter getting off the ferry showed he was wearing a large backpack, but if you think this is the same tent you saw on Maui, it's unlikely he had room in his pack for anything else, like a portable lab."

The two women regarded the black garbage bags glistening in the sun as it dipped in and out of the clouds racing overhead.

Jennifer's concern seeped through into her face. "People find this trash on the sides of roads or in the parks, or in their rental units when they're cleaning up after the renters have gone. Most of them have zero idea of how dangerous it is. Besides the explosive nature of the chemicals the meth chefs use, a lot of this stuff can even be radioactive."

Kali nodded. "It's being dumped all over the place." She sighed and glanced over at the mother and little boy. She pulled out the detective's shield that hung on a chain beneath her shirt. "Okay. I don't think this will take long. Here's hoping this poor kid is allowed to speak without his mother drowning him out."

She walked over to the officer who was standing patiently as the boy's mother continued to argue. She absolutely refused to join the other people who were heading to an area where small transport buses had been gathered to bring people into the city.

As Kali approached, she signaled to the officer that she wanted to speak privately with the woman. He nodded and stepped to one side with the child. Immediately, the woman turned her indignation on Kali.

"We're not leaving," she said. "They told me we have to leave everything here and go with them." She looked at the meager possessions stacked in and around her shelter. "This is all we have in the world. I'm not leaving without it."

"I understand," said Kali. She recognized that the woman was simply distressed and frightened. "But I'll need you to be quiet for a minute and listen to me." She spoke evenly. "A man has been found dead very close to where you sleep. Your son might be able to help us figure out what happened, and it's vital that you let him speak. Do you understand?"

The woman looked nervously at the blue tent, just visible from where they stood. Police had already taped off the area.

"I saw them carry him by," said the woman, more quietly.

"Did you speak to him, or see anyone in or around his tent?"

"No." The woman shook her head. "He just got here last night. He walked past us, carrying his stuff. He said hello to my son. He seemed . . . okay. You know, like a normal person. Not a serial killer that might shoot us all up in the night. I try to pay attention."

"Your son might have walked over to talk to the boy in the tent at some point. Do you know if he did?"

The woman shrugged. "I don't think he did, but he was here by himself, playing, when I went to fill our water jugs this morning up near the public restrooms."

"Will you allow me to ask him a few questions? It could be really important."

The woman seemed deflated. "I guess so. I mean, if there's something we can do to help."

Kali gestured to the police officer, who walked over holding the small boy's hand. The woman reached out and stroked the child's hair.

"It's okay for you to talk to this lady," she said. "I'll be right here with you."

"Hi," said Kali. "My name's Kali. What's yours?"

"Justin," he said. "Are you a lady policeman?"

"I am," she said. She knelt down slowly, so that he didn't have to look up at her. "I was just wondering if you ever talked to that boy in the blue tent."

Justin looked at Kali, his face serious. "He was asleep. I didn't want to wake him up."

"When did you see that he was sleeping?"

"This morning. I thought maybe he wanted to go for a swim with me. He wasn't old like everyone else here. He was like a big brother would be. I was going to tell him the water is nice. I like to swim before a lot of people go out there, but my mom won't let me go alone."

"That's a smart thing for a mom to do. The waves can knock you over if you aren't careful."

Justin nodded. "I know. But I only go to the very edge, so that my feet can get wet."

"I like to do that, too. I like to squish my toes in the wet sand."

His face brightened. "It makes a funny sound when you pull them out."

"Before you went over to the tent and saw that the boy inside was sleeping, did you see anyone else go over to talk to him, or maybe leave some things near his tent?"

The little boy squinted his eyes, thinking hard. "No. Nobody else went to say hello to him. Just me. I would have heard if somebody walked past our house."

Kali felt her heart twist. This child viewed the stretched, worn tarp and its scant protection as a house. She stood up, extending her hand. He reached out, and she shook his hand gently.

"Thank you, Justin. You did a very, very good thing today. It was kind of you to help me. I'll bet your mom is super proud of you."

Justin smiled. He looked toward the tent, then up at Kali.

"Is he awake yet? Maybe I can go and say hi to him now."

Kali and the mother exchanged glances.

"No, I'm sorry, but he had to leave," said Kali. She smiled, trying to be reassuring. "He isn't there now."

The child's face revealed his disappointment. "Do you think he'll be back later? I have a kite."

"I'll help you fly your kite," said the mother. "We'll do that later on. Right now, why don't you go and get your jacket, and your kite, and that book about the trains? We're going to go for a ride on one of those buses over there."

Justin nodded, then walked away toward their makeshift shelter.

"Thank you," said Kali. "I appreciate your help."

The woman looked toward the buses. "I really don't want to leave," she said.

"I understand," said Kali. "You may not believe me, but I really do. The shelter is a nice one. You'll get a safe, comfortable space to sleep, and hot meals. There will likely be other children there, too. Maybe Justin can find someone to play with while you're there."

She stepped away, and Kali saw the worry etched on her face.

"Good luck to you," Kali said. "To you both. I hope things get better."

CHAPTER 30

Jennifer dropped off Kali in front of the hotel's main doors, then sped off on her way back to Sand Island to help with the activity there. The medical examiner had already promised to be in touch as soon as he'd conducted his initial exam, so Kali called Walter to fill him in.

"You think it was an overdose, or are we looking at someone helping Carter on his way into the next world?"

"I have no idea," she said. "He was just lying there, stretched out on his back on top of a sleeping bag inside the tent. There was an empty plastic snack bag with what appears to be powder residue. We assume meth. No obvious signs of a struggle. A lot of footprints around, but not much else. He had a backpack with a spare pair of shorts and two shirts, a wallet, and a couple of books. Old paperbacks. There was an empty plastic water bottle on the sleeping bag near his feet."

"Okay," said Walter. "So that's Trey Carter—lost and found. What are your plans?"

"I'm going to go over to the Wela Wela Cave tonight. Jennifer says Vice doesn't have it on its radar. They've got an investigation underway monitoring a couple of other city clubs they're pretty sure are being used as distribution centers, but Wela Wela hasn't popped up, except that they're running girls there. They may be underage."

"Just what the world needs," he said. "Do they think the other clubs are handling locally produced product, or is it coming in from out of state?"

"They aren't sure, but she says the volume suggests it's coming from somewhere else. If Wela Wela is involved, someone has worked out a system that's kept them from being detected so far."

"Okay. You taking anyone with you?"

"No, just dropping in to get the lay of the land and see if anything indicates it's worth pursuing in connection with Trey Carter or Maya Holmes."

"What about those directions on the restaurant receipt about calling first and mentioning the Geology Club?"

"I'm going to leave that alone for the time being and just look around. See what the place is like. Vice has that info now and will likely pursue it."

"I don't like the idea of you going alone."

"Afraid the strippers will gang up on me?"

"Never underestimate a motivated group of strippers."

She smiled to herself. "Everything there okay?"

"Seems like. Other than the fact that everything for miles smells like wet dog."

"Sorry. Can't help you with that." She chuckled. "I'll call you later."

She showered quickly and changed her clothes, doing her best to look like she might just be out for the night and was stopping in for a drink. Her blouse was tight and low-cut. She put on a short jacket to camouflage her shoulder holster, added several layers of eyeliner and mascara to her eyes, and left her hair hanging long and loose.

The valet flagged a taxi for her, and she had the driver drop her off at the edge of Chinatown on a corner several blocks from the club's address. She walked slowly toward it along a sidewalk littered with trash. This part of the city was more run-down than the glossy central tourist zones, and she passed several small warehouses and overgrown lots strewn with litter and the evidence of human occupation. The few people loitering in these areas ignored her.

As she drew closer to the club, the sound of music could be heard. It was electronic, pulsing aggressively against the walls that separated the club from the sidewalk. There was a small neon sign that read WELA WELA in a blacked-out window, but nothing else to indicate the destination. As she approached the entrance, she saw a man standing just inside, his muscular arms crossed against his wide chest. He was taller than Kali, and out-weighed her by at least eighty pounds. As she turned toward the door, he stepped out of the doorway and stood in front of her.

"What do you want?" he asked. His voice was heavily accented, but she couldn't identify it.

"To go inside and get a drink," she said, scowling. "You got some problem with that?"

"Private club," he said.

"That why you hung a lighted sign in the window?"

"Like I said, private club."

She tossed her hair over her shoulder.

"I'm thirsty," she said.

The door guard looked at her, running his eyes from her face to her bare legs and high-heeled sandals, making a decision. "You looking for trouble? We got our own girls here. Owner doesn't take to outsiders trying to push their way to the front of the line. Besides, you might be a little too wholesome for our particular clientele."

Her skin crawled.

"Yeah. I'm so flattered," she said. "All I want is a drink, and I want to see who's here. You understand?"

He threw back his head and laughed. "Let me guess. Boyfriend? Husband? Girlfriend? You start any crap in there, and I'm going to be the one to finish it."

"Just looking," she said. She reached out and touched his arm. "Promise."

He stepped away from the door, still grinning.

"Just remember—up to you how you leave," he said. "Play it wrong, and it just might be in a wheelbarrow. You got time for one drink, then you go home and cry into your pillow there. Understand?"

"Sure," she said. "I understand."

Inside, the air stank of sour beer and carpets soaked in dirt and alcohol. The music was nearly unbearable, but she resisted the impulse to cover her ears. A long stage jutted into the middle of the room from the rear wall, surrounded by a counter that was built along the underside of the stage floor. Bar stools lined both sides, and clusters of tables filled the spaces between the stage and the sides of the room. The bar itself was located along the back wall, and in the dim light, Kali identified several doors leading into the building's recesses on the opposite side of the street entrance.

There was one bartender, a tired-looking woman in a skimpy dress. On the stage, three poles spanned the distance between the low ceiling and the stage floor. Two were occupied by dancers, and Kali noted how young they appeared. There were few patrons. Two men and a woman sat together at a table toward the rear of the room on the bar side, and two men sat spaced out along the bar stools at the stage. They didn't appear to be together.

Kali breathed in the sour air. To her it felt like the kind of place someone might come to die. She walked slowly toward the bar. The back door leading into an alley behind the bar shelves was open, and she could see several people gathered outside, smoking under the street lamps. The music was too loud to hear their conversation, but from the glimpses she was able to catch as they moved around, it was a group of three young women.

She sat down, twisting her stool to an angle that took in both the bar and the stage, with the front door visible. She placed her left elbow on the edge of the wooden rail edging the bar. The once-gleaming wood was sticky, and she was careful to keep her arm out of reach of whatever it was that had adhered to the surface.

The bartender turned and saw her. She walked over, clearly disinterested.

"What can I get for you?" she asked, her voice bored.

"Vodka and pineapple juice," said Kali.

"Tall glass?"

"Sure," said Kali. She watched as the woman scooped ice into a glass and measured a shot of vodka from the cheap bottles in the well attached to the counter next to the sink, then added luke-warm pineapple juice from an opened carton sitting on top of a small refrigerator. When the woman slid the glass in front of her, Kali instinctively recoiled at the rancid odor.

"You don't look familiar," said the bartender.

"I'm not," said Kali, grimacing. "Just over from Maui to see my sister, and couldn't take the company anymore."

"I get it," said the woman. She glanced idly at the dancer on stage, who wasn't even making an effort to find the rhythm of the pounding music.

Kali's eyes automatically followed her. As far as she could tell, the dancer was only using the pole to hold on to in order to stay upright. She took a small, tentative sip of her drink, hoping the alcohol in the vodka would kill off whatever bacteria was swimming around in the warm pineapple juice. She tried to not think too closely about the condition of the ice and what might be floating in the rubber hoses that fed the ice maker.

The bartender drifted away to refill a beer for a man who had walked up to the far end of the bar. Kali caught movement from the corner of her eye and turned slightly. At the back door, the group of girls had shifted, and one of them had stepped into the additional light cast by a bulb over the back door. Kali started, gripping her glass. She took a long breath, then stared intently at the thin figure. It was someone she knew—the rush of familiarity was accompanied by a surge of anguish. It was Makena Shirai.

As she was deciding whether to go out the front door and make her way around to the alley where Makena stood, or to simply bypass the bartender and force her way out through the back door, Makena stubbed out her cigarette on the door frame and came inside. Makena walked past the bartender, toward the restroom doors on the back wall of the room, near the corner of the stage. The bartender, clearly familiar with her, gave no notice.

Kali waited until Makena had gone through the door of the women's bathroom, then climbed down from her stool and followed her. The door swung into a cramped space with separate bathroom stalls positioned opposite a single sink with a dirty mirror above it. Makena was there, peering into the mirror, adding a fresh coat of bright pink color to her lips. A small, woven shoulder bag swung against her side as she moved. Kali noted how her shoulder blades protruded sharply from the sleeveless halter top of her short dress, and how thin and childlike her arms and legs were. Her dark brown hair was pulled away from her face, and her sunken eyes gave the impression that she was far older than she actually was.

She turned toward the door as Kali stepped inside. As she registered who it was, her eyes grew wide . . . then narrowed in annoyance.

"Hello, Makena," said Kali.

"Unbelievable," snapped Makena. "You followed me here?"

"No," said Kali, truthfully. "Just one of those lucky coincidences you hear about."

Makena's eyes raked over Kali. "Funny. You look like you're out for a big night. Finally found someone to hook up with?"

Kali's eyes flashed. She felt an urge to step forward and slap the sneer off the younger woman's face. She looked at the emaciated arms, riddled with needle tracks from ongoing drug use, at the poorly nourished body and the worn clothing, and wondered where everything had simply fallen apart. Certainly Makena had been given a multitude of opportunities to make other choices. Kali felt a deep sense of failure sweep over her. She wondered if it was somehow her fault—if she had tried too hard to fill the gap left behind by Mike's death, or if she simply hadn't tried hard enough.

"Uh-oh," said Makena. "Touch a nerve? Or are you about to give me another clean-up-your-life-Makena speech?"

"Would it do any good?"

Makena turned back to the mirror, wiping a small smudge of lip color from her cheek beside her lip.

"I don't need your help," she said. "More to the point, I don't want your help."

Kali tried to keep the frustration from her voice. "What are you even doing here? You're nineteen. You're not supposed to be in a bar."

Makena swung around. This time, she was the one consumed with fury. "Twenty. I'm twenty. Guess my last birthday just slipped your mind. I wondered why you didn't send a card."

Kali was momentarily silenced. Then her own anger returned. "As if I'd know where to find you. And you're still underage."

Makena shoved her lipstick into her shoulder bag, then turned to Kali and held out her arms, waggling her fingers dramatically.

"Did you bring your handcuffs with you on your date?" she asked in a mocking voice. "Why don't you just arrest me?" When Kali made no answer, Makena dropped her arms and shook her head, the gesture infinitely sad. "This is your problem, Kali. You're always a cop first and a person second. Just like my father."

Before Kali could respond, the bathroom door opened, and the bartender stuck her head inside. She glanced at Kali, then spoke directly to Makena.

"Your next date is here," she said. "You'd better get a move on."

The woman left. Kali looked at Makena. She

stood there, her small figure taking up almost no space, her posture defiant, challenging Kali to interfere.

"Makena . . ."

"What are you really doing here?"

Kali shook her head. "Not any of your business."

"Oh . . . I get it. If you weren't looking for me, you're on a case. I guess I should have figured that out to begin with. If you were on some date, that would mean you've finally gotten over my dead dad, and we both know that's not ever going to happen."

Kali was going to comment, but a sudden impulse took hold, prompted by Makena's drug addiction and her presence in Hawai'i's world of shadows. "I'm looking for a witch," she said.

Makena's response took her by surprise. She stepped backward, a look of profound fear registering on her face. Then she pulled her shoulder bag close and pushed past Kali on her way to the door.

"You don't want to do that," she said, speaking low. "I've been hearing stories. You know I don't believe in that stuff, but there's been talk about a witch in the islands, one that's not afraid of killing."

Kali put out her hand, stopping Makena. She saw finger bruises on the girl's upper arms, and could tell from the size and width that a large man had likely made them.

"What do you know?" she asked.

"That's all. A bad witch."

"A man or woman?"

Makena shook her head. She seemed suddenly nervous, her earlier bravado completely evaporated. "I don't know."

"A witch who makes drugs?"

Makena pulled away and pushed against the door. "That's the rumor," she said. "A witch that conjures drugs out of the sand, and kills anyone who gets in the way."

CHAPTER 31

In the morning, Kali had breakfast and checked out from the hotel. Jennifer came by to give her a ride back to the ferry port and share the details so far gathered on Trey Carter. The coroner's report confirmed that the cause of death was a heart attack, probably brought on by drugs. There was meth in his system, and analysis on the residue in the plastic bag found in his tent was conclusive: a pure batch of methamphetamine in powder form, a large quantity of which the dead boy had inhaled by snorting, and which remained in his body. Kali asked that a copy of the report be sent to Stitches for comparison to what she'd found in the university students.

The discussion about a witch being connected to the local drug trade had intrigued Jennifer. "I remember some of those witch stories from when I was a kid," she said. "My parents were very superstitious, so I took it with a grain of salt—I guess I figured they were trying to scare my brothers and me into behaving, or the boogie man would get us."

"Effective?"

Jennifer laughed. "Only marginally, I'm afraid."

"Did you learn the stories about the akua noho?"

Jennifer frowned. "That's the Sitting God, right? Yeah, that one was scary. The shapeshifter who could possess anyone it chose."

"And that person—once possessed—became a kind of god themselves," said Kali.

For the duration of the ferry trip back to Maui, Kali tried to block the image of Makena in the nightclub, instead focusing on the old stories she'd learned, trying to see the connection—if there even was one—between the murder of Maya Holmes, the drug traffic, and the old legends.

By the time they reached port, she'd come to no conclusions. Instead of heading directly home, she drove to the hospital to visit George. She stopped in at the gift shop on the lobby level and bought the day's tabloid newspapers to bring to him. When she reached his room, he was sitting up in bed, supported by a number of pillows. The television in his room was on; she saw that it was a popular show that explored the possibilities of past and present alien visitations to Earth.

George looked up at Kali as she came through the doorway, a large smile on his face.

"This is a great show," he said. "I've never seen it before, but one of the nurses told me about it. The experts say that maybe the reason we see all these UFOs in the sky and in the water is because they're from a civilization that's keeping track of how we develop."

"We might be in serious trouble, then."

He looked up at the screen. "That could be. Maybe they think it's not a good idea for us to go to Mars or back to the moon, and want to make sure we don't do that. Maybe they think we behave so badly, we should all just stay home."

"I think I'd have to agree," she said. She walked over to the visitor's chair and sat down, holding the newspapers she'd brought on her lap. "Maybe we're some kind of entertainment to them. Could be the people who live on some other planet pay big money to take trips across the universe, then they just sit in their spaceships and watch us blow things up and spread our trash across every possible surface."

"You mean like intergalactic tour buses?"

"Exactly."

"Hmm." George squinted at the television screen. "I guess I'd rather find out they were getting ready to teach us something that would make us better."

"Well, I'm all for that. I'll volunteer to be on the welcoming committee if that's the case."

George grinned again. "Or maybe they're out scouting for exotic snacks, and we're on the tasting menu."

She laughed. "How are you feeling?"

He held up his bandaged arms. "Some burns,"

he said. "But nothing serious. I've been getting oxygen treatments, too. Because of the smoke. But I'm doing good."

"I brought you some reading material," she said. "Do you want me to put it on that tray next to your bed?"

"Thank you! Maybe you could put them on that counter by the television," he said. "The nurses are going to feed me soon; that way I won't spill anything on them."

"How's the food?" she asked. She saw that despite his smile, he looked weary.

"Pretty good. It's nice to not have to cook for myself."

Kali was struck suddenly by the thought of George being on his own. She knew he'd been a widower since she was a teenager, but she was so used to seeing him at his store, busy and surrounded by people, that she'd never given any real thought to what his life might be like beyond that. And now his store was ruined.

He was apparently thinking about his store as well.

"I heard the big window in the front break, and saw something come flying through and skid across the floor," said George. "It landed under the shelves in the front, the ones where all the cleaning supplies are stacked."

He closed his eyes, remembering.

"The fire investigator told us it was a homemade incendiary device," said Kali. "It was pretty sophisticated, with some kind of super accelerant instead of the alcohol that's usually inside."

He nodded. "A Molotov cocktail, right? It sure made a big fire. But there's some good news, too. My sons came over from O'ahu and boarded up the store and met with the insurance people. It's not as bad as it looks, except for the roof and one side of the store along the outer wall. The insurance is going to cover some improvements, like a new dairy case and flooring. I'm going to get some of that fancy vinyl planking for the floor—the kind that looks like wood but is easier to keep clean. The boys are staying to help with the repairs, and to make sure the contractors get things moving."

"That's great news, George."

"And pretty soon, my good friend Detective Kali Māhoe is going to call me and tell me she's caught the bad person who started the fire."

"That's my hope, too." She looked him over, concerned. "George, I'm really worried that someone did this because I asked you to keep your ears open for any witch news."

His face scrunched up as the gears of his mind turned. "That might be," he said. "But you aren't to blame for what other people do. I asked, but I didn't hear anything."

"Who did you talk to?"

"Just put the word out that I was interested in learning a little local herb-craft that might help me even up a score."

"Did anyone approach you?"

"No," he said.

Kali looked at the bandages on his arms, and felt a rush of responsibility. "I shouldn't have asked you to do that. I'm afraid it looks as though the fire was directly connected."

"Maybe," he said. "Who knows? Bad people do bad things. It might be because I told someone to wait longer than they wanted to, or didn't have the right brand of potato chips, or they just didn't like the way I look. It's not your fault, Kali. It's just a dangerous world."

A tall, young nurse came into the room, carrying a tray. She smiled brightly at George and nodded to Kali.

"Okay, George," said the nurse. "You can flirt with the ladies after you've had something to eat. I brought you soup and a piece of chocolate cake. How does that sound?"

"That sounds pretty good," he said.

Kali stood up to leave. "I'll check in on you tomorrow. I'm going to arrange a special ceremony for you. Meanwhile, please let me know if there's anything you need, okay?"

"Okay," he said. "But I'm already getting a new floor and shelves, so I think I have everything. Except, if you see a UFO tonight, you have to break me out of this joint so I can see it, too."

"I promise," she said.

She took the stairs to the lobby level. As she was approaching the front doors, Mrs. Bailey came in, carrying a huge bunch of flowers.

"Those are beautiful!" said Kali, stopping to admire them.

"They're from my garden," she said. "I picked them for George."

As she drove out of the parking lot on her way home, Kali thought of the pretty nurse and Mrs.

Bailey with her flowers, fussing over George. She felt better, but not as good as she'd feel when she finally slapped handcuffs on whoever had thrown a fire bomb through the window of a kind old man's store.

CHAPTER 32

Kali watched as Walter and Elvar maneuvered a wide, flat wooden dolly from the driveway to the space next to the burned hale in her yard. She'd cleared away the collapsed roof and the singed palm fronds, and taken down the frame that had once supported them. The sawhorses that had held the canoe had buckled, damaged by the flames. Now the burned canoe sat on the ground, exposed, looking desolate and unloved.

She stood to one side as the two men lifted the charred remains and placed it on the dolly. They secured it with several long bungee straps, pulled taut across the top of the canoe and hooked on either side to the dolly's edges.

Walter glanced at her. "You ready?" he asked.

She nodded.

The two men slowly pulled the dolly and its sad

burden through the thick grass and across the sloping yard. Each time it became bogged down, Kali helped lift it and move it forward.

There was little conversation. It took them nearly a half hour—even working together—to get the dolly to the small dock where the Gingerfish bobbed in the water. They'd waited until the tide was up and the water was just a foot from the surface of the dock. The bow of the boat was already facing out toward open water, so Walter jumped onboard, uncoiling a towline fitted with a hook on one end.

There was a blanket stretched across part of the boat deck. Walter pulled it away, revealing a raft made of narrow planks, altogether about two feet wider than the canoe. The raft was resting on small plastic float barrels that were attached to the bottom along each side, with a large, hefty eye hook on one end of the wooden platform.

Elvar joined Walter on the boat, and together they lifted the raft over the side and heaved it onto the dock. Next, they unleashed the canoe and lifted it from the dolly and onto the boat dock, resting it carefully on the float platform. After they had used the same bungee cords to secure it to its new resting space, Walter threaded one end of his towline through the eye hook, making a mooring hitch that could be quickly released.

When he was through, he, Kali, and Elvar stood at the end of the platform, surveying their work.

"Well, so far, so good, said Walter, "but now's the tricky part. We've got to get this into the water behind the Gingerfish without flipping it over or the canoe coming loose and sliding into the sea."

They considered the possibilities, settling on sliding it slowly on the short end, off the dock and into the water. Kali held her breath, her heart pounding as the end of the raft disappeared under the water, pressed down by the weight of the canoe, before popping back up above the surface.

Walter climbed back on board, double-checking that the towline was secure.

"All good," he said. He looked up at the sky, then at Kali. "We should take advantage of the weather being relatively clear right now," he said. "It's going to get messy soon, so . . ."

"I'm ready," she said. She looked at Elvar. "Are you coming out with us?"

He shook his head. "No," he said. "I would feel as though I were intruding on something very private. I'll stay here and make sure the line doesn't get tangled as Walter pulls away from the dock. I can hold the end of the raft until the towline has played out."

She smiled at him, grateful.

"Thanks, Elvar. For all of this. It's kind of you."

"It was my pleasure to help." He looked at the canoe, at the blackened edges of the partially carved hollow, at the once-beautiful line of the prow. "I am sorry for this loss. I know this canoe had great meaning for you, and I hope the person responsible for its destruction will be found."

She nodded. There was nothing else to say, so she climbed onto the deck. The boat's engine rumbled to life, and Walter eased slowly away from the dock, allowing the towline to play out gradually. Elvar kept it from becoming twisted, and the little raft followed the Gingerfish out into open water. From the deck, Kali watched as Elvar's figure slowly faded away.

After they were about a mile from the shore, Walter eased back on the throttle, and the boat slowed.

"What do you think?" he asked. "Do you want to go out a little farther?"

She looked up at the gray sky. The wind had picked up, and she knew the weather was going to worsen the later the day became.

"No, this is good," she said. She slipped off her shoes. She'd worn her bathing suit beneath her clothes, and pulled off her shorts and sweatshirt, leaving them on the cushioned seat on one side of the deck. She climbed onto the stern and stopped for just a moment, then dove cleanly into the water.

Walter watched as she surfaced and began to swim to the floating raft, her long, sure strokes cleaving the water. She reached it, grasping one side. With one hand, she stroked the wood of the ruined canoe.

"Here you are," she said, softly. "In the water, at last. This is where you were meant to be, out on the ocean. I'm sorry that I'll never know the joy of sailing in you. I'm sorry that Mike couldn't keep his promise to you."

She loosened the caps on the plastic floats and removed them, then pulled on the mooring knot. The raft was free. She moved her legs, treading water, feeling the salt spray from the small waves splash against her lips, giving her a taste of the deep briny flavor of the ocean. The raft slipped away. She knew it was only a matter of time before the floats filled with water, and a large enough wave washed over the raft so that it sank beneath the gray, moving surface of the sea. Right now it rode the ripples, moving farther and farther away from her.

She watched for a few moments longer, then turned and swam back to the Gingerfish. Walter was waiting to pull her back up onto the deck. They sat for a few more minutes, watching as the raft was pulled away by the current.

Walter started the engine.

"Are you okay?" he asked.

She turned and smiled at him.

"I'm okay," she said.

Walter turned the prow back toward shore. For just the briefest moment, the heavy gray clouds parted, and a brilliant flash of sunlight lit the surface of the wide, rolling sea. Then the darkness moved back in.

That evening Kali sat on the front steps of her house, watching a small black cat slink through the grass next to the lanai in pursuit of something small. The cat belonged to someone in the neighborhood, though she hadn't yet discovered who. It was supremely uninterested in the fact that Kali's property was covered in the scent of a large dog, and came and went as it pleased. The cat had discovered that the low flowering shrubs that ran along the bottom of the house were inhabited by large, colorfully striped garden spiders, and had taken to hunting them.

Hoping to distract it from killing the harmless

spiders, she called to the cat, but it ignored her. Looking past the feline, she saw that the space exposed by the burned hale was illuminated against the lighter sky behind it. She wrapped her arms around her knees, feeling an unusual sense of disconnection. Being besieged in a place that should have been a shelter against the outside world was unsettling. She thought of Justin and his mother boarding the bus, leaving behind what had become their home.

Her eyes swept the yard, confirming that the security cameras were still in place, and that an officer had been stationed at the end of her driveway. The footage the cameras had so far collected revealed nothing useful. Knowing they were there did little to comfort her; instead, she felt an even deeper sense of invasion.

She knew that the attack on George's store was no mere coincidence. In her mind, she laid out the puzzle pieces: the rainbow tree, the drugs, the lava dust in the lungs of Maya Holmes, fire and mayhem at every turn, the legends of sorcery that were manifesting all around her. She shivered, then stood up and went inside.

CHAPTER 33

K ali reached across her desk to lift the buzzing phone. Charlie Holmes's name was displayed on the screen. There was no chance for her to say anything. His breathless voice came across the line.

"I found it," he said.

Kali tensed. "Found what?"

"Her laptop."

A sense of elation washed over her.

"Where was it?" she asked.

"Where I might have never looked for it," he said. "It was in one of her puzzle boxes."

Kali frowned. She knew she'd looked through the jigsaw boxes herself, and that the SOC officers had done so before she'd even made a visit to the condo.

"Which box? They were all searched."

"Not this one," he said. "It was in my room, on top of some books piled on the floor near my desk. I didn't put it there. The thing is, I don't like those puzzles, and would have never had one of Maya's jigsaws in my room to begin with. So when I noticed it today, I thought it was odd—but figured one of the police officers had put it there by mistake when they had finished looking around. Anyway, I picked it up to put it back in Maya's room, and the box felt oddly heavy. When I took the lid off, her laptop was inside on the bottom, underneath all the puzzle pieces. She must have been trying to put it somewhere she thought would be safe."

Kali felt her pulse quicken. If Maya had had the prescience to hide her computer, she must have been worried that someone might be after it.

"Don't try to boot it," she said. "We'll send someone for it right away. What are the chances you know her password?"

"Pretty good," he said. "We both had so many passwords to keep track of, just like everyone else these days, that we made a master list of the important ones. We each kept a copy. Bank accounts, logins for different things, and our access passwords for our personal computers."

She tried to keep her excitement in check. It was still a long shot that there would be anything useful to find.

"Does your list include e-mail logins?"

He hesitated. "I'm not sure . . . I think her social media logins are there. I'll check."

"You're my hero, Charlie," she said. And she meant it.

* * *

The digital forensics team went to work immediately once they had the computer in their possession. In the office, Kali paced back and forth as she awaited a call from computer forensics investigator Olin Janosky. Several hours had gone by. She was jittery with the amount of caffeine she'd consumed when she heard the ringtone on her computer alert her to the incoming screen call.

"Aloha, Detective." Janosky's deep voice came across the computer speaker. He held up Maya's laptop in front of the camera so that Kali could see it. "I have your digital artifact here. Lots of technical data on the desktop. I'm not an expert in the field of marine research and development, but some of what we found are hundreds of pages of code that may have some relation to that area of study."

"Can you decipher it?"

"It's in Python, which is a pretty common code language, but it's been heavily encrypted. We'll need a password, or a key in order to decrypt the pages. We'll keep working on it. I assume it's potential evidence?"

"It's very likely something that the victim was working on, possibly connected to the research lab where she was employed," said Kali. As quickly as the thought arose, it was replaced by another: It seemed odd that Maya would have those files on her personal laptop, rather than on her work computer.

Janosky's voice interrupted her line of thought. "There are also diagrams, including a schematic that looks like a design for altering a robotic sensor, as well as published studies of various kinds, many of them theoretical in nature. One of the documents on the desktop appears to be a draft of a proposal for some type of underwater robotic device connected to mining. That one is a text document we're assuming was written by the owner of the computer. I'm sending you copies of everything right now, along with transcripts of the e-mails. We're still looking through everything, of course—but you requested these as soon as we could get them to you, particularly those with name and e-mail address matches to the list you provided."

"Did anything jump out at you?"

Olin looked thoughtful. "The victim appears to have had a nominal social media presence, limited largely to photographs of animals and nature. Her Instagram account is the most robust. She didn't have many followers, but she herself followed about three hundred separate accounts that focused on running, fitness, nutrition, nature, and public personalities related to science."

"That seems a little odd for an attractive, physically active young woman in her twenties, wouldn't you say?"

Janosky's shoulders lifted and fell in a shrug. "It takes all kinds."

"Yeah. I suppose it does," said Kali. "Do we have a cross-reference yet for e-mail contacts and phone records?"

"Incomplete, but yes. What we have so far is on the way to you."

"Thanks for the rush on this."

"No problem," he said. "More to come." His face

was abruptly replaced by the department's official logo screensaver.

After the call was over, Kali sat at her desk, waiting for the documents to show up on the internal network. She read the proposal with interest. Maya had addressed it to Davos O'Connor. In it, she described a project she'd been working on in her spare time that involved an alteration to a sensor used on the ROV that was deployed into the ocean's depths to locate mineral deposits. The proposal asked O'Connor for his support and involvement in the development of the enhanced sensor, alluding to a profitable partnership. Maya didn't go into additional detail, but said she had completed the code and would be willing to let O'Connor view a sample to prove that her research was correct. The proposal was dated for the month previous to Maya's death.

Next, she scanned the e-mails as they began to populate her screen. The personal exchanges were largely with her parents and Charlie. There were numerous newsletter subscriptions that were connected to her health and fitness interests. Among the e-mails were some between Maya and Trey Carter, encouraging him to come with her on walks, or to go and see the animals at the conservation center where Charlie worked. There were several dozen back-and-forths with Jody about meeting up for runs, or what times were most optimal for ocean swims. In several recent e-mails, there were a few direct references to Davos O'Connor, including one in which Jody referred to him directly as being a "jerk," and that Maya should try to just ignore his "insufferable arrogance."

Maya's e-mail response to this had been benign. She'd written: His head has always been bigger than most doorways, but I knew that coming in. When he was my advisor, he always made me feel like he was doing me an enormous honor. I just really wanted to stay in Hawai'i, and this job seemed like a great opportunity. Guess we'll see!

Kali pondered this exchange. She'd already decided—quite independently—that Jody's assessment of O'Connor's character was entirely accurate, but she had to wonder just how unpleasant O'Connor might have made things for Maya. Being a jerk didn't necessarily equate with being a murderer—sometimes, it might make someone a victim.

She swung around in her chair, making a plan. Time to bring the egotistic Dr. O'Connor in for one more visit. She wouldn't let him know they were already looking for Vance Sousa. This time, her conversation with O'Connor would be a full-on interrogation, police station style.

CHAPTER 34

Davos O'Connor looked like a damp, angry rat that had been cornered by a pair of patient mountain lions. He sat in the interview room's deliberately uncomfortable metal chair, hands gripping the edge of the table in front of him, his hair and face damp with perspiration. Kali and Walter faced him from across the table. He'd been advised of his rights, and had declined the presence of an attorney after stating that to have a legal representative would imply that he felt guilty of something, which he assured them he did not.

Neither Kali nor Walter was moved by his declaration.

"You seem to be of the opinion that you've been accused of a crime," said Kali. Her voice was without inflection.

O'Connor reached up with both hands and

loosened his tie, tugging the knot free. He glowered, his eyes spitting fire at them.

"Do you have any concept," he said, "any concept at all, of how much you've already damaged my standing at the laboratory? Now, on top of everything else, you've had me dragged away in front of my subordinates by officers in uniform."

"Dragged?" asked Walter. "Do you mean dragged as in what happened to Maya Holmes when she was lugged hands-bound through the forest, hauled into a tree, and left there hanging for birds to pick apart? That kind of dragged?"

O'Connor swallowed his sharp retort, whatever it may have been. Then his wrath flared again, and it came out. "You know exactly what I mean. You already know my whereabouts at the girl's time of death. Your attempts to intimidate me, I assure you, will get you nowhere."

"Whereas your attempts to avoid answering our questions are likely to get you an overnight stay in jail," said Kali. "And we've only verified part of your alibi. Just because the neighbors saw you in the yard now and then, and your car was in the driveway, doesn't mean you were home at the exact time Maya Holmes was violently murdered."

She watched as he flinched.

"You weren't particularly nice to Maya, were you?" she asked.

"Nice? I was her boss." He leaned forward, hands flat on the table before him. "Why don't you tell me how nice I should have been? These days, if you so much as offer a woman employee—or any employee, really—a cup of coffee, you can be accused of sexual harassment."

"So you overcompensated by bullying her?" asked Walter.

"I was always, without fail, professional in my interactions."

"Public opinion seems to disagree," said Walter. "Pushing around your underlings appears to be the way you run things at your research center."

"Pushing people to do better, and pushing them around, are not the same thing," said O'Connor in a petulant manner.

"It certainly shouldn't be," agreed Kali.

"Was it just Maya Holmes?" asked Walter. "Or did you also take the same attitude toward the other women on your team?"

O'Connor tilted his head toward Walter, eyes narrowed. "I suppose," he said, "that you're referring to Jody Phillips. What ridiculous tale has she had to tell?"

"She hasn't said anything," said Kali. Her calm voice held the unmistakable air of authority. "But it's interesting you would immediately assume that she had. Is there something you'd like to get off your chest?"

"I would like," said O'Connor, sitting back in his chair, "for you to get to the point, whatever that might be, so that I can get back to work and try to do some damage control with my team."

"Tell us about them," said Walter.

"You've already talked to all of them. Why badger me?"

"Perspective," said Walter.

"And there's always the chance you know something you aren't even aware of," added Kali. "Don't you want to be helpful?"

They watched him. He seemed to be giving serious thought to what they'd said.

"Okay," he said. His voice was less belligerent. "Ask your questions."

"Let's start with the last time you physically saw Maya," said Kali.

"I've already told you. Thursday afternoon before she died. She was at the lab, picking up some storage containers for the samples she was going to collect the next day and during the weekend."

"Why was she going to do this alone, without anyone to help?" asked Walter.

"It was what she always did. She was just gathering rocks. We wanted to be able to run some tests on a new system I've been working on to enhance the efficiency of mineral identification."

"I was in your office," said Kali. "It was full of rocks. You needed more?"

He looked at her with an intense dislike. "Yes. We'd already run tests on what we had. We were looking for a wider variety before we started more intensive underwater trials."

"And you weren't concerned when you didn't see her on Monday?" Kali asked.

"Why do you keep asking me the same questions?" he roared. He took a deep breath, then spoke more calmly. "I was in meetings, I was working. When I didn't see her on Tuesday, I just assumed she was working from home, or was elsewhere in the building. I don't feel the need to keep people on a strict schedule. Many of them have studies, and some are volunteers. To a large extent, they are free to come and go as their time works best for them, unless we have already determined a day and time for a test or some other function, such as a meeting."

"I see," said Kali. "Why don't you explain exactly how the other unit at the research lab interacts with your own. The one run by Byron Coolidge."

O'Connor made a small, dismissive sound. "Byron doesn't run anything. As I've already tried to make you understand on countless occasions, I am in charge of CMMR. I am the director. I make the decisions. Byron is working on his degree, and as such is available to me to carry out various experiments connected to my research. More to the point, his lab team is assisting in the development of an advanced fuel system that will allow our underwater robots to function independently. Right now, they must be tethered to a ship's power."

"What you're saying, then," said Walter, "is that without Mr. Coolidge, you wouldn't be able to further your own agenda or complete your project. Is that correct?"

O'Connor bristled. His earlier aggression returned. "I assure you," he said, "with very little effort, I could find several dozen doctoral candidates who would fulfill the same purpose."

"When I visited Mr. Coolidge's laboratory, the other people there seemed to be working for him under his direct supervision," said Kali. "Vance Sousa and Gloria Marsh."

"Both are working on their own degrees, and assisting Byron for credit," said O'Connor. "Marsh is useful, but is also a dull conversationalist, not to mention needlessly aggressive. Sousa is extremely talented, but he's a liability."

"Oh? And how is that?" asked Walter.

O'Connor shifted in his chair. He hesitated before answering. "He's volatile. Behaves unpredictably. But then, many brilliant minds present with unconventional behavior. I overlook it to the best of my ability, as I don't have to be in his company very frequently. Byron finds him handy."

"Handy. That's quite a commendation," said Walter.

O'Connor refrained from digging himself deeper.

"What about this battery system Mr. Coolidge's team is working on for you?" asked Kali.

Again, O'Connor shifted in his seat. He looked uneasy. Kali pressed him, taking advantage of his sudden lack of composure.

"We can find this information through other means," she said. "But since you're here, what exactly are the qualifications of the people working with Mr. Coolidge? Their specific areas of study?"

"Chemical systems," he said, his voice gruff.

Kali watched as O'Connor grew increasingly uncomfortable. "What type of chemicals?"

"Alternate fuel sources, primarily," said O'Connor. "We're looking for efficiency at scale so that our robots can be deployed for extended periods of time without being recharged. Again, cost savings."

"I see," said Kali. "I guess it's nice you have access to so many capable people." She nodded at Walter, then turned to O'Connor. "You'll have to excuse us for a moment," she said. "I'll let you know if we have any more questions."

They got up, leaving O'Connor sitting at the interview table, staring at the metal surface. Outside the room, Kali took Walter's arm.

"Chemicals again," she said.

Walter looked at her. "Yup," he said. "You thinking what I'm thinking?"

"I believe so," she said. "Let's let him go. I want him to be able to reach out to Byron Coolidge. Put a tail on them both and see if one of them leads us to wherever Vance Sousa is. We know there's no meth lab at CMMR, but there's one somewhere, and Sousa, at the very least, is involved in it. This whole thing has a great big stamp of crazy on it."

"Do you want to ask him outright if he knows where Vance is?"

"No. Better to let him think we got what we wanted from him and that he can stop worrying about us. Right now he doesn't seem to be aware that we know Vance is missing."

"You think they're all somehow connected to Maya's death, or that they could also be involved with meth production?"

"I don't know yet. It's highly likely it's at least one of those things, and possible that it's both. But only one of them is running the show. O'Connor is already an authority figure among them, so he's a good candidate. He certainly seems to love pointing out that he's in charge of everything."

They went back into the interview room. O'Connor looked up.

"Before you go," said Kali, "could you tell me if you can think of a reason for Maya Holmes to keep copies of her work files on her own private computer?"

He started. "So you found it?" he said, doing his best to hide his surprise.

"Just answer the question," said Walter.

O'Connor began to perspire again. He raised a hand to wipe his forehead. "Anything created on the laboratory premises is the physical or intellectual property of CMMR. It would be both inappropriate and unethical for any members of our research teams to keep files or documents belonging to CMMR on their own electronic devices," he finally said. "Is that an answer?"

"It is," said Kali. She turned toward the door, standing to one side. "We appreciate your help." Then she added, "You're free to leave for now—though it's possible we'll see one another again."

He pushed back his chair, scraping the floor as he stood. He straightened his tie and stalked past her. "Perhaps," he said. "Though I sincerely hope, to the deepest core of my being, that I never encounter either one of you again for as long as I am breathing."

"Interview ended," said Walter. He stated the time, then switched the recorder off. They watched as O'Connor stomped away.

CHAPTER 35

Barely an hour after O'Connor had departed, the duty officer buzzed Kali's desk.

"That woman is back," he told her. "Jody Phillips. She wants to see you, and she's all wound up about something."

"I'll be right out," Kali said.

She walked toward the reception area. Jody was standing by the door, watching for her. As Kali drew closer, Jody held up her phone. She was clearly agitated.

"What's going on, Jody?"

"This. Oh my God, this," said Jody.

She thrust her phone out to Kali. Kali took it, gazing curiously at the screen. There was a page open in the browser, and she read rapidly, not comprehending the significance. Jody's jaw was clenched, her face flushed.

"Can you believe it?" she asked.

Kali shook her head. "I don't know," she said. "I'm not sure what I'm looking at."

Jody grabbed the phone from her and scrolled to the top of the page. Kali saw a title: The Journal of Applied Marine Robotics and Sea Mining Technologies.

"This paper was published today," said Jody. "See the date? I didn't even know it was coming out, but look at the names of the people who are cited as authors."

Kali looked more closely. Beneath the journal title was a headline that read REVOLUTIONARY MINERAL IDENTIFICATION SYSTEM TARGETS DEEP SEA VEINS AND DEPOSITS, and just above the date were the names Davos O'Connor and Byron Coolidge. Her eyes met Jody's.

"Tell me what this means," she said.

"It means," said Jody, her voice trembling with outrage, "that O'Connor and Byron have stolen Maya's work and published it as their own."

"How can you be sure that this is Maya's work?"

"Because she talked to me about it. She'd been working on this theory on her own, about how there had to be a way to develop a new application for the sensors we use on our underwater robotic vehicles that would enable them to detect and differentiate between different types of mineral deposits. Not just in locating valuable minerals such as cobalt, manganese, and copper, but pinpointing the mineral deposits accurately so that they could be extracted without unnecessary damage to the surrounding ecosystem."

Jody searched Kali's face, waiting for a response.

"I thought that was what your whole team was working on," said Kali. "I'm sorry, but you're going to have to explain this in a little more detail."

Jody took a deep breath. "So right now, for instance, when we mine for cobalt crusts on seamounts, we strip them. What Maya was developing was a way to avoid doing that by identifying really large deposits. She knew that if we only mined the big ones, it would mean we could reduce the amount of damage done to sea geography and habitat like we cause now when we mine every small mineral deposit we come across. It wouldn't completely eliminate the damage, but it would definitely help. Plus—and this is really important—we wouldn't be searching blind anymore, hoping to bump into something. The sensors would detect the big deposits and tell us exactly what we'd found."

As Jody grew more agitated, Kali reached out and put her hand on the other woman's arm.

"Just breathe, Jody. I understand the potential, and I hear what you're saying, but where's the proof that this was Maya's invention, and not O'Connor and Coolidge who developed it? It's pretty much what he's already described to us as the purpose of his current program at CMMR."

"You don't understand! She went to him with it," said Jody. "She tried to talk to Dr. O'Connor about it, but he laughed at her. She laid it all out for him, but his response was to treat her like a misbehaving child. Finally, he agreed to look at what she'd done so far, but it was as though he was just trying to placate her."

"And?"

"Well, after he saw her calculations, he told her

that she could keep doing it, and that if she made any real progress, to let him know and he'd consider further evaluating her work."

"Did O'Connor let you know that this paper had been published today? Or did you hear about it from Byron Coolidge?"

Jody shook her head. "No. Neither one of them. I don't think they know, or they would have been blasting it across the universe. It's a big deal. They were both bragging that they had a paper coming out in a few months, but I just tuned it out when they talked about it. It's unlikely there were two papers in the works, so this probably just came out earlier than they expected. That happens sometimes."

"Without them knowing?"

"Sure. The editorial staff probably gave them a projected publication date, but if they had an unexpected gap to fill in an issue that was coming out sooner, and this other paper was ready to go, they may have used it to plug in a hole."

Kali nodded. "Okay. If I showed you some files, would you be able to tell me if they have anything to do with Maya's research and what you're describing to me?"

"You found her computer! Yes, yes, of course." Jody gestured wildly. "This system is going to change everything, and that means it's going to be worth a fortune. Maya will never get the credit she deserves, and O'Connor and Byron will get all the glory and riches. I could murder them both."

"Interesting choice of words," said Kali. She knew that a fortune was too often exactly enough to kill for.

* * *

Jody sat next to Kali's desk, leaning forward. She peered intently at the computer screen. Walter, looking mystified, stood beside her and watched as the pages of code came up. Together they stared as lines of letters and numbers and punctuation marks scrolled by.

"It's like a secret language," said Walter.

"Exactly like a secret language," said Jody.

"Do you understand what any of this means?" asked Kali.

Jody sat back, looking frustrated. "I'm sorry, but I really can't do much with this while the files are locked," she said, regretfully. "Did you ask Charlie if he might know anything about how to get into these files? Did he say anything about a password or a key? To clarify, a key would be a separate digital file used to open these pages."

"He's already given us what he had as far as passwords, but forensics said none of those worked for these files. Charlie said he didn't know about any other passwords, and didn't seem to know anything about a separate digital file like you're describing."

There was a flash of doubt on Jody's face. "I wonder," she said softly, looking up. "Do you think these documents could be connected to her death?"

Kali shrugged. "Hard to say," she said, her tone noncommittal. "But thank you for taking a look." She paused. "By the way, how closely do you work with Gloria Marsh?"

"Gloria." Jody made a face. "Minimal contact, at best," she said.

"Mutual dislike, as well?" asked Kali.

Jody shrugged and looked away, embarrassed by her own response. "I wouldn't go that far. Just nothing in common anymore. She's not generally very social. Maya wasn't either, really—at least not with a lot of people. But we had fun training together."

"And dishing about the people you worked for?"

"I suppose you could call it that. Blowing off steam, maybe."

There was the sound of someone typing on a keyboard in the next room. A phone rang, and the noise of passing traffic could be discerned through the open window.

Jody glanced at Walter, then looked away. For a moment she bit her lip. Then she turned to Kali. "If you want, you could send me copies of these files," she said. "I've got some time. Maybe I could figure out a way into these documents."

"Thank you," said Kali. "That might be helpful. We've got people working on it here, but I'll let them know you're willing to be a resource."

Reluctantly, Jody stood up. "Sure. That would be fine," she said. She looked around the station, examining the surroundings. "You know, I thought the inside of a police station would be larger."

"This is just a satellite station," said Walter. He gave her a brief smile. "Come on, I'll walk you out. Someone told me there's a cherry red '67 Mustang parked outside. Is that your car?"

She nodded, appearing to relax.

Walter shot a quick glance at Kali, then led Jody toward the exit.

Kali watched them go. She turned back toward her desk, thinking hard. She wondered what it was that was flitting back and forth, like a wisp of fog, just out of reach in the back of her mind.

CHAPTER 36

"What do you want to do about this academic paper that was just published?" asked Walter.

"I'm not sure," said Kali. "We've already talked to O'Connor about as many times as we can without charging him with something, and he's already told us he was working on this very thing, so it's no surprise he published a paper on it. I don't see why he would have mentioned the journal to us—he's made it pretty clear he doesn't think cops are intelligent enough to grasp the subtleties of his work."

"Their whole team was working on the same thing, though. So how come he gets the credit?"

"Yes, but . . ." she said, assembling her thoughts. "It's not uncommon for the head of a research group to be cited as the lead person on a work of this kind, so that's probably why O'Connor's name appears before Byron Coolidge, but it does seem like the others should be listed as well."

Walter rolled his eyes. "More posturing? Don't these people have anything more interesting or important in their lives?"

"Maybe not."

"We're nearly a week into this and still no break," said Walter, his frustration evident. "Outside of knowing that Vance Sousa is involved, that is. We still don't know for sure where any of these people were after noon on Saturday—Jody Phillips, Gloria Marsh, Byron Coolidge, or the good Doctor O'Connor."

Kali listened as he rattled off his list.

"Wait a minute," she said. "That's it—it's the names. Jody calls O'Connor by his last name, but always refers to Byron Coolidge by his first."

"So?" said Walter. "O'Connor is her boss. Coolidge is a colleague, and from the obsession that all these people seem to have with their degrees, Jody outranks Coolidge in that department. She already has her PhD, and he's still working on his."

"That's true, yes," said Kali. "But it's the way she says it that's bugging me. It feels like there's a whole lot of familiarity there."

"Small group of people. I guess it wouldn't be surprising if there were some fraternizing going on."

Mentally, Kali reached out again, trying to lock down the half-formed thought.

While Walter was going over some paperwork with Hara, Kali called Charlie to see if he had any ideas about an additional password for the encrypted files on Maya's computer. He didn't answer, so she left him a message and turned her attention to the lab and autopsy reports. Nothing had been revealed by a more extensive examination of Maya's car, and the material in her lungs had been identified as a finely pulverized type of volcanic rock dust commonly used in gardens. The crime lab technician had made a note that it was highly crushed basalt-based scoria that formed from cooled magma, and had no markers to differentiate it from a wide variety of brands available at garden centers across Maui and the other Hawaiian Islands. The report noted that the actual blend of dust would also be difficult to trace to any one particular lava flow.

Soil samples from the crime scene, however, had revealed that the same material in the victim's nose, throat, and lungs had been spilled onto the ground at the base of the tree. Kali sat back in her chair, picturing the girl's last moments: having her hands bound, being dragged from the hot stones, unable to stand fully on her burned feet, then forced to breathe in the dust until she could no longer breathe at all. She imagined the terror as the girl fought her captors, and the recognition that her life was coming to an end.

In her mind, Kali saw the rope being thrown over the branch and secured, then wrapped around Maya's neck before her body was hoisted into the majestic tree. There were figures there, but they were faceless, nameless—just shadows going through a pantomime depicting a monstrous and deliberate act of evil.

Then what? she asked herself. What did the people who murdered Maya Holmes do next—dust off their hands, go home, cook dinner, make love, then fall safely asleep in their own beds? She found the idea ludicrous, and yet something like this had almost certainly taken place.

She walked over to Walter's desk, pulling up a chair. Hara was seated next to him on the other side. Both men stopped what they were doing and turned to her.

"You have an idea?" asked Walter.

"Not exactly," she said. "I just want to talk. We have three different sets of footprints from the crime scene. One is already a match for the print outside my house, which I'm still guessing belongs to scary Vance. Based on the indicators, including shoe size and weight profiles, we're looking at two heavier people and one light person with slightly smaller feet. We've been thinking that means three men of different sizes, but what if it's two men and a woman?"

"No reason it wasn't," said Walter.

Kali turned to Hara. "Do we have shoe sizes and weight profiles for Gloria Marsh and Jody Phillips?"

He shook his head. "No, ma'am. But I'd guess they're about the same general size, though the girl with the red hair is shorter and heavier."

"Get that information, please."

"Should we be collecting shoes from all of these people?"

Kali shook her head. "The chances that someone kept the pair of dust- and mud-covered shoes they wore at a murder scene is about zero. We can't even find Maya's own clothes or shoes. But it might be worth a look. Let's get the details on the two women, and see if anyone can be eliminated. If not, we'll start looking through closets."

Hara rose and went back to his own desk. Kali saw him searching for contact details, then pick up his phone.

"The Marsh woman claims she barely knew the victim, and the Phillips woman appears to be her only friend," said Walter. "You think someone's lying?"

"I think everyone is lying," said Kali.

"Why was Maya killed?"

"I thought it was drugs," said Kali slowly. "Either she was involved, or was causing trouble for the people making and/or distributing them. We know she was trying to help Trey Carter clean up his life, and we know she likely wasn't popular with whomever it was Trey was dealing with. She may have had direct contact with that person. Now I wonder if she was killed because O'Connor wanted to steal her work."

"Could be both. Trey worked at the lab, and that's a link to the meth."

"Highly likely. It's just tying all these people together that's the hard part. Well . . . that and positively putting someone at the scene." She looked at Walter's computer screen, reading to herself from the statements made by the people connected to the dead girl. "We've absolutely got to find Vance. We have his description tied to the attack on George's store, we know he's mixed up in drugs, and he's also working at the lab. Plus I'm convinced he's the one who was rearranging my bras and panties and started the fire in my yard."

Kali glanced toward the back of the room, where Hara was printing documents.

"And the girl, Gloria Marsh?" asked Walter.

"On the surface, she's not very friendly with the others," Kali told him. "Maybe we can use that."

Hara rejoined them, carrying the pages he had retrieved from the printer. He looked expectantly at Walter.

"Do you want me to give you a summary, Captain?"

"Go ahead," said Walter.

"Gloria Marsh reports herself as five foot four inches, and weighs one hundred fifty pounds. That matches pretty close—within five pounds—of her driver's license information. She wears a size eight shoe. Jody Phillips is five foot six inches and says she's one hundred thirty pounds. Also within five pounds of her driver's license. Her shoe size is eight and a half."

"That's well within range of what we know from the footprints," said Kali.

"Yes," said Walter, "but Vance Sousa is somewhere in that range as well. What do we have on him, Hara?"

"Only the information on his license, sir. We don't have his shoe size right now, but he's listed as five foot six inches, and one hundred forty-five pounds."

Hara sat down at his desk and waited.

"Okay," said Walter. "Right now I have a great big headache thinking about the lack of solid alibis. We have O'Connor on CMMR's security camera footage on Friday until late in the day, and most of Saturday. On Sunday, his neighbors confirm that he was in his front garden with a weed trimmer, and that his car was there until Monday morning."

"Everyone else, including Jody Phillips, is also in and out of the security camera footage on Friday, and everyone used their key cards to enter the building on Saturday morning between eight and nine o'clock," said Hara. "All of them were gone by two o'clock that afternoon."

"Right. So where did they go?" asked Kali.

"You mean, where did they say they went?" Walter scowled.

"Byron Coolidge entered the CMMR building that morning and went into the lab run by Dr. O'Connor," said Hara, reading from his printout. "He left the building at just before two in the afternoon and went home. Neighbors confirm his car in the driveway and lights in his windows later on. Vance Sousa and Gloria Marsh both claim to have been at their separate residences, but no one there can confirm their statements. Marsh's building supervisor says he stopped by to give her a package that had been delivered to the office by mistake, but can't remember if it was at lunchtime on Saturday or later in the afternoon. On Sunday, Marsh has receipts from grocery shopping and a ticket stub from an afternoon movie she saw on her own. Some film about an earthquake disaster."

"It seems as though whoever's guilty would have tried to establish a pretty firm story, don't you think? We've heard people make up some incredible tales, and killers working together nearly always have a story." Kali chewed it all over. "What about Vance Sousa?"

"The couple living across from him in his building went over to his apartment to complain about loud after-hours music and a bag of kitchen garbage sitting outside his door that some animals had gotten into and spread around. That was Saturday night, but it was after midnight."

Walter swung around in his chair and looked at his computer screen, scrolling down the page on view. He looked up at Kali. "Your buddy Vance took the ferry over to Lāna'i Island on Sunday and spent the day there. The ferry attendant says she remembers him vividly. Her word, not mine. Seems like he spent most of the trip over and back dancing around on deck and annoying the other passengers."

"It poured that day," said Kali, frowning. "I wonder what he was doing over there?"

"Snorkeling, apparently," said Walter. "That spot where all the spinner dolphins congregate in Hulopo'e Bay. Guess rain isn't a big deal if you're underwater and already wet."

"According to Stitches, Maya Holmes was dead by Saturday night. Maybe the killers took the day off on Sunday."

"We don't have a lot of data on the family for these people, beyond O'Connor being divorced and the others living alone," said Kali. "I'm going to look into that. Ex spouses, partners, significant others."

They sat together, contemplating the accumulated facts. A traffic call came in about a flash flood blocking traffic near a bridge on the Hana Highway, and Hara jumped up to deal with it. Walter leaned back in his chair.

"I thought you had a meeting with Chief Pait this afternoon," said Kali, watching him.

"Not till later." He grunted. "I'd rather get a couple of teeth pulled without any anesthetic." He looked toward the coffeepot on the other side of the room. "You want some coffee?"

"Not right now," she said, pulling out her phone. "I'm going to try again to reach Charlie Holmes."

CHAPTER 37

A faint sense of uneasiness gripped Kali as she listened to the voicemail prompt again. She waited for the beep, then left another message.

"Charlie? It's Detective Kali Māhoe calling again. Could you please get in touch as soon as you can? Either this number or my private number is fine. I need to speak to you immediately."

She read off her private number again, then ended the call. She'd already left a half dozen messages, none of which had been returned. The marine rescue center had told her Charlie was still taking some personal time off, and they hadn't heard from him, but would ask him to get in touch if he stopped by or checked in with them.

There was no real reason to worry, but she couldn't shake the feeling that something was amiss.

"I'm going to drive over to the condominium where Charlie lives," she told Walter. "I've been calling him all afternoon, but he hasn't responded to any of my messages."

Walter turned from the counter, where he was stirring cream into his coffee mug. "Be careful," he said, more than a little concerned.

Kali stood in the entrance to Charlie's condo. The front door was partially open, and it was a mess inside. Dishes had been tossed out of cabinets, drawers were flung open, and the sofa cushions had been ripped apart. Shredded foam stuffing from inside the cushions was scattered around the room. The knickknacks from the living room shelves were on the floor.

She called Walter. "We're going to need a team over here," she said. "Charlie's gone, and all signs point to him having left not on his own terms."

"Not good. Too many people connected to this case are disappearing." He sounded grim. "I don't like the sound of this."

"Neither do I," she said.

"Forced entry? Blood anywhere?"

"Not that I've been able to see so far," she said. "The door is open, but it doesn't look as though the lock is broken. I think he let someone in, or was followed here and someone rushed him at the door and got inside." She looked around the bedroom. "They've done a number on the interior, that's for sure. Whoever did this was looking for something, and was pretty motivated to find it."

"The computer, you think?"

"Seems likely. No one connected to any of this knows that the computer has been found except for Jody and O'Connor, so I suppose we can assume it wasn't them."

Inside the bedrooms, it was more of the same. Anything that had been on a shelf was now on the floor. Drawers had been pulled out, and the mattresses on the beds were askew, as though someone had searched beneath them. She walked back into the kitchen, then stopped short. There was blood on the floor by the refrigerator. She stooped to examine it, touching one corner gently with her pinky finger. It was sticky, but had yet to fully dry.

By the time the forensics crew arrived, Kali was beside herself with worry. There were no immediate clues suggesting who had been there or where they'd gone. The neighbors on either side of Charlie's residence weren't at home, and no one who answered any of the other doors had noticed strangers on the premises.

Kali walked up and down the row of condos, her anxiety growing. She stood at the end of the walkway, watching the light traffic on the quiet neighborhood road that fronted the building.

Acutely aware that Charlie might be running out of time, she checked in with the forensics team, then drove back to the station. Walter had just finished with his meeting with Chief Pait and was sitting at his desk with a glass of water and bottle of aspirin.

"How did it go?" she asked.

"Oh, you know. The usual orders. Round up all the criminals. Eliminate the existence of illegal drugs. Stop people from driving too fast, shoplifting, littering." He turned to her, a pained expression on his face. "Oh, and he wants me to fix the weather. He said we've had enough storms for this year."

"So you'll be busy for a few days," she said, trying to smile.

"Yeah. So back to Charlie Holmes. We're treating this as a likely abduction, and we've got everyone looking for him. Did forensics come up with anything while I was with the chief?"

"Not yet," she said. "The blood on the floor worries me."

"It's worrying all of us." He looked at her closely. "When is the last time you actually slept?"

She shrugged. "I'm okay. I'd be better if . . ."

Her phone buzzed, and she pulled it from her pocket. The caller ID revealed that Mark Shore, the park ranger, was on the line.

She held the phone out so that Walter could see. He stood up from his desk.

"Hi, Mark. What's up?"

"Sorry to bother you," Mark said, "but we've got a problem up here. One of the part-time rangers found a weird makeshift structure up in the high ground off a path leading to where that poor girl was hanging, and when he went to investigate it, some crazy guy jumped out of the bushes and clocked him. The ranger's okay, but he was on his own and didn't want to have another run-in with this nut, so he came back to the station."

"Do we have a description?"

"Skinny guy, dark hair, lots of tattoos. And . . .' Mark hesitated. "Buck naked, too. The ranger's not sure, but he thinks he's seen him up here before. At least, the ranger says he looks like a guy who volunteered on a trail cleanup a while back— but that guy had clothes on, so it's hard to say."

"We know who he is," said Kali. "Regard him as dangerous and don't try to approach him. And please wait at the ranger station—we'll be there soon."

"Well, be careful. The ground is unstable. We've already had one small mudslide, and it could get worse at any minute."

"Understood," she said. "We're on our way."

She rang off, looking at Walter. "Road trip. We'll need Hara, too. We just got a location on Vance Sousa."

CHAPTER 38

Dressed in storm gear, Kali and Walter took the Jeep. Hara followed in his cruiser. They left the vehicles at the trailhead parking area at the base of the mountain. The ground was thick with fresh mud, and the footing was difficult. They climbed as quickly as they could, following the path that led past the ranger station and toward the rainbow tree.

Kali moved quietly along the higher ground beside the path, moving cautiously in an effort to stay concealed. She used her left hand to steady herself against the trunks of the trees lining the trail, while her gun was tightly gripped in her right hand, ready in case Vance made a sudden appearance.

In the forest on either side of the path, hidden

by the dense undergrowth and towering trees, she knew that Walter and Hara were covering her, moving silently in a flank formation. Stealth was essential—she knew they all understood that the element of surprise might be the only thing that made a difference today between Vance being taken alive or not. She pushed aside the thought that it also might be what determined whether she and Walter and Hara made it home safely this evening.

Now, coming through the foliage, she could discern the sound of chanting. She slowed her approach and moved carefully into the shadows along the trail's edge. They were still some distance below the clearing with the multihued eucalyptus. A narrow path twisted away from the main trail, and the sound seemed to be emanating from there. Warily, she followed it, and a small opening came into view. At the back, an enormous rock formation jutted into the space like the prow of a great, stony ship, blocking out much of what was left of the pale daylight beyond the forest's border. She stood behind the trunk of a massive pine and peered into the gloom.

There was a flutter of movement at the top of the outcropping. She could make out a crude hut on one side of the surface, clumsily built from palm fronds and pine branches, and wondered if it was meant to be a prayer hut. Near it, a male figure moved among the shadows, and a male voice chanted something that sounded like random, muddled words. There appeared to be a second person seated against a boulder. The dim light illuminated the stone backdrop, and a fire sprang up on the top of the rock. Kali watched as the standing figure fed a few branches into the flames. He lifted something, which she saw was a book. He raised it toward the sky, then began to tear the pages from it. A few fluttered in the air, landing on the ground at the base of the rock. The others fell into the fire, feeding the flames.

He stood in front of the inferno, repeatedly crouching and stretching his body upward. She crept closer. The figure moved into a patch of light. It was Vance, his naked body covered in painted symbols that obscured many of his tattoos. The second person, seated against the stone, made no movement as Vance's voice rose in volume, the nonsensical words of this chant growing louder. As Kali watched, Vance began to dance in front of the fire. His movements were jerky and fitful, as though his limbs were being manipulated by strings, or by something far beyond his control.

Kali glanced to her left and right. She could distinguish Walter and Hara, each about twenty feet away on either side, parallel to her. She raised her arm and made a fist with her hand, forming the wait signal, then watched for their response. In turn, each of them acknowledged the silent command, raising their own hands and giving her a thumbs-up.

Slowly, Kali emerged from behind the tree, gun drawn, Vance's figure clearly in her sight line. He seemed unaware of her presence. She waited for a few seconds, trying to determine who the second person was, and if they were conscious. There was no movement. She stepped closer, then called out.

"Come down from the rock, Vance!"

His dancing ceased abruptly. He looked down from the sloping ledge. The rim was about seven feet above the clearing floor, and Kali watched as he slowly straightened and gazed down at her. His face seemed distorted—his eyes were wide, unblinking.

"Kneel before me!" he commanded, spreading his arms wide.

"I said to come down!"

He swung his head toward her in an unnatural movement. She felt a chill at the back of her neck, coursing down her entire spine.

"I called you here, priest," he snarled. Then he leapt sideways, spinning across the surface of the rock, bouncing on his ankles with bent knees. Again he began to chant, waving his arms above his head.

Kali signaled to Walter and Hara to move in slowly. She stepped to her right, doing her best to get a better view of the person propped against the stone face of the massive rock.

"Is that Charlie up there with you, Vance?" she shouted, but he didn't seem to hear. She moved closer to the outcropping, looking for a foothold or access point. She could hear rustling to her left, and knew that Walter was closing in.

Suddenly, Vance gave a dreadful scream. He leapt into the air in front of the fire and whirled around, again facing Kali. He gyrated, pounding his chest. The markings on his body and face made no sense to her, but the illusion they created was of a fiend.

"You have entered my house at my command!" he called to her. "I am a Kane, and you have no power here. You will do my bidding." He reached down and picked up a long branch with leaves clinging to twigs along its length, then thrust it into the flames of the fire now roaring behind him. The tip of the branch blazed, and he brandished it above his head, then whirled it in a wide arc that came within a few feet of Kali's head.

To her right, she saw Hara break cover, slipping into the open space before the rock. Walter was on her left, and the three of them spread in a shallow curve. Each of them directed their firearm at Vance.

Above them, Vance had picked up the torn book from the rock and turned away. He was facing the fire, chanting and half-dancing, half-lurching once again.

"Cover me!" Kali said to Walter. "If he's got Charlie, I've got to get to him. Vance has lost his mind."

"You're not going up there alone!" said Walter. "Hara, I can't make that climb fast enough—follow Kali, and don't take your eyes off Vance for a second."

Hara gave a sharp nod. He moved directly behind Kali, watching as she found a sloping area that led past the hut and onto the rock. He kept his gun trained on Vance, searching for secure footing on the slick rock surface.

Kali climbed swiftly, coming up on the side where the other figure was still visible, an unmoving mass in the flickering light of the fire. She drew close enough to see that it was definitely Charlie. His hands were tied in front of him, and blood covered one side of his face, dripping from a cut on his forehead. She couldn't see whether or not he was breathing.

"Charlie!" she called as loudly as she dared. "It's Kali, Charlie—can you hear me?"

There was no response. Charlie's head was slumped forward against his chest. In the shadowy light of the flames, she couldn't be certain if he was awake, or if he was even alive. She squatted, inching forward, trying not to draw Vance's attention. Vance appeared to be in some kind of trance state, the senseless words spewing from his mouth in a constant stream, the sounds punctuated by his juddering movements. His eyes had rolled backward into his head, and even as she watched, he dropped his burning branch and began to pound his chest with both hands, his fingers clenched into fists.

Kali glanced to her side, making note of Hara's progress up the rock face. It was now or never. She sprang forward, kneeling by Charlie's side. Reaching out, she pressed her fingers to his neck beside his windpipe, finding the carotid artery and feeling for a pulse. He made no move, but she detected a weak pulsing rhythm. She did a quick scan of his body, looking for injuries. Beyond the cut on his forehead and a series of bloody scrapes, there wasn't anything immediately apparent. She raised his eyelids one at a time, noting the dilated pupils.

With her free hand, she reached out, trying to determine what had been used to bind his hands. As she ran her hand over the knots, Charlie stirred and moaned. His eyes fluttered, and she saw him move his feet as if searching for footing.

The material binding his wrists felt like a thick twine, and even as the thought occurred to her that there was no time to try to free him before Vance realized what was taking place, she heard the sound of wild laughter, then saw Vance bend and reach for his flaming branch. In what seemed to her less than a fraction of a section, he was above her and Charlie.

"Who do you think you are?" he thundered, his fevered voice echoing against the stone. "Do you think that you can stop me, that you can stand on the devil's wing? Do you think that you can meddle with the plans of a god without paying a price? I'll burn you, priest! I'll turn you into dust and ash!"

Even as the last word left his mouth, he swung the branch downward toward Kali. Instinctively, she raised her arm to protect her face, and tried to aim her gun at Vance. She pulled the trigger, and the bullet glanced off of the granite. The heat of the flames scorched her arm, and she could smell burnt hair. Vance was chanting again. He raised the branch a second time, this time swinging the flame lower. Kali dropped to the ground, throwing her arms around Charlie and pulling him down with her. She heard Charlie groan and felt her cheek strike the hard ground. Rolling quickly to her back, she tried to lock her aim on the demented, moving figure on the boulder's rounded peak.

Even as she fought to lock Vance in her sights, she heard a crack as a firearm discharged close by. Vance's body arched backward, his chanting interrupted. There was a brief moment in which he stood, legs apart, arms spread wide, the branch in one hand and the other raised toward the heavens. Then he fell backward, out of her sight, silenced. She turned to her left and saw Hara. He was standing in a classic fighting stance, knees flexed, one foot slightly offset, and his arms extended in front of him, with both hands gripping his pistol.

As Hara lowered his weapon, Kali saw his arms begin to shake. He stood up straighter, then turned to her. He seemed unable to move.

"Are you all right, Detective?" he asked. She heard the strain in his voice.

"I'm fine." She tried to smile. "Thanks to you." She knew that this was the first time he had fired a shot at another human being, and that he was wrestling with that truth. "We need to get help for Charlie."

He nodded, then looked toward the forest behind the rock above them. They could hear the crashing of underbrush, and knew that Walter was making his way around from the back. The flames of the branch sputtered out as it lay on the hard surface of the boulder. Kali could see what was left of the book lying beside it. It was her grandmother's, torn beyond repair. She felt her stomach clench with anger and grief.

Hara looked at Kali and Charlie, unsure.

"Go!" said Kali. "But toss me your utility knife first."

Hara pulled his knife from his duty belt and threw it to her, then sprang forward, disappearing into the foliage. Moments later, Kali could hear Walter's voice, followed by the sounds of something being hauled through the underbrush. As she worked to cut away the heavy twine around Charlie's wrists, she saw Walter and Hara pull Vance into the clear space that he'd so recently used as a stage. This time, it was Vance's hands that were securely bound. He was standing, mumbling incoherently. Blood flowed from a bullet wound in his right shoulder.

Walter pushed Vance into a sitting position on the ground while speaking into his radio. Hara stepped up beside Vance, fixing his attention on the naked, moaning figure.

Walter turned to Kali.

"Help's on the way. We'll get this jerk down and tie him to a tree trunk, since he seems to have an affinity for that sort of thing. We'll be back up as quickly as we can to help you get that kid down. What kind of shape's he in?"

"I'm pretty sure he's concussed," said Kali. "There's a head injury, plus cuts and scratches." She looked into the forest. "This place—Vance—this isn't all of it, Walter. I can feel it in my bones. This idiot wasn't on his own, and if I'm correct about meth production somehow mixed up in this whole thing, there's got to be a factory somewhere close by."

Walter nodded. "Agreed. But first things first. You hang tight, and we'll be as fast as we can."

Walter turned to Hara. "Is the suspect secured, Officer?"

Hara looked from Walter to Vance, and back to Walter. He spoke with certainty. "Yes, Captain."

Walter nodded, his face grave. "Outstanding job today, Officer Hara. Outstanding."

CHAPTER 39

Kali knelt beside the stretcher, searching Charlie's face. He was mumbling. His eyes opened, staring wildly about him. They found Kali's face and tried to focus, but it was too much. His lids closed, and his head turned to one side. Kali nodded to the medics that they could begin the trek back to the waiting emergency vehicle parked below. She was about to turn away when she heard Charlie say something. She bent over him, her face close to his. He was clearly distressed, and his lips moved as he attempted to form words.

"What is it, Charlie?" she asked. "You're safe now. What is it you're trying to say?"

Again the muddled sounds left his lips. Kali listened hard, trying to make sense of the words.

"Did you say cave?" she asked, unsure.

He repeated the word.

"Try to nod your head, Charlie, if you're saying cave."

His head moved, ever so slightly. His eyelids fluttered again.

"Okay," she said. "I'll find the cave. And then I'll come and see you."

"No," he said. His voice was weak. "Stay away . . . from the cave."

As the medics lifted the stretcher and turned away, she hurried back to Walter, who was giving direction to several officers who had responded to the call.

"He said something about a cave, and to stay away from it. See if you can get through to Ranger Shore," she said, her mind working fast. "Find out if there are any caves in this area, particularly close to where we are right now."

"Are you sure that's what he said?"

"Yes, I think he was trying to tell me there's a cave or cavern somewhere close. It might be where Vance has been practicing his black magic. I'll be right back."

The first part of the response team who had taken control of Vance had already started down the slope toward the parking area. She caught up with them, calling out for them to wait. When she reached them, Vance looked at her and grinned. He was no longer struggling, but it was clear he was still being affected by whatever substance he'd consumed.

"Where's the cave, Vance?" she asked. "What's in it?"

His head lolled to one side, and his dark eyes flickered. "You should know."

She looked at him, disgusted. "Tell me where the cave is, and tell me what's inside."

"Something more powerful than you," he sneered. "Your magic means nothing here."

He closed his eyes and began to chant again loudly. She could get nothing more from him. The two officers holding him by the arms jerked him forward. He lifted his feet, forcing them to bear his full weight. His voice grew louder and more defiant. Kali stepped back, nodding to the officers to take him away. She turned and ran back up the path to the spot where she'd left the others.

Kali walked quickly around the perimeter of the rock formation, checking for openings or any kind of fissure they may have overlooked. There was nothing immediately obvious, and she felt her frustration rising up, engulfing her.

Walter and Hara met her as she was making her way back to them. Walter was on his phone.

"Mark says no caves, at least nothing like the Ka'eleku Cave just north of Hana, but there is an old lava tube," said Walter. "It was blocked off years ago to keep kids and hikers from getting inside after parts of it began to collapse. Someone got hurt in there a while ago, and they were in pretty bad shape before a hiker heard them calling for help. The park service moved loose rocks in front of the opening, and no one's been inside since."

"Someone's been inside," she said. "Did he tell you how to find it?"

Walter looked at his phone. "He just sent a map. It's downloading now. Mark says we're nearly on top of it, that it's not far from this big rock face."

Kali swung around, facing the silent stone.

There was nothing that looked like a stack of boulders that had been deliberately moved. Behind her, Walter and Hara stood staring at the greenery that had rooted in the crevices of the craggy surface. A thought flitted through her mind. She wondered, silently, if Vance had placed some ancient curse upon it that would require a magic word or an incantation that would unlock a secret opening.

A raindrop struck her forehead. She shook herself, and the strange thoughts dissipated into the humid air.

"I don't see anything here," said Walter.

He peered intently at his phone screen. Kali and Hara moved closer. Kali compared the outline of trails and geographical features on the map sent by Mark with her immediate surroundings. The large rock formation was a prominent feature. To one side, a corridor of trees and shrubs separated the huge rock from the path they were on—which connected to the larger trail—and the high spaces above with the clearing where Maya had been killed. On the stretch approaching the clearing with the rainbow tree, several smaller paths on both sides intersected with the main trail.

Visually, Kali traced the main track to a thin black line denoting a winding path that plunged off to the right, less than a quarter mile from where the team now stood. This path headed downhill for a short distance, then made an abrupt left turn and began to climb. It was at this juncture that Mark had drawn a circle, indicating the location of the blocked mouth of the lava tube.

"That's probably where Vance was holding Charlie, and where Maya was before she was taken up to the firewalking stones," said Kali. "If the part-time ranger who ran into him today is correct and Vance is someone who volunteered on a past trail project, it might be when Vance first stumbled on the lava tube opening."

"Secret headquarters?" asked Walter, frowning at the map image. "Seems like one of the rangers would have noticed something out of the ordinary."

"Not necessarily," reasoned Kali. "Mark has only a small team tasked with covering a huge area. And when I hike, I use the same trails repeatedly. I have favorite spots and views like everyone else, and if the weather is iffy, I like knowing what to expect as far as terrain and elevation."

"Yeah, but Vance doesn't look much like the athletic type," said Walter. "He would have had to have several other people with him if it was him who brought Maya up here, and it's also unlikely he got Charlie up here on his own."

"Charlie was incapacitated. And so was Maya. Both of them had been subdued, at least to some degree. It's unlikely either one of them was able to put up much of a fight."

"Okay, so say that's how this played out today— they were subdued, and Vance had help. That suggests the other person, or persons, is still somewhere close by. We certainly haven't seen anyone else on the main trail, and no one got past the rescue crews."

"There could have been several people who became aware of us thanks to all the noise made by Vance. They could be hiding in the forest. The vegetation is pretty thick."

Walter looked at the path ahead of them. He turned to Hara, who was standing tensely, waiting for direction.

"Okay, everybody," said Walter. "We all know the situation. According to the ranger's notes, the lava tube has one entrance. The other end, which originally came out closer to the coast, has been damaged, and a lot of it has caved in. That means there's one way in and one way out." He looked down at his phone. "According to the ranger, there's a stretch inside the tube starting at the entrance that's about seventy feet long and has a slightly downhill angle. The ceiling of the tube is about nine feet in height at the tallest point, and the width is roughly nine or ten feet across at the widest spot. The rangers were last inside over two years ago, so conditions may have changed a lot."

He looked at Kali, his countenance grim. "The tube is unstable. This has the potential to get ugly."

"Yeah. I expect it will," she said. "But it's already been a pretty ugly day. So let's get this over with."

CHAPTER 40

Dusk was rapidly descending over the forest, the change in light accelerated by the thick cloud canopy that had formed in the dampness. Despite the map and Mark's detailed directions, accessing the old lava tube wasn't without its challenges. The heavy rains had left the ground in poor condition. Deep puddles and stodgy mud made the going slow, even as the viscous, constantly altering terrain also obscured whether or not the path had been recently used.

Unable to wait for more reinforcements, Walter, Kali, and Hara moved quietly along the twisting, narrow path. After about ten minutes, Kali, who was slightly ahead of the others, caught sight of the sharp turn outlined on the map, and saw a rough stack of boulders and large rocks that seemed too symmetrical to have been an act of nature.

She gave the halt sign, and everyone stopped, stilled in their tracks. Above them the wind rustled through a multitude of leaves and branches. Kali could hear songbirds jostling for nighttime positions among the trees, and caught the flicker of the wings of the golden-hued Maui creeper as it fluttered from one tree to the next. Through the dense fern undergrowth, she saw the glint of eyes. A small axis deer stared back at her. She tilted her head, listening for any sound that didn't belong there. The deer bounded away, perhaps recognizing some omen of what was about to take place.

Stepping forward with her gun drawn and her other hand held palm up, she crept toward the rocks alone, and was startled to see that there was a narrow space behind them, as though they had been moved from their original formation and reassembled to allow access into the space beyond. The mouth of the lava tube was clearly visible.

There was a faint glow of light emanating from within, but she could detect no sound. Kali backed up carefully, and gestured for Walter and Hara to move in closer. Walter pointed to Hara, indicating that he should remain outside the cave's entrance to sound an alert in case anyone approached.

Together, their weapons drawn, Kali and Walter stepped cautiously into the dim, cool opening of the ancient lava tube. It sloped slightly upward, and the hard surface beneath their feet was dry. Just enough light filtered toward them from some unknown source ahead that eliminated the need for flashlights.

Side by side, they moved ahead guardedly, ever deeper into the mountain's stony belly. The light grew slowly brighter. Shadows flickered along the walls ahead. They passed a pile of empty antifreeze containers and battery package wrappers. Several feet farther along, the wall was lined with empty glass containers. She turned to Walter, who nodded in acknowledgment. He mouthed the words Here's your meth lab, and she dipped her head in agreement. They both knew the danger that surrounded them, and how combustible the debris could be. Kali's apprehension mounted as she noted the carelessness with which the rubbish had been discarded.

The tunnel bent to the right, widening slightly. Here several dozen plastic garbage bags filled with more trash had been left behind. The tops of several of the bags were opened enough for them to glimpse the contents: dozens and dozens of used paper coffee filters stained with a crimson-colored residue, and multiple empty packages of a drugstore brand of sinus tablets containing pseudoephedrine. There were several large bags of cat litter, and Kali knelt to look at a larger bag propped among them. The lettering on the front of the bag read Volcanic rock dust for landscaping. Kali's throat constricted as the significance of the bag's contents struck her.

Now that they were some distance from the lava tube's entrance and the fresh breezes that cleared away any unusual scents, they could smell chemicals in the air, dominated by the unmistakable aromas of ammonia and ethanol. Both Kali and Walter knew that the cat litter had likely been mixed with the rock dust to try and mask the overpowering odors of the meth-making operation's debris.

There was no time to dwell any further on the implications. From somewhere ahead, Kali and Walter could hear humming, the words muffled by the distance. The sound was familiar. They paused, listening and watching. The tube bent again, and as they stole forward, the voice became clearer. Kali recognized it immediately. It was Byron Coolidge.

In the light cast upon the walls of the cave, she could discern his figure as it moved in and out of sight on the far side of the curving rock. Crouching slightly, Kali inched forward. She could feel the warmth from Walter's body just behind her. She made herself ready, and turned slowly, making eye contact with Walter. He nodded. Together, they stepped forward into the opening ahead.

"Freeze!" roared Walter as Kali covered Byron with her weapon. "On the ground! Now! Hands on your head!"

Byron swung around and faced them, his face flooded with amazement. He was wearing a protective mask, which he pulled down under his chin. Recognizing Kali, he took a sudden step to the side and looked around wildly, as though preparing to flee farther along the length of the lava tube.

"Don't do it!" she shouted in warning as she saw him twist. "ON THE GROUND!"

Hesitantly, Byron lowered himself to the floor of the cave and stretched out on his stomach. On either side of him, long folding tables had been set up against the sides of the cave. Beneath one were several propane tanks and hoses that led to a portable camp-style cookstove on the table's surface. Two burners were lit, and on each burner, a large glass cooking pot sat above the flames.

Kali registered this fact the same time as Walter, and both of them looked with concern at the stove. The stench of chemicals was nearly overwhelming. They both knew too well the potential for the chemicals to combust. Kali tried not to think of how Mike had been faced with this same scene: a confrontation with paranoid meth cooks who had taken his life instead of surrendering. Her heart clenched at the thought, and her rage mounted at the realization that Walter, whom she also loved, should be faced with this same danger now, years later, on a mountain that should never have been touched by this degree of crime or waste or grief.

Without turning his head, Walter spoke to Kali, his voice terse. "Shut off that stove and then cuff the professor, please. I have you covered."

Kali moved warily toward Byron. "Put your hands behind your back."

Silently, he inched away from her on his belly, closer to the stove. She realized that he could reach it more quickly than she could get to him.

"Don't come any closer," he said. "Or I'll kick this table, and then . . . ka-boom."

"Move away from it now," she said. "Get up slowly and stand over there facing the wall, across from Captain Alaka'i."

Byron was sweating profusely. Kali could see his chest rising and falling rapidly as his body reacted to the stress of what was happening. She saw him glance up at the cookstove as if making some internal calculation. He looked up at Kali.

"I said get up and face the wall," Kali said. "Now."

Byron rose suddenly on one knee, then took a half step toward the stove. He shook his head. "I wouldn't try to shoot me in here," he said. "If you miss, the bullet will ricochet off the rock and hit something in here. Some of the chemicals. We'll all blow up."

His eyes were wide. Kali could see the distorted pupils. She knew that if he was high, he was also unlikely to be reasonable.

"I'm right, you know," said Byron. He began humming again, a disjointed tune that Kali didn't recognize. "The pots—what's in them isn't stable."

She tried to keep the fear out of her own voice. She knew that what he said was true.

"Maybe I like my chances," she said. "Either way—bullet, explosion—you're going down. For this, for Maya Holmes, for Trey Carter."

Byron laughed, the sharp cackle magnified by the rock.

"Is that what you think? That I'm some evil mastermind assassin?" His voice was shaky, and again he glanced at the cookstove. "I promise you, you're looking in the wrong place."

"Is that right? Then point me in the right direction," said Kali. "You can start by telling me about how you stole the work of a young woman, then killed her to cover up your theft."

"Ah," said Byron. "You've been talking to the green-eyed Jody Phillips, haven't you? Or, as Vance likes to call her, his Pahulu. It was Jody who found out what Maya was working on and saw the potential. At first, Davos wasn't sure, but I recognized the opportunity right away. A brilliant innovation that would change undersea mining forever. Jody and I convinced Davos to come on board . . . and Jody worked on Maya to learn the details of her invention."

"By pretending to be her friend?"

"By becoming obsessed with her. She was perfectly content until she caught sight of Maya and her beauty. Followed her around like a puppy dog, even though Maya made it clear she wasn't interested. But Maya was kind. And stupid. She offered Jody friendship, but that just wasn't enough. Jody wanted to be Maya, but of course she couldn't. Not with that scar. Not even close. Maybe Jody really thought she was in love, and maybe Maya broke her heart. Maybe it was simple envy—but whatever it was, Jody wanted to make her pay. And she did, when she helped Vance shove her pretty face into that bag of dust."

Byron took another infinitesimal step closer to the stove. Kali moved at the same time, keeping her gun trained on him.

He smiled at her. "Is it becoming a little more clear to you now?"

"It is," said Kali. "You, Jody, and O'Connor continued to use Maya for her invention, and you encouraged Jody to get as much information from her as possible. You needed to publish that paper so that everyone would think the mining device was yours, and Maya had to die before the paper came out. But then you cut Jody out of the loop, didn't you? You didn't include her as an author on the paper, and you didn't even mention her as one of the supposed developers of the technology you'd all stolen from Maya Holmes. Seems like a serious miscalculation for a couple of smart guys like you and O'Connor. Jody knew the paper's publication meant that if you sold a patent, she'd never see a penny out of your little scheme."

"The whole thing sounds more like a soap opera than a respectable research facility," said Walter as he adjusted the grip on his handgun. "Jealous Jody scheming to help take away Maya's work, you and O'Connor scheming to deny Jody credit when it was published, and Vance working like a puppet for all of you, slowly losing his mind to the effects of all that nice, fresh meth you and he were cooking up."

"He overheard us talking about the financial potential of Maya's invention. And his zeal for legends and myths was a useful distraction, at least at first," said Byron. "You've met him. The rumors of a witch turned out to be pretty accurate, wouldn't you say?"

"He wasn't interested in a share of any profits?" Kali asked, moving infinitesimally closer to Byron.

Byron shrugged. His lips twitched. "You should ask him, I guess—if you can get a coherent answer out of him. It was the drugs that he valued. As far as the invention, Jody screwed up—Maya should have had those files on her work computer where we could access them, but they weren't there. Who knew they'd be stashed away on her laptop, and that she'd have created a lock to keep them from being readable by anyone else?"

"She must have suspected Jody and the rest of you all along," said Kali, watching him closely.

"Possibly so." He laughed. "But it's all just a set-back. Jody and Vance will get the password out of Maya's silly brother."

"Charlie's safe. And Vance has a bullet hole in him," said Walter. "So you can tell us the rest of the story from your jail cell. It's time to go."

"And leave all my beautiful work behind to spend the rest of my life in a prison?" Byron looked around. He shook his head. "I don't think so."

Kali's apprehension grew. She needed to keep him talking until he was out of range of the stove. She looked at the burners, where whatever was in the large glass pots had risen to a frantic boil.

"Why the drugs, Byron?" asked Kali. "You said you're going to make a fortune off the patent for Maya's invention."

"Sure, eventually," he said. "In the meantime, I'm making a fortune off the weakness of others."

"Are you using the Wela Wela Cave in Honolulu as a distribution center? Or do you have Vance doing that for you? Maybe that's how you control him—using him as your errand boy."

Byron laughed. "Control him? Stage direct him, maybe. But Vance is his own unique animal, as you must have realized. All wrapped up in his magic and his legends." Byron looked suddenly serious. "The distribution is strictly local. But I think he actually enjoyed killing that girl. At least, it seemed that way, from where I stood. Vance is the one who dreamed up a way to do it that would scare people away from this part of the forest so as to help keep our little laboratory secret. And Jody was only too happy to help."

"Along with Gloria and O'Connor?"

"Gloria?" Byron shook his head, amused. "She doesn't have a clue about what's been going on right underneath her perky little nose. And we knew that Davos wasn't brave enough to be part of our meth project. He would have been a liability. He's just wrapped up in getting that patent secured for the new sensor. If he knew about our pharmaceutical enterprise, he might have turned us in, so we kept it from him. The information, and the profits."

He looked around and sighed. Then he moved again. Kali and Walter each realized at the same instant what it was that he planned to do. In a flash, he moved and blocked the stove. Neither Kali nor Walter could take a shot without risking hitting the bubbling concoctions on the stove. Byron leapt to the side, deeper into the darkness of the tunnel as it dove further into the mountain. As he fled, he kicked out with his foot, aiming for the table holding the gas stove. He struck the edge. One leg of the table crumbled, and the pots began to slide on a trajectory toward the stone lava floor.

Instinctively, Kali flexed, prepared to follow him.

"Don't!" Walter shouted. He grabbed her by the wrist and pulled hard. "Turn around and run! Run!"

They did, sprinting for all they were worth on the uneven rock footing, careening into the solid walls, slipping as they made the first turn away from the lab and back into the darkness of the tube. Kali felt the air around her body contract, then expand with a violent, furious energy. She knew that Walter was there, somewhere close in the black-

ness, but there was no time to say anything. There
was only a sudden lift, as if gravity had retreated
followed by a mighty, crashing boom. Then came a
complete and terrible failure of light, and Kali lost
track of where the tunnel ended, and where she
began.

The blast hurled Kali and Walter from the inner
tunnel to the entrance of the lava tube. They
landed facedown in the scrabble lining the floor
their breath knocked out of them. Kali pressed her
hands against the rock and slowly pushed herself
into a crouching position. She looked for Walter
and saw him spread on the ground a few feet away
motionless. As she crawled forward to his side, she
heard the sound of the rock above her and behind
her groaning, knowing it was a matter of seconds
before the entrance to the tube collapsed.

"Walter!" she yelled, shaking him vigorously
He moaned, rolling over onto his back. "What the
hell . . . ?"

"Explosion," she gasped. Then she added, "Lava
tube."

The words registered. He looked up, and a blast
of dust shot downward from a widening crack in
the curved ceiling above him.

"We've got to get out," Kali said, her voice
nearly drowned out by the sound of rock crashing
in behind them.

She stood, legs shaking, helping Walter onto his
feet. He limped forward a few steps, and his right
leg buckled beneath him. There was movement at
the opening of the tube, and Hara was suddenly
there.

"Captain!" he said. He looked at Kali, noting that her face was covered in dust and blood.

"I'm okay," she said. "Help Walter."

The rock groaned again, and Hara grasped Walter under his arm from one side while Kali supported him from the other. They pulled him forward, past the entrance, past the first stand of trees and pile of boulders. There was a colossal cracking sound, and together they dove behind the rocks as the lava tube collapsed upon itself, the grass-covered earth above it caving in, leaving nothing but a deep impression and a blast of debris settling in its wake.

For a moment, no one said anything.

"Was there anyone in there, sir?" asked Hara, breaking the silence. He stared at the place where the cave's opening had once been.

"There was," said Walter, coughing. "A very bad man making drugs."

"Not anymore," said Kali. She wiped a streak of blood from her face. "And I'm pretty sure not ever again."

CHAPTER 41

Hindered by the rain and the slippery footing, Kali, Walter, and Hara finally made it to the path. Walter was limping badly. Both he and Kali were dazed and bruised, and covered by a fair amount of mud. Kali and Hara took turns supporting Walter on the narrow trail. They half slid, half scrambled back down the mountain to the parking lot and finally reached their vehicles.

"Hara's car or my Jeep?" Kali asked, aware of how much Walter's leg hurt.

"I'll go with you," said Walter. He turned to Hara. "Stay in touch the whole way. We'll go ahead. The Jeep has higher ground clearance, and if the roads wash out I'd rather we were in front of you so you don't get caught."

Hara nodded. He helped Walter into the passenger side of the Jeep, then ran to his cruiser. Kali waited until she saw his headlights come on, then started the engine and edged out onto the main road. There was already about two inches of flood-water on the road, and she could see the accumulated rainwater moving in a steady current as it swept across the paved surface.

"This is bad," she said.

By now the rain was coming down in sheets. Walter radioed the main station and reported the explosion. He requested that Davos O'Connor and Jody Phillips be picked up as soon as possible and taken into custody.

"I wonder what being arrested for conspiracy, grand theft, and accessory to murder will do for O'Connor's precious reputation," he muttered as he fiddled with the Jeep's radio system.

"Drug charges, too. He had to know what Byron was up to."

The radio crackled, and Hara's voice came across.

"We've got alerts for road washouts from here to the bridge, sir," he said. "The ground on the slope along the highway has been tagged as highly un-predictable. There's a small landslide just on the other side of the road to the station."

They hit a bump in the road as the tires struck a downed branch that had been obscured by the mud and water. Kali glanced at Walter, who was gripping his leg just above the knee.

"Sorry," she said. "There's a lot of debris on the road."

He scowled at her. "You need to replace the shocks and struts. Really, the whole suspension. And the seat covers, which are covered with dog hair. And this communication system. The sound is terrible." They hit another bump. "Although I guess it would be a fitting wrap-up to a really awful day if your relic of a car decides this is when it finally wants to fall apart."

Kali didn't reply. Ahead they could see the headlights of another car moving slowly along the road toward them. Water sprayed out from the wheel wells as the Jeep navigated the flooded surface. As the other car became more visible, Walter pulled himself upright in his seat and pointed at the oncoming vehicle.

"Look!" he said. "That's her car coming toward us. Vintage Mustang, cherry red."

"Whose car? What are you talking about?" asked Kali.

"Jody Phillips. That's her car, remember? I walked her out to the parking lot when she came in to help with the computer program."

Kali slowed as she drew closer to the Mustang. The other vehicle swerved slightly and slowed. It was clear the driver was having difficulty maintaining control on the flooded road.

"What does she think she's doing?" asked Kali.

"Heading up to the prayer hut to help Vance try to force information from Charlie that he probably doesn't even have."

"Tell Hara to block the road behind us. I'm going to pass her, then box her in."

In a minute, they'd drawn even with the red car. Kali could see Jody huddled over the wheel. She seemed unaware of who was in the Jeep as Kali and Walter slowly passed her. In her rearview mirror, Kali could see that Hara had turned his car across the roadway, preventing her from passing. As she watched, he flipped on his rooftop flashers.

Once she was about thirty feet past the Mustang, Kali slowed nearly to a stop, then turned and maneuvered the Jeep around. She pulled up close behind Jody's car, doing her best to block her from the other direction.

There was no movement from inside the car, and nowhere for it to go. They sat for a moment, watching.

"You stay put," said Kali, reaching for the door handle. "Tell Hara to use the speaker to tell her to step out of her car, and for him to approach at the same time as I do—and to do it carefully. We don't know if she has a weapon."

Hara's voice came over the car's megaphone, instructing Jody to step out of the vehicle. There was no response.

"I'm going in," said Kali. In front of her, she watched as Hara exited the cruiser, gun drawn. She pulled out her own firearm and edged out of the Jeep, moving quickly to the back of Jody's car. She couldn't see anything through the windows.

Without warning, the engine of the Mustang roared and began to reverse. Kali jumped out of the way and watched in amazement as the back tires slipped onto the soft verge, then spun and moved forward onto the road, angled for the front of the Jeep. The Mustang fishtailed on the wet pavement and sped forward, hitting the opposite shoulder in the narrow space in front of Kali's car, smashing the Jeep's headlight. The Mustang raced away through the rising water, back in the direction it had come.

Hara ran up, splashing through the rising water. "There's no way she can maintain that speed in these conditions," he said. "I'll call for a road-block."

"I'm going to try to catch up," said Kali. "Follow me, but be careful—I've already got an injured Walter. I can't have you get hurt as well."

She climbed back into the Jeep, turning care-fully.

"Are you going to add criminal charges about your headlight?" asked Walter, tightening his seat belt.

"You bet I am." She put the Jeep into gear. "But this is where my four-wheel drive trumps the showy sports car and the high-tech cruiser. You'll need to hold on."

The Mustang was already out of sight ahead along the winding road. Kali drove as fast as she dared, fighting the urge to go faster. She listened to Hara as he gave an update. A roadblock was being put in place at the next intersection six miles ahead.

There was no need. As they rounded a curve, they could see the other car's taillights, but the car was stopped. The road ahead of it had disappeared beneath a giant wall of mud. The hillside had caved in and blocked the road. Jody had driven into it, and the Mustang was trapped in the deep, viscous soil and uprooted foliage that covered the surface.

Kali pulled to a stop and waited. They could see Jody struggling to climb through the passenger side window, which had narrowed to an impossible width beneath the crumpled hood and roof of the Mustang.

"Does she think that even if she can make herself small enough to get through that space that she can run away from us on foot?" asked Walter.

"I'm not sure what she's thinking, but it looks to me like she's stuck in that window."

It was true. As Hara drew up behind the Jeep, Kali got out and approached the Mustang. Jody's head, arms, and upper torso were outside of the car, exposed to the pounding rain.

From the corner of one eye, Kali saw Hara helping Walter out of the Jeep. Walter limped over, leaning on Hara's shoulder.

"I don't want to miss this," he said.

The three of them stood watching as Jody struggled in the window.

"Would you like some help?" asked Kali.

Jody seemed uncertain of how to respond. "I didn't realize the road was covered," she said, breathlessly. "Now I realize why you had it blocked the other way . . . I'm sorry I didn't pay attention. If you could just help me . . ."

"Would you be kind enough to get the pry bar out of the Jeep?" Kali asked Hara. "We should offer assistance to this citizen in distress."

"Yes, ma'am," he replied, hurrying to the Jeep.

Kali stepped into the mud covering the roadway, drawing closer to Jody. "Looks like you were heading toward the park trails, Jody. It's not really the best hiking weather, is it?"

"I . . . well, I had the idea that maybe Charlie had gone up that way," Jody offered. "He's obsessing again about Maya . . . and now that he knows where she was found, I figured that's where he'd go . . . It only seemed right that I should try to help you find him—I knew the weather was turning bad, but I thought I could get up there before it really hit." She looked at them, trying to push the wet hair out of her face while holding on to the doorframe.

"Right," said Kali. "I suppose you thought you could take shelter in the lava tube if necessary."

Jody looked at her sharply, comprehending. She began to struggle again, but Hara walked up with the pry bar. Walter nodded to him, and Hara carefully examined the damage to the car door.

"Stay still, miss. I'm going to pry the top of the window frame open if I can."

She clung to the door, and Hara inserted the pry bar near the top of the window, using his weight to wrench it upright. As he did so, the door sprang free, and Jody pulled herself back into the interior. There was no expression on her face.

"Shame about this car," said Walter. "You'll have to leave it here, but we'll give you a ride." He turned to Kali. "Guess we'll have to take the long way around."

"Guess we will," she said. She turned to Jody. "Step out of the car. Right now. I'm tired of being out here in the rain and mud."

Jody climbed out. Kali moved up next to her, holding her handcuffs.

"Did you get her to meet you at the supermarket down in Kahului?" asked Kali. "What did you tell her—that you were there to help her with the samples, and that the two of you would take your flashy car?"

"So what if I did?" Jody hissed. Her voice was filled with bitterness. "You didn't have to be around her, you know. But I guess the gifted, beautiful girl isn't so smart or pretty anymore."

"Maybe," said Kali. "It sure sounds like you're still jealous, though."

Jody's face was a stone.

"Face the vehicle," Kali said. "Jody Phillips, you are under arrest as an accomplice in the murder of Maya Holmes, as an accessory in the manufacturing of illicit substances, and a whole bunch of other things, too." She turned to Hara. "Please inform Miss Phillips of her rights and assist her into the back of your cruiser. We'll be right behind you on the road." She looked at Jody. "I'm afraid you're in for a bumpy ride."

CHAPTER 42

Nearly three weeks had passed since the arrest of the people connected to the death of Maya Holmes and the theft of her technology. The rain had finally worn itself out, and the day was warm and clear. On the far side of the lanai at Kali's house, Walter manned the grill, wrapped in an old chef's apron, singing as he cooked. Nina and their daughters were in the front yard, putting out bowls of potato salad and pineapple coleslaw—except for Suki, the youngest, who was enthusiastically chasing Hilo up and down the slope leading to the sea.

From the shade of the lanai, Elvar watched Suki in amazement. He stood next to Kali, gripping a large plastic container filled with iced chocolate cupcakes that Birta had prepared.

"I've never seen a child with so much . . . energy," he said.

Kali laughed. "Yeah, and that's how she is presugary-dessert. Wait till you see what she's capable of after she's had a couple of those cupcakes."

"After I eat a couple of cupcakes, I generally want to take a nap," said Elvar, still watching as the small girl and the enormous dog took turns leading the way up and down the lawn.

Hilo slowed to a jog, then stopped in the shade of a tree, folding his legs beneath himself. He sank to the ground. As he rolled over onto his side, Suki caught up with him and began to dance around him in circles.

"She's even got Hilo tired out." Elvar's voice was full of admiration. "Look at him. He's clearly calling for a time-out."

He was right. Hilo flailed his legs as Suki dashed around him in a circle, calling his name in her high-pitched voice. As they watched, she sat down on the ground beside the dog. He rolled over onto his back, and Suki began to tickle his stomach, laughing in glee as his legs twitched in response.

"Elvar, can you give me a hand?" called Walter. "I need you to keep an eye on this batch of burgers while I set up the last table."

Elvar handed the cupcake container to Kali and went to assist Walter. A car drew up in the driveway, and Kali watched as Charlie Holmes got out. He walked shyly toward the lanai. He was gripping the handles of a large shopping bag, and Kali could see bags of chips poking out the top. She smiled and waved to him with one hand, gesturing for him to join her on the lanai.

"Hi, Detective," said Charlie, coming slowly up the steps.

"It's just Kali, please," she said. "I'm really glad you could make it. I heard you're leaving in a few days, and I hoped to see you before you went."

"Yeah," he said, hesitating. "I think my parents would like to have me come home to San Diego for a while. I've had an offer for a full-time job at the National Wildlife Refuge there, and I've decided to take it." He looked around wistfully. "I'm really going to miss this place, but after everything that's happened . . . well, it's time to go, and the refuge is doing important work. It will give me the opportunity to make a positive difference in the lives of the animals I love."

She nodded. "I think it's a good decision. And you can always come back to visit." She smiled at him. "Did I hear correctly that Maya is going to get the recognition she deserves for her invention?"

His face brightened. "Yes. Now that we have the password to the files on her computer, we can prove it was all her work. My parents found a patent attorney to help. If the patent sells, my mom wants me to promise to go back to school to get my doctorate degree." His eyes were filled with sadness. "In honor of my sister."

"She'd be really proud of you, Charlie. I'm glad you were able to get into those files."

He looked at her, grateful. "The password was octopus. I should have thought of that right away, but it wasn't until I was back in the condo, cleaning up the mess that crazy guy made, and I found the stuffed octopus, that I had the idea it might be the word Maya used."

"Your sister was a brilliant woman."

He smiled and extended the shopping bag. "I wasn't sure what to bring, so I picked up some chips and buns and some hot dogs. And some ice cream. Is that okay?"

"That's perfect," she said. "I'll put the ice cream in the freezer. Why don't you put the buns and chips over there on the table with the other food? That lady by the table is Nina, Walter's wife, and the girls are Walter's daughters. They'll show you where everything should go. Grab something cool to drink and come back up here. There are plenty of comfy places to sit here on the lanai."

He reached into the bag and extracted two half-gallon tubs of ice cream, then handed them to Kali. She gave him the cupcakes in exchange.

"Yum," she said approvingly, glancing at the label on the ice cream. "Pistachio is my favorite." She laughed, reading the other label. "And so, as it happens, is maple walnut. Good job!"

He looked at her in surprise. "Maya loved pistachio, and maple walnut is my favorite. Guess I don't have much imagination."

"You have exactly the right amount, I'd say." She took the sweating tubs into the kitchen as Charlie walked tentatively toward the group on the lawn. She stowed the ice cream in the freezer, then stood watching from the window as Charlie introduced himself to Nina. While they were chatting, Suki galloped up, running to Charlie and hugging his legs. She was saying something, but Kali didn't have to hear the words to know she was doing her best to entice him to play chase with her.

Through the window, she could smell the food cooking and hear the sound of ukulele music. She went out to join the others. Birta had arrived from next door. She was standing with Nina, laughing at something she had said. Beth and Lara were setting out napkins and paper plates, arguing about on which side of the plates the forks should be placed, and if the napkins should be folded in triangles or halves. Hara drove up in the middle of the discussion, and both girls immediately dropped what they were doing to run to the car to greet him.

Walter walked up next to Kali, strumming his ukulele. "What is it with him? Every female who doesn't even get excited when the storm alarms go off somehow falls into some kind of enchanted swoon as soon as Hara appears. I don't care if she's eight like Lara or eighty-eight like my neighbor, Mrs. Wilson."

"Jealousy is unbecoming in a man of your age, Walter. Plus we just learned how dangerous that emotion can be."

He snorted. "Jealousy? I'm just trying to figure it out . . . while telling myself I shouldn't shoot him in the foot for having an effect on my girls." He looked at her, curious. "Are you as immune to his looks as you pretend to be?"

"Absolutely not," she said. She patted Walter on his arm. Her eyes darted briefly to where Elvar could be seen flipping burgers on the grill. "But he's not really my type."

"True dat," said Walter. He nodded toward the front lawn, where Kali had set up lawn chairs. George was there relaxing in one, and Mrs. Bailey was sitting beside him. Birta had joined them, and the three of them appeared to be engaged in an animated conversation. "Get a load of that," he said.

"What are they talking about?" asked Kali.

Walter raised an eyebrow. "Turns out that Mrs. Bailey and George share a passion for weird things in the sky, deep-sea monsters, and everything in between. Even more remarkably, that tough lady that lives next door to you—Elvar's sister—belongs to some local UFO watch group. They're over there comparing stories."

"You're kidding . . . Birta?" asked Kali. She was amazed. Blunt, down-to-earth, and practical were all ways she would have described Birta, but an interest in otherworldly things was a definite shock.

Walter's smile faded. "You shaking off all the Maya Holmes drama yet?"

"Mostly," she said. "Trey Carter was a straight-up overdose, according to the autopsy. The residue found in the bag of drugs in the tent near his body doesn't match the profile of what Byron Coolidge was cooking up, so it appears that Trey must have bought something locally before he reached the camp where he died. And I saw the statement from Gloria Marsh. She heard all the hullabaloo about that damn journal paper, too. She says O'Connor and Byron Coolidge were beside themselves with worry about the publication date, but she didn't know why. Apparently, they'd pitched it, using an outline of Maya's research, thinking they had

plenty of time to find her computer and get any re
lated files off it—but the publication date go
pushed up by several months, and they only foun(
out about it when Jody saw it in the journal an(
confronted O'Connor. Evidently, she threatene(
to spill the beans."

"So they panicked." Walter looked thoughtful
"They tortured the girl to get the information the
needed to build a prototype of her invention, bu
she didn't give it to them. And Vance, who was s(
methed up that he really thought he was som(
kind of sorcerer-god, created a little too mucł
drama, bringing attention to himself and that par
of the forest instead of scaring people away like h(
intended."

"And then there's the greed component. Byror
thought he could make a fortune on one side witł
his meth production, while O'Connor thought h(
could get away with claiming Maya's invention a
his own." Kali shook her head. "In his statemen
he swore he has the rights to it because she wa
working for him when she invented it."

"And Jody Phillips is just a crazy jealous persor
who thought that if she got the files and the plan
from Maya, then she'd get a cut of whatever cam(
of its sale," added Walter.

"I guess scientists aren't all as clever as the
think they are," said Kali. She looked across th(
lawn at Charlie, who had pulled up a chair and wa
talking to George. "Maya suspected something, o
she would have never hidden her computer i
Charlie's room like she did."

"Seems like." He looked toward Charlie. "Kin(

of interesting that Gloria Marsh—the most aggressive and least likable out of that bunch of unlike-
able people—wasn't part of either the murder or
the meth project."

"You sound a little disappointed."

"Just surprised. She's in the clear on all of it,
apart from being a pain in the rear end, and so far,
O'Connor's not being charged with either the
production or distribution of illegal substances."

"Impossible he didn't know."

"What was that you told me about the number
of rental convertibles zipping around this island?
Improbable, but not impossible."

She smiled briefly, then gazed out across the
green lawn, spread out in a softly undulating slope
toward the sea.

"You know, Walter, I don't think I'll ever be able
to look at or really appreciate one of those rainbow trees ever again. Such a beautiful thing to be
witness to such evil."

He reached out and squeezed her shoulder.
"You need some music to wash those thoughts
away." He looked at her with understanding, smiling gently. "George told me you're planning a
blessing ceremony for his store, now that it's re-
paired and ready to reopen. He seems pleased by
that."

"Yes," she said, thinking about what would take
place. She would use salt water gathered from the
sea in front of her house to cleanse George's
space, so as to release any remnants of negative energy that might be lingering from the attack. A traditional lei woven of dark green maile leaves

would be laid across the new threshold of his store and untied before George entered the restored space for the first time. It was important to her that George feel that the terror of that night had been completely discharged, and that he could once again welcome his customers without being haunted by what had happened. For the briefest of moments, she wished there was some simple ceremony that might help bring Makena's troubled young life into balance. Then she shook her head, releasing the thought. This wasn't the time to dwell on problems.

Walter studied her for a moment. Then, lifting his ukulele, he wandered toward the table where the food was set out. Picking up the tempo of the tune he was playing, he sang along in his comforting baritone.

The afternoon was relaxed. It was clear that everybody was enjoying the company of everyone else. The sky had cleared just in time to reveal the golden hour that heralded the impending arrival of sunset. Every last cupcake and drop of ice cream had been finished off, and Kali walked across the soft grass to the steps of the lanai, heading inside with a few odds and ends that would need to be washed so that their owners could take their containers home with them. She was standing in front of the sink, squirting a honeysuckle scented dish soap into the running water, watching as the suds sprang up in the sink, when she felt someone walk up behind her. She turned, expecting to see Walter. Instead it was Elvar who was standing there.

"Oh," she said, surprised. "I thought you were Walter."

"No," he said. "I told Walter to go home. His kids are tired." The corner of his mouth moved slightly, as though he were suppressing a smile. "They're also covered in chocolate and ice cream and dog hair, but he'll need to sort that out on his own."

She waited.

"I thought maybe I could help you clear up," he said, gazing steadily at her.

"Really? Seems like you've been doing a lot of dishes at this sink lately."

Their eyes locked. She looked at him, taking in his strong jaw and kind eyes. Outside, the sound of music and laughter had grown faint. The happy gathering was winding down, and before too long, Charlie would have said his goodbyes and Hara would have left to go home. The girls would be carried to Walter's car and strapped in, already half-asleep. Mrs. Bailey would drive George home, and Birta would fuss over putting away chairs and wiping down tables.

She turned back to Elvar, understanding that she was making a choice. She knew he was waiting for her to make a decision.

"Okay," she said. She smiled and reached toward the counter, lifting a dish towel and tossing it to him. "I guess the job's all yours, then. Let's see if you're up to it."

He caught the towel and stepped up beside her, close enough that his arm was brushing hers. The light filtered softly through the open window, filling the room with warmth. Kali could see the space in the yard where the grass had yet to grow back from the fire, but it was okay. She was getting used to the idea that the canoe had sailed away, out of reach, and that it was time for her to plot a new journey of her own.

CHAPTER 1

The midmorning sun hammered down on the old pineapple field's rutted surface, imparting a relentless, blazing glare. The ocean breeze had failed, on a colossal scale, to deliver a cooler version of tropical air over the lip of the coastal cliffs and down into the Palawai Basin plains of Lāna'i Island's central region. It was hot, and it was early, and it was going to get hotter.

Detective Kali Māhoe peered once again into the recesses of the freshly dug trench at her feet. She'd been in, out, and around the hole for most of the morning, and her sleeveless green T-shirt, tied in a messy knot just below her breasts, was soaked with sweat. Streaks of dirt partially obscured a tattoo encircling her upper left arm, depicting a stylized, slightly geometric interpretation of a thrusting spear.

At the bottom of the hole in front of her was an old refrigerator, its door flung open and partially resting on the mound of red-tinged dirt that had been created during its excavation. There was a small backhoe parked close by, on loan from the island's community cemetery. It was close enough that she could feel the additional heat radiating from the surface of its recently used engine.

The area around the open ground had been enclosed by crime scene tape, while a makeshift tarp on poles covered the hole, tenting it from the unlikely possibility of wind interference on this unusually still morning, and fending off the sun's glare for the benefit of the police photographer. In place of the abundant natural island light, bright, artificial lights had been set up around the perimeter, angled to illuminate the depths of the hole.

The tarp had proven completely ineffective at providing any semblance of shade. In the trench, Maui medical examiner Mona Stitchard—commonly known as "Stitches," but only behind her back—was kneeling beside the refrigerator, taking measurements and making notes in a small book. Her hooded, sterile white plastic jumpsuit clung to her arms and the sides of her face, held in place against her skin by a layer of perspiration. Kali could see that her narrow eyeglasses were sliding down her nose.

Kali studied the peculiar contents of the open refrigerator, then took a long swig of water from a bottle hooked onto her belt, leaning her head back as a few drops trickled down off the edge of her chin.

Police Captain Walter Alaka'i walked up and stood beside her. He regarded the refrigerator with curiosity, his frown giving way to a row of creases in his wide brow. "Well, I gotta say this is definitely a new one. Any brilliant initial thoughts you're not sharing?"

Kali shook her head, considering the question. "Sorry. Nothing yet, beyond the obvious, slightly bizarre component."

She looked away, across the field, and then back down into the hole. What she didn't say was that she was keenly aware of a residual sadness and loss still clinging to this space, filling the molecules of earth around her feet, newly disturbed after untold years.

Stitches glanced up at Kali and Walter.

"Well, I suppose we all like a challenge." She waved her arm at a fly buzzing by her face. "And this should certainly be interesting."

The three of them regarded the derelict refrigerator. It was an older General Electric model, with a single, large main compartment and a smaller freezer door on the top. The shelves from the main compartment were missing.

"My mother had a refrigerator like this one," said Walter, pointing at it with the opened bottle of water he was holding. "And a matching stove. She was crazy proud of them. Horrible shade of yellow, if you ask me."

"Technically, the color is harvest gold," said Stitches. "Hugely popular from the 1960s all the way through the '70s."

Walter frowned at her.

"You think it's been here that long?"

"Hard to say," she answered, shrugging. "Though it doesn't seem likely someone would bury a new one."

She stood up, passing her medical bag to Kali with one hand and stretching out the other toward Walter, which he grabbed and pulled. Emerging from the depths of the trench with impressive composure, she tugged the plastic hood away from her face and hair, now plastered wet against her head. She peeled off her jumpsuit with relief, and stood beside them, taking off her glasses to clean them. Walter passed her the bottle of water he'd been holding for her. She replaced her glasses and took the bottle, drinking from it gratefully.

There were a number of people milling about the area surrounding the trench, each involved in either further securing the scene or attending to some detail: Tomas Alva, Lāna'i's only full-time cop, officially part of the Maui County Police Department; a police photographer busily loading equipment into the back of his car; the crime scene team from the main station in Wailuku on Maui; Burial Council officials who were required to attend the scene of any uncovered grave that might have a cultural tie; and a terrified-looking young couple who were clearly tourists, huddled by a rocky outcropping at the edge of the field. They were dressed in matching brightly patterned Hawaiian shirts, and on the ground beside them were two metal detectors, their long, narrow handles clearly visible.

Looking over at the couple, Kali sighed. "I guess

I should go and talk to them one more time before the woman passes out or starts wailing again," she said.

The offer sounded half-hearted, even to her own ears. Stitches glanced at her. Walter regarded her with a raised eyebrow.

Kali glared at them. "Seriously? Surely both of you can see she's one wrong word away from another bout of hysteria," she said in a defensive tone. "And yes—before anyone points it out, I'm fully aware I'm not at my best with over-excited twenty-somethings."

Both Stitches and Walter turned toward the young couple, considering.

"Probably put a big dent in her day, right?" said Walter, his smile lopsided. "They're just kids on vacation. Not every day you go looking for buried treasure and turn up something like this."

Kali exhaled. "Okay, okay. Point made."

Walter's grin widened. "One of these days, you'll realize I'm always right."

Kali snorted. "Playing the uncle card?"

He reached out and patted her lightly on the shoulder. "I can safely say that not only are you my *only* niece, you're absolutely, without doubt, my favorite one."

He turned to Stitches, who had begun to wad her used jumpsuit into a ball.

"You all through here?"

She nodded. "For now. I'll know more, of course, once we've moved everything back to the morgue and I can do a proper examination." She surveyed the long-abandoned appliance in the hole. "Meanwhile, good luck with the search. Hopefully you can find something that will be useful in ascertaining an identification."

"Well, we've searched as much as we can with the fridge still there," said Walter. "Maybe there's something still hidden beneath it. We'll see, I guess." He wiped a few drops of sweat from his brow with the back of his hand. "I'm going to head back to Maui after we get the body and fridge loaded up on the launch."

Stitches had already walked off, making her way toward a waiting car that would take her to the harbor for the roughly nine-mile boat crossing back to Maui across the Au au Channel. Walter strode toward the backhoe, gesturing to the driver. The engine turned over. Parked beside it, a truck fitted with a flatbed also roared to life. The drivers of both vehicles made their way slowly toward the open hole, guided by Walter.

Kali peered once more into the depths of the trench. Lying inside the no-longer-gleaming harvest-gold refrigerator, dressed in a pair of rotting overalls, was a skeleton, its bony hands folded neatly across the chest. It was lying on its side, both legs bent at the knees, feet pressed together. She had the impression it had been placed there with great care—even reverence, perhaps. She looked more closely. Her initial feeling suggested to her that whoever had performed this strange burial had possibly cared about the dead person in some way.

She supposed it looked like a small man, but it was difficult to tell. Resting on the corpse's narrow shoulders, in lieu of a skull, was a large, ornately carved wooden pineapple, a macabre adornment that gave no sense at all of who the long-dead figure might have been—or how he'd come to be resting here, in a dormant field of fruit, bereft, headless, and utterly alone.

CHAPTER 2

It was well after noon by the time Kali had compiled her notes with details about the burial setting and finished her final interview with Brad and Jan, the tourist couple. As she'd predicted, the woman had broken down into a fit of wild crying midway through her account of the morning's events.

Brad had been more pragmatic, even a little excited.

"We thought maybe we could find some old coins, you know? Something to take home as a souvenir that didn't come from a gift shop."

Kali refrained from pointing out that removing a historic artifact from the islands wasn't likely to be looked upon kindly by the authorities. She watched his face, fascinated by the difference be-

ween his reaction to the discovery of a body, and
hat of his girlfriend.

"When the metal detector starting going off, we
lug around the spot and kept hitting metal. Jan
hought it might be a treasure chest, but I figured
t was probably some old piece of harvesting
:quipment that got covered up." He patted the
;irl on her leg, as if consoling her for the loss of an
imaginary fortune.

Kali frowned. "And when you realized it was an
)ld refrigerator, why did you keep digging?"

He grinned. "Well, why would someone bury a
'efrigerator? I mean, maybe something important
1ad been stashed inside of it. You know, valu-
1ble—not just a pile of old bones."

He fumbled as he saw the expression on Kali's
ace. "I mean . . ."

"You mean that the body of some long-dead
1uman being, perhaps a local person, is of no pos-
ible concern, or any value." She watched as he
quirmed. "Correct?"

"Well, no, of course not. It's just that . . ." He
ooked from Kali to Jan, and back to Kali. "Jan
:alled 911 right away, you know? I mean, a body,
ight?"

"Yes, a body. Exactly right."

Jan made a fresh sobbing noise. "I didn't want
o open it," she said, making an effort to keep her
'oice from breaking. "In the movies, opening the
)ox buried in the remote field never turns out to
)e a good thing. I knew there was something bad
n there. I just knew it."

"The skeleton belonged to an actual person,

you know," said Kali. "A living human being wh
probably had a family and friends."

"And at least one enemy," Brad joked.

Kali swallowed her irritation at his shallow re
sponse, doing her best to temper her character as
sessment with some degree of kindness. She
turned to the woman, ignoring Brad.

"You could look at it this way: Thanks to you
maybe someone will finally find some peace an
closure knowing that their loved one has been
found."

The woman grasped at the thought gratefully.

"Well, glad to have helped, of course. I mean
anything we can do . . ."

"You're absolutely sure you didn't find anything
else?"

Exchanging glances, Brad and Jan shook thei
heads. They looked directly at her with no appa
ent subterfuge.

"No," said Jan. "Nothing at all."

Kali waited, but they just sat there, dishevele
and sweaty. The woman's shoulders sagged. Ka
noticed a small tear in her shirt, as well as so
stains on her beige sneakers. "I'd appreciate a ca
if anything occurs to you."

Again the couple looked at one another, befor
Jan spoke.

"So, it's okay if we go back to Maui tonight? W
have a flight home to California the day after t
morrow. Should we cancel it? Will you need t
hold us for more questioning or anything lik
that?"

Kali suppressed a smile. There were, she though

simply too many police shows on television these days.

"I don't think that will be necessary, but we'd appreciate it if you could keep all of this to yourselves until we've been in touch," she said, keeping her voice even. She could tell they were more than ready for cold showers and the hotel bar, where they'd most likely retell their story over and over, no matter how many times she might ask them not to. "Just make sure Officer Alva has all of your contact information before you leave." She lent them a more serious gaze. "Just in case."

The refrigerator, still holding the body, was carefully lifted from the ground and loaded onto the flatbed truck. To give them space to work, a command center for the police and crime scene crew had been set up near the parking area. The surrounding area was searched diligently, the soil sifted for any small item that might shed some light on the moment when the refrigerator had been covered and abandoned. As the day lent itself toward dusk, more lights were set up around the now-empty hole. Armed with a bucket, sieve, and small shovel, Kali helped turn over the loose earth meticulously.

She could see the undulating landscape of the pineapple field rolling off into the distance, shrouded by the growing shadows. Tomas Alva stood just outside the line of light, waiting patiently. Like Kali, he was covered in dirt.

"We're going to shut this down for the night,"

he said wearily. "Probably take forever, but we've
got a team using ground-penetrating radar coming in the morning, and a crew to start digging up
the rest of the field if necessary . . . in case the
head's nearby."

It won't be, Kali told herself. The pineapple suggested that the burial had had some sort of ritual
significance, and it was unlikely that a head had
been relegated to a separate box and conveniently
planted somewhere in the vicinity. She kept her
thoughts to herself. It wouldn't hurt the SOC crew
to spend a few days with backhoes and shovels.
The last thing she wanted to do was keep anyone
from feeling useful.

She felt Tomas's eyes on her. They'd known one
another for years, and she suspected that he'd
likely read the gist of her thoughts. He said nothing, only grinned tiredly.

"I'll give you a ride into town when you're
ready," he said.

She brushed herself off, succeeding only in
making her hands dirtier than they already were.

"I'm going to make a mess of your car seat," she
said, somewhat apologetically.

"Can't get any dirtier than my seat will be," he
said. "Come on. Let's get you settled, and I'll go
and see if there's any supper left for me at home."

They walked to the car and climbed inside. For
a moment, Tomas sat with his head back against
his headrest. He reached forward slowly, turning
the key that had been left in the ignition. As the
car's engine rumbled softly, he backed out of the
makeshift parking spot and pulled onto the narrow track leading to the two-lane main road.

They rode in silence for a minute. Then Tomas turned to Kali. "Can you think of any reason someone would replace a head with a wooden *hala kahiki?*"

She considered his question. "Well . . . it's an obvious way to conceal the victim's identity, at least in the short term," she offered. "But I think it's more likely there was something significant about the choice. Why not a real *hala kahiki?* It's not as though there's a pineapple shortage here. Market shelves are full of them."

"That's what I was thinking. Seems like someone went through considerable effort to find a wooden one."

Not if the person's death had been planned in advance, and the carved pineapple had been conveniently at hand, she thought. That scenario suggested a premeditation that might somehow tie to the image of this particular fruit. "I don't love these cold cases," she said instead. "It's bad enough when we know who the victim is to begin with, but when we have to figure out who it is before we can hunt for a reason, I start losing sleep."

"Maybe," Tomas responded, his voice thoughtful, "it was a natural death, or an accidental one, and the pineapple was an afterthought."

She looked at him sideways. "Natural death by decapitation?"

Tomas shrugged. "Yeah, it does sound a little crazy, doesn't it? What about an accident, maybe with some of the equipment, and someone wanted to hide it?"

It was Kali's turn to shrug. "I'm sure stranger

things have happened. But in all likelihood this wasn't just an accident."

They drove the rest of the short distance in silence. Darkness had almost completely fallen as Tomas pulled the car up in front of the entrance of the Hotel Lāna'i in Lāna'i City.

She unclipped her seat belt and opened the car door, already anticipating the magic of a long shower and late dinner.

"Mahalo for the ride," she said, climbing out. "I'm heading back to Maui early, but I'll be in touch before I leave."

"*Pomaika'i*," called Tomas, using the Hawaiian word for "good luck." He gave a wave as he pulled back out into the street, taillights fading as the road curved away into the night.

Kali turned, gazing at the small plantation-style building that housed the hotel. It was painted a soft yellow and surrounded by blooming foliage. She climbed the front steps, stopping halfway with her hand on the rail, scanning the tranquil setting in appreciation. The designation of "city" was stretching things more than a little bit, she thought. The tiny town was hardly more than a pretty square bordered by a few shops and restaurants, with beautiful residential neighborhoods spreading out beyond.

Never the tourist magnet that continuously drew hordes of visitors to Maui and O'ahu, the island of Lāna'i had become identified with the sweet, prickly crops of fruit growing in orderly rows across its face. The small hotel had once served as private lodging, and was modest in comparison to the two enormous resorts located in other parts of the island.

While the nickname Pineapple Island had eventually become popular, promoted in newspapers, magazines, movies, and television, Kali knew that the island's dark history had little to offer in the way of sweetness. Lānaʻi, so green and peaceful, was steeped in dark myth and violent legends that whispered of man-eating spirits that stalked the living.

"I wonder how many of the tourists who make their way across the channel know about the Lānaʻi monsters?" murmured Kali, half to herself.

"Probably none of them," answered a male voice.

Kali started, surprised that anyone had heard her. A very old man was standing on the porch above her, partly in the shadows near the rail, looking out toward the dangling moon, which was surrounded by faint, glittering stars. She halted her ascent up the stairs just before the stranger.

"Do you think it would make a difference to them if they did know?" she asked.

The old man shrugged. "I doubt it," he said. "Just fodder for T-shirt slogans, I would think. No one believes in anything anymore unless they can see or taste it."

She mused over his words, and the abundant truth in them. "Or unless it touches their own life directly," she added.

"Exactly so," he said. He bowed slightly in her direction, then turned back to the rail, resuming his observance of the moon's widening glow. "You must excuse me. I have an agreement with Hina, you see, that I will, whenever possible, greet her as she arrives to light the night."

Kali was surprised to hear him speak the name of Hina. *The Hawaiian goddess of the moon.*

"That's quite an honorable agreement," she said, her voice carrying a genuine respect. "I'm sure, Grandfather, that she looks forward to seeing you each evening."

The man smiled broadly, evidently finding her use of the title *grandfather* friendly. They stood together in companionable silence for several minutes, looking at the sky as the cool night breeze whispered across their faces. As she turned toward the door, she noticed the deep lines around his eyes; there was old grief written there, but laugh lines as well, deep crevices that came from a lifetime of many smiles. For a fleeting moment she wondered what her own face revealed, and if others might someday look at her and see nothing but regret or the disillusionment that regularly arose from constantly dealing with the results of the cruelty and selfishness of her fellow humans.

"*Aloha ahiahi,*" she said softly to the man, nodding her head. As he returned the gesture, she opened the door quietly and passed into the hotel foyer, imagining the imminent comfort of climbing beneath the fresh, cool sheets of her temporary bed, where she might dream, all the while bathed in Hina's silvery light.